WHEN THE BLACK LOTUS BLOOMS

When The Black Lotus Blooms

From a carven green jade box
he took a handful of shimmering
black dust, and placed it in a
golden brazier which stood on a
golden tripod at his elbow.

In Stygia, that ancient and evil
kingdom that lay far to the south,
he had seen such black dust before.
It was the pollen of the black lotus,
which creates death-like sleep and
monstrous dreams; and he knew
that only the grisly wizards of the
Black Ring, which is the nadir of evil,
voluntarily seek the nightmares of
the black lotus, to revive their
necromantic powers.

—Robert E. Howard
   from
   HOUR OF THE DRAGON

⁊⦁

WHEN THE BLACK LOTUS BLOOMS

edited by
Elizabeth A. Saunders

introduction by
Robert R. McCammon

cover/design by
Jame A. Riley

UNNAMEABLE PRESS
Atlanta, 1990

Acknowledgements

Cover/design © 1990 Jame A. Riley and Unnameable Press; "Foreword" © 1990 Elizabeth A. Saunders and Jame A. Riley. "Introduction" © 1990 Robert R. McCammon. "Ninfea" © 1990 Kay Marie Porterfield. "The Rift in Autumn" and "Armada Moon" © 1990 Thomas E. Fuller; "The Dancer in the Dark: Interlude Three" © 1990 Thomas E. Fuller, from his unpublished novel. "For Ray," "The Pursuit of Happiness" and "Trip" © 1990 Michael N. Langford. "A Scent Like Silver" © 1990 Susan MacTabert. "The Grey Smudge," "Marker" and "Grey Men" © 1990 the Estate of Joseph Payne Brennan. "Marine Passage: Two Mothers" © 1990 Jane Yolen. "Skeleton Key" © 1990 Scott H. Urban. "A Case Study" and "Precursor" © 1990 Donald M. Hassler. "Assassination Festival" © 1990 Marvin Kaye. "Door Closing" © 1990 Wendy Webb. "Midnight Visit" and "The Strange High Armadillo in the Mist" © 1990 Gerald W. Page; "Waygift" by Gerald W. Page © 1977 Aurora Publishing, for FUTURE PASTIMES, reprinted by permission of the author. "The Lon Chaney Factory" © 1990 Brad Linaweaver. "Ballad of the Faithful Wife" and "Not By Blood Alone" © 1990 Millea Kenin. "Dream" © 1990 Bobby G. Warner. "A Trick of the Night," "Graveyards in the Dark" and "Carousel" © 1990 Sharon K. Epperson. "Drifting Atoms" © 1941 Weird Tales, renewed 1990 Mary Elizabeth Counselman; reprinted by permission of the author. "Dream People" © 1990 John Grey. "Late Bloomer" © 1990 Janet Fox. "Siren Strains," "Gothic" and "The Old Marsh Road" © 1990 Jame A. Riley. "On The Blue Guillotine" © 1990 Gregory Nicoll. "Red Rover" © 1990 Glen Egbert. "The Wind Has Teeth" © 1990 G. Warlock Vance and Scott H. Urban. "Pinto Rider" © 1990 Charles L. Grant. "Snow Dove" © 1990 Brad Strickland. "The Window" © 1990 Elizabeth Conklin. "La Belle Dame" © 1990 Jack Massa. "The Egret" by Michael Bishop © 1987 Playboy Magazine, reprinted by permission of the author. "Moving" © 1990 James Robert Smith.

All illustrations are © 1990 by their respective illustrators. The inset illustration detail on the cover is by Gustave Doré. The Lotus design and Unnameable Press logo are trademarks of Unnameable Press. All rights reserved. Nothing can be reprinted or reproduced by any means from this collection in whole or in part without prior permission of the author or illustrator. Brief passages may be quoted in reviews stating book and story title and author. All other contents © 1990 Unnameable Press.

FIRST EDITION

published by
Unnameable Press
P.O. Box 11689
Atlanta, GA 30355-1689

Trade Softcover
ISBN 0-043227-05-5
Limited, Signed Hardcover
ISBN 0-943227-06-3
Limited, Signed Deluxe Hardcover
ISBN 0-943227-07-1

Contents

And there came to him a sudden gleam of
understanding. This before him was the
Black Lotus, symbol of the evil that waits
for men in sleep. It was casting a spell
upon him that would lure him to death.

from
BLACK LOTUS
by Robert Bloch

The timelessness of common dreams was not
his lot; centuries passed on leadenly, and
he knew every second of their length as he
lay within the tomb of his fathers; enmauso-
leumed upon a slab covered with stone that
was carven with demon-given basilisks.

from
BLACK LOTUS
by Robert Bloch

ε&

Foreword

ELIZABETH A. SAUNDERS
AND JAME A. RILEY

Well, here we are, folks — the Lotus has bloomed at last. If you are a serious collector of dark fantasy books, you have no doubt heard all the reasonable excuses for delays in the publication of a book and have probably been offered several that didn't sound at all plausible. The truth is, Small Press is a labor of love — and an expensive labor at that! The work is hard and we (at least) feel that the results are worth the wait. We hope to bring that same satisfaction to each of you who have waited with us.

Unnameable Press has increased the level of quality in each publication, from the first letterpress folios to *All The Devils Are Here*, released at the Confederation WorldCon in Atlanta, 1986. *When The Black Lotus Blooms* has gone far beyond that production, thanks mainly to the support of people who believed we could make that leap. Thank all of you sincerely for your assistance in making this real.

Small Press has traditionally been the frontier for the new and interesting — and ofttimes for the bizarre and strange. It can be a cutting edge in Science Fiction and Dark Fantasy. We are trying to combine that edge with a return to classic traditions of presenting Horror and Dark Fantasy, a return to an outlook that counts the world of spirit more important than violently separated blood and bone. We are also trying to return to the great Art Nouveau traditions of bookmaking, to the idea of the book as an important art form. The turn of the century was a time when ideas of organic beauty began to combine with ideas of the beauty of machines, and much of beauty was born.

The concept of *Black Lotus* evolved from the dimly remembered Golden Age story of a man confronting the unknown limits of a Lovecraftian world. The image was that of the black lotus and its use by the sorcerers and powerful evil priests of the Hyborian world. The exact literary reference has been elusive. At the time of this writing, we are beginning to wonder if the 'memory' is actually a dream from a childhood where Clark Ashton Smith and Frank Belknap Long were a part of every day. We have, however, located a couple nice references from a couple of great sources and want to thank Robert Bloch and the estate of Robert E. Howard for permission to use them.

The Black Lotus — sleep, death, dreams . . . nightmares. These are potent images that speak to something in most of us — and are the gifts of the lotus. We hope we bring you something that will bloom in the darker recesses of your mind . . . then we will have accomplished everything we hoped.

There are many people without whose help this project would never have been completed. We would like to thank all of the contributors to this book for their patience (and belief that this book would see the bookstore shelves), Tristram Coffin (may your feet dance forevermore), Worldcon Atlanta, Inc., Dan Roberts of the nimble fingers, Thomas E. Fuller of the nimble mind, Charles and Betty Saunders for blooms of a strange variety (and much else), Brad Linaweaver of the nimble pens (both red and black), Ellenina Riley, Diane Vail, Valeria Baker, Barbara McAdams, and Edwin Attaway. Thanks to Pete and Tim Brown at The Darkroom, Irma Terry and Jim Jeschke at American Composition and Bob Kreger at BookCrafters for making this so easy in the final stages. Most importantly of all — thanks to all the people who have given encouragement and support during the evolution of this book. ❧

Introduction

ROBERT R. McCAMMON

This is art.

Yes, it is.

Between these covers are fantastic word paintings. Some of them are drawn with heavy strokes, some with the most ethereal of touches. Some are pastel, some are oil; some are dappled with light, others with darkness from the palette of midnight. They are all worthy of consideration and contemplation, hanging as they are in the gallery of imaginings.

This volume is particularly exciting to me because it has a definite "Southern" bent. Many of the writers in this book live in the South, and I've read and enjoyed much of their work in other publications. I am proud to say that my Southern writer friends represented in these pages have "arrived". They may not be household names yet, but they are working in the fire of truth and the blood of intensity, and they will forge their mark on the vast landscape of dark fantasy.

Occasionally I'm asked a question of why I believe Southern writing to be different from the writing of other geographical areas. Southerners grow up, whether we realize it at the time or not, in the territory of magic and mystery. We can leave our houses and be walking in a woodland usually within minutes. And I don't mean those little tracts of trees and grass that pass as "woodland" in a lot of other places, but honest-to-God-take-the-wrong-path-and-you're-lost forests, with no houses or roads or signs to remind you of the comforts of civilization. We can drive down the backwoods route not very far from our front doors and find ourselves at the edge of a swamp, where at night there will be no lights but the stars. We can wander the route through towns that are marked on no map, and we can find ourselves in conversations with people who have chosen a particular time to remain rooted in and for whom the modern world ceases to exist. We never know what might be around the next curve of that uncharted, sinisterly thrilling route, and we follow it for the love of going one more mile into the unknown.

The quality of Southern folklore also contributes to our storytelling aspirations. From childhood we bask in tall-tales, tales of blood vengeance and fouled honor, tales of swampy cemeteries giving up their dead and houses with rooms no human can enter without going mad. All Southern towns seem to have an epic behind their names, places like Murder Creek, Alabama; Fearsville, Kentucky; Transylvania, Louisiana; Talking Rock, Georgia; Skinem, Tennessee; and House Red, Virginia. Growing up in the South, we understand the connection of generations, of ancient voices speaking from the past to the present through family diaries and cryptic notes written in the margins of old yellowed Bibles. We know the story of the murdered slave whose spirit walks at night through yonder woods, his mouth sewn shut to forever keep the master's secret; we know the story of the black horse that snorts foam and rides endlessly with a dead man strapped to his saddle; we know the tale of the weeping stones, and the lament of the lady in white for the soldier who died for Dixie.

Every southern town has a haunted house, a deadly curve, a witch's tree, a bottomless lake, or a graveyard with stones so old they cannot be read. Every Southern town carries stories within it as gifts of their native land.

Being born and living in the South also exposes us to a high level of violence. Like the Wild West, the South is a place where guns are commonly in view and their owners are not slow to use them. We live in a land, whether we admit it or not, of redneck tempers and brute force, where a barroom brawl can escalate into a shootout or knife fight as fast and mean as an Elvis sneer. This is a land where the columns of elegant old plantations were built by the brand and whip, and gentrified men shot each other over a lady's perfumed glove.

Here we cling to what was. We understand how the past fits into the present, and how that in turn will interlock with the future. Our heritage of folklore and imagination is the common earth between the ages, and as Southern writers all the work we do is based on that solid red clay.

WHEN THE BLACK LOTUS BLOOMS is a work of art and a symphony of voices. Each writer or artist has a definite style, pace and rhythm; a definite and unique vision of what was, what is, and what may yet come to be.

Stories like James Robert Smith's "Moving", Gregory Nicoll's "On The Blue Guillotine", Jame A. Riley's "The Old Marsh Road", and Michael Bishop's "The Egret" are prime examples of Southern writers working from the iridescent pool of regional folklore. They have added their own vision and voices, and the results are fascinating, terrifying, and wonderful.

Brad Linaweaver's "The Lon Chaney Factory" sparkles like gothic greasepaint. Janet Fox's "Late

Bloomer" is a fearful hybrid of horror and beauty. Glen Egbert's "Red Rover" is a muscular masterpiece, and "The Wind Has Teeth" by G.Warlock Vance and Scott H. Urban will freeze your blood . . . if you have any.

For a walk on the bizarre side, "The Strange High Armadillo In The Mist", by Gerald W. Page, takes us west of the river into Harold's realm. A monstrous door beckons in the 1941 Weird Tales reprint "Drifting Atoms", by Mary Elizabeth Counselman. Marella is entranced by her swimming pool in the haunting "Ninfea" by Kay Marie Porterfield, and the masterful Charles L. Grant writes about darkness, light, and a lucky shot in the soul-stirring "Pinto Rider".

There is a wealth of talent, ideas, visions, horror, dreams, and nightmares in *WHEN THE BLACK LOTUS BLOOMS*. To take a bite is to enter the world of the fantastic, and one bite will be the first taste of a feast of wonder. ❧

. . . O night-black lotus flower, that groweth
beneath the River Nile! O poisoned perfumer
of all darkness, waving and weaving in the
spells of moonlight! O cryptic magic that
 worketh only evil! . . .

from
BLACK LOTUS
by Robert Bloch

Ninfea

KAY MARIE PORTERFIELD
illustration by
HARRY O. MORRIS

Marella has sensed the presence of something unusual beneath the tepid water of her swimming pool since the night a month ago she first slept in her new home. Late at night she walks barefoot across the deep carpeting of her bedroom and gazes out at the large rectangle of moonlit water in her courtyard. Fingertips pressed against the glass, she feels an urge to slide open the patio doors and take a nocturnal swim, gliding across the turquoise-tiled pool with powerful strokes. She cannot swim or even float. In fact, her heart beats faster when in the proximity of an expanse of water larger than a bathtub. It was the pool, strangely enough, which convinced her to buy this Spanish home built in 1925 — far too big for a woman alone.

In the lunar light that bathes the wrought iron furniture and the water with liquid silver, she thinks she sees a dark, amorphous shape expand beneath the water's surface, as if a bottle of India ink has been emptied into the pool. She slips outside and switches on the underwater lights. They cast wavery shadows, and the whole courtyard becomes a submerged landscape, potted orange trees undulating like plastic sea plants in the aquarium she owned as a child. The pool however is empty. Marella shakes her head, latches the door, and makes a mental note to drive to Santa Barbara in the morning to have her eyes examined.

When she sleeps, music quivers and darts through her dreams like an elusive school of fish. Two of the songs she

15

can remember her grandmother singing — "Yes, Sir! That's My Baby!", "Sweet Georgia Brown." Ice tinkles in footed crystal which clicks when it is carelessly set on a glass-topped table. Laughter, the scent of gardenia perfume, and the smoke from Cuban cigars weaves across the courtyard.

The next morning as she drives the six miles to town, she finds herself humming "Five Foot Two, Eyes of Blue."

She stands five foot eight in her stocking feet and her eyes are gray-green flecked with sienna. When the optometrist tells her they are in perfect working order, she decides she has been working too hard and takes the rest of the day off from the book she is writing, the second in a three-book teenage romance contract. She eats an omelet at a sidewalk cafe and window shops until her calves tingle, pleasantly tired.

On the way to her Volvo, she passes a vintage clothing store and pauses to look at a sequined chiffon scarf in the window. Impulsively, she buys the spangled, crimson and flame colored whimsy. The shop owner suggests that its previous owner was a flapper. His knowing smile tells her he assumes she has made her purchase for the effect it will have on the man in her life.

There is no man in her life — only the men in her romance novels which she has faithfully churned out on her word processor, three a year for the past five years. Ironic that the romance market should sicken along with her marriage, she thinks for the hundred and twenty-ninth time as she drives home. She vows she will write something substantial and significant as soon as she has fulfilled her current contract. Her writing has not been going well at all; perhaps this time she will keep the promise.

That night Marella turns on the underwater lights and the overhead courtyard lights before, her body exhausted, her imagination restless, she slides between the sheets. An hour passes before she is drawn to the doorway to stare at the pool. She sees nothing beneath the surface of the water, and feels ridiculous at letting her imagination run away with her outside the parameters of a book contract. She turns off the yard lights, and despite her best intentions to return to bed, steps outside to darken the pool, just to see what will happen this time, A slight breeze caresses the water's skin, raising liquid goosebumps which dance on the surface. As she stares at the pool, a murky cloud swells in the water, swirling like smoke — to her monochromatic night vision, pearl changing to the color of ashes, now charcoal. In the distance, a glass windchime tinkles.

Marella takes a tentative step toward the edge to better see, then flicks on the light and retreats to the safety of her bedroom. Perhaps she should make an appointment with a therapist. In her haste and agitation, she forgets to lock her door.

When sleep finally comes, she dreams of a man in white flannel pants and a dark, double-breasted jacket. The points of his shirt collar are rounded and fastened with gold studs that wink at her like eyes. Perched atop his dark hair, which is combed back from his forehead, is a straw boater hat. He smiles and extends a hand to her, leads her through a throng of guests to an art deco chair by the pool. He seats himself across from her, so close that although their knees do not touch, she can feel his warmth through her silk stockings.

The two of them are an island as waiters flow around them bearing trays of drinks while people talk of Herbert Hoover and prohibition, of the scandalous book, *Lady Chatterly's Lover*, and broccoli, an interesting vegetable now grown in Santa Clara. Henry Beaumont is producing a talking film with singing and dancing; he calls *The Broadway Melody* a musical. And aren't the paintings at the new Museum of Modern Art in New York City wretched eyesores? Now that you mention New York, tell me, what do you think about the stock market?

She spots a thin woman, bobbed hair nearly covered by a cloche. At her throat is a scarlet hued scarf that flows down her pallid shoulders like blood. It is the same scarf Marella purchased that afternoon. How unsettling it is to be upstaged at her own party, for this has suddenly become her party — it is her pool, after all. She touches her own throat lightly, fingertips skimming flesh, and realizes her neck is bare tonight. Her gentleman friend gives her a look which says this woman is of no significance, which says he would like to move his lips slowly over her throat. Marella feels her pulse thrum beneath her skin.

Waves of conversation surround them, ebbing and surging with a gentle rhythm. There is no need for Marella and her gentleman to speak. There is only need to look deeply into his lapis eyes as the band plays Rudy Vallee's theme song, "My Time is Your Time." When he leans forward she wonders if he will ask her to dance. Instead, he reaches for her right ankle and lifts it to his thighs. With a sinuous gesture he slides the pump from her foot and strokes the length of her silk-stockinged arch with his thumb. Marella leans back smiling at the sky spanned with paper lanterns of rose, magenta and mauve. The air she breathes is gardenia perfume. "Ninfea," he calls her with his mind, water lily, water nymph.

When she calls the therapist the next morning, she considers keeping whatever lives in the pool a secret. It and her dream visitor are intertwined, she knows. "I'm having a block with my writing," she finally tells Dr. Wert. She has chosen him from the Yellow Pages. He informs her of an opening tomorrow morning due to a cancellation.

In the afternoon when José, the pimple-faced pool

man, makes his weekly visit, she discusses the murky state of the water the last two nights. At first he takes offense, accusing her of saying he does not perform his job. She assures and soothes him. Eventually he agrees to test the water for algae. There is none. Neither have there been any dead birds or squirrels which might decompose and foul the water. No one has swum in the pool since she purchased the house.

Marella persists until José goes to his truck to look up the symptoms she has described, in a handbook of swimming pool maladies. He returns to tell her the text mentions nothing about seductively swirling mists which beckon in the night. He suggests that Marella hire a psychic or exorcist and starts to leave in a huff. Halfway to the door, he turns and apologizes to her, offering to call his cousin in Encino who reads tarot cards. Marella politely declines.

Dr. Wert is a Jungian, it turns out the next morning. He makes much of her decision to move to California when she reveals her fear of water to him in an attempt to make him smile, but he ignores her when she confides that she chose her new residence solely on its distance from New York and her ex-husband. He raises his eyebrow when she tells him how much she revels in her solitude, how essential it is to her livelihood as an author. She neither likes nor trusts him, she concludes after fifteen minutes. He is too stony faced and sober in his manner. To make matters worse, he doesn't smoke a pipe.

After half an hour, Marella has confessed her dream since it takes place by the pool, but she keeps the pool's phantom resident and her nightly illumination experiments a secret. Dr. Wert suggests that the male figure in the straw hat and white flannels is herself, her animus, actually — the male part of her psyche. The meeting may symbolize some sort of psychic integration; she is healing from her divorce. The swimming pool, a classic symbol of the subconscious, is important, as well. He leaves her to draw her own conclusions about how it relates to her fear of water. She will need to set up a series of standing appointments to work on that. Marella puts him off.

Her writer's block is not discussed, but when she leaves his office, she feels cured of it. She is so relieved she stops at a music store and buys a Bobby Short tape so she can listen to "Tiger Rag" while she works.

At home she sets aside her partially completed manuscript to begin a historical saga about the man in the boater hat and the gold collar studs. Mr. Animus, she will call him. It sounds very Italian, very mysterious and romantic. Mr. Animus, she plots, is the sensitive, yet masculine scion of a self-made wealthy family of immigrants. Mafioso, she amends. His family is connected with Al Capone's gang in Chicago, but he, a paragon of virtue, has escaped to California where he meets a hazel-eyed starlet who lives in a tastefully ramshackle Spanish style mansion much like her own house. Marella decides to make Mr. Animus everything she wanted her ex-husband to be for her, everything he was not. She will end the book with the wedding to end all nuptial ceremonies. She considers the possibility of a sequel covering the stock market crash.

After sitting for three hours in the sickly green glow of her word processor's screen without marring it with a single word, she gives up to bask in the late afternoon sun. The pool glistens like an aquamarine. For dinner she opens a tin of caviar and spreads it on water crackers, delighting as the cold, salty food slides down her throat. Tomorrow she will go to the library to research Southern California in the twenties and possibly the history of this house. She will investigate the possibility of signing up for swimming lessons and she will look in the Yellow Pages under "Psychics." Tonight she will dream.

Marella leaves both the courtyard and the pool unlit when she goes to bed, smiling at her previous childish attempts to keep whatever lurks beneath her subconscious at bay with high intensity nightlights. No sooner does she close her eyes than her Mr. Animus is seated on the garden chair in front of her, the ball of his thumb yet massaging her arch. He grasps her instep firmly as he massages the tendons in her foot and strokes the sinews of her libido.

"Tell me about yourself." Marella is empty of the tales she must spin like webs simply to live. She wants him to invent a book for her — one which ripples and flows without sharp edges or hard surfaces. "Tell me your story," she begs him with her eyes.

"Later, Ninfea," he mouths silently, and he turns to watch the dancers with deep set eyes. They do the Charleston, introduced years ago to the Paris cabaret scene by a Negro entertainer, Bricktop. It is late and their movements are far less energetic than when the party began hours earlier. The beaded fringes of the women's dresses click together as their bound-bosomed torsos dip and weave in the light from the Japanese lantern. Knotted ropes of pearls slide against flame colored satin. An ivory opium pipe is lit and passed.

Her foot secure in his lap, Marella dozes. When she awakens the courtyard is deserted. She gazes at Mr. Animus beneath her lashes, catching a shadow of despondency brushing his unguarded face. Does he know she's studying him? "Tell me your story," she begs him with her mind. His fingers trail absently up her stockinged calf to the back of her knee, sliding up the inside of her thigh to the exquisitely sensitive place where her stocking ends. "Tell me."

A tear slides from the corner of his eye and down his cheek. Once more he turns his face from her, this time, it seems, to memorize each tile in the pool, each irregularity in the mirrorlike surface of the water. He wills her into a torpor with his touch, and her heart slows though she is close to the water. The spaces between her breaths grow wider. She sleeps again, as if his sadness were a more potent drug than that made from poppies.

When in her dream Marella awakens, she awakens from it, also. For a moment she is disoriented. Her gaze wanders to that portion of the pool she can see from her bed. A layer of milky mist hovers over the surface of the water, its tendrils as intricate as seaweed. Marella spots movement in the mist, watches it part, catches a glimpse of Mr. Animus, his body naked and flashing in the moonlight. His back toward her, he seems unsure of himself, then enters the water silently. Although she knows he is swimming, she cannot hear the churning of the water, only the sound of the windchime in the distance, the sound of Rudy Vallee from the gramophone he has placed in the chair where he sat earlier.

With extraordinary clarity, she hears his regular breaths, hears the summons of his desire. He has prepared for this rendezvous. On her poolside chair rests a dark blue plate with two ripe amber pears, their skins so thin over aromatic flesh that Marella senses they ache as she does. Beside them lies a bone-handled paring knife, a drop of blood on its silver tip. Reflected in the blade, the moon is a glowing pearl.

Covering herself with a tissue-thin kimono, she stands before the mirror, combing her hair, tying her antique scarf in a tight headache band about her temples; she prepares to join him.

By the time she crouches at the edge of the pool, her

toes curling around the still warm tiles, he is lying motion-less on his back, hands clasped across his broad chest. He grins up at her with teeth white as moon dust, and she studies the whorls of dark hair on his chest and thighs. The men she has invented for her books pale beside this man who smells of caviar and pears.

He is wreathed in the cloudy liquid which so con-cerned her yesterday. It swirls about him like ribbons tied to his wrists. The flowing tendrils are red, they smell of salt and the sea. No matter. His penis points her way to him like a fleshy arrow. She feels herself opening, swelling out-ward like a gardenia blossom, her perfume wafting toward him. "Tell me your story," she begs him with her body.

Carried by an invisible current and shadowed by the wavering ribbons, he drifts away from her, to the middle of the pool. "Come here and I'll tell you," she reads in his unblinking eyes. The scarlet-tinged water is as warm as amniotic fluid. She imagines it embracing her, caressing her limbs.

"My time is your time," Rudy Vallee croons. Then the needle sticks in a groove of the record. "Isyourisyour isy-our."

Time stands still, trapped by the tiny spike of metal, until Marella arcs her body toward him and breaks the spell. She slides through the water like a foetus, like a fish. Ninfea.

When she fails to answer the bell the next morning, José uses his key and slips into the courtyard through the garden gate. All is silent except for the wind-stirred wavelets that gently pat the tiles of the pool. Beneath the reflected clouds that shimmer on the surface, a cloud of scarlet water floats, beckoning; while discarded on the bot-tom, the crimson scarf snakes and bleeds itself transparent and useless as a dead skin. ❧

The Rift In Autumn

THOMAS E. FULLER

Summer is retreating, falling back in on itself.
The defiant greens attempt to hold fast.
Attempt to comply to the seasonal imperative
That decrees this time, this cycle, is theirs.
But like tattered armies serving a dead king
They are forced from fastness to fastness
And their empty fortresses are filled to overflowing
With the triumphant paper armies of Autumn.
And still they come.

They blot the sky, malignant millions,
Wildly riding the apostate Apple Winds
Through the shuddering length of the Rift.
An insubstantial invasion deliriously burying
The defeated defenders in graveyards of color.
The Autumnal Gardens are dying,
Bleeding ten thousand captured Falls out
Into the vanquished summer air.
And still they come.

And the Twelve Cities, scattered like diamond dust
Along the silvered banks and islands of the Sheen,
Waken fully to the extent of Autumn's betrayal.
The vague unease has turned from apprehension to panic
And the people stand in blank amazement
As the fragile foolscap dragons blanket
Their streets and fill their parks to flaming capacity.
And still they come.

The elegant cloud carracks fight to rise
Over the drifting veil of spangled leaves
Only to plummet down broken-backed as their
Waxed silk wings and filament-wire frames
Collapse like badly made card castles.
The gaudy carnival barges plow the Sheen;
Their blunt bows splashing through leaves
Like lethargic ice breakers in the tropics
Until their ancient engines jam tight
And they are left abandoned on the Sheen,
Leaf frozen in aging Autumn hues.
And still they come.

And the temples are crowded with people
Who never crowd temples.
And the ancient prayers are chanted
By people who never chant prayers.
And there are those who stare at stained glass,
And those who stare at the distant balconies
Of the Palace of Night and Light
Shrouded by the Autumn blizzard of the Leaves.

And still they come.

ॐ

A Scent Like Silver

SUSAN MAcTABERT
illustration by
BOB GIADROSICH

When Lucinda broke the Silver Psyche hanging over her vanity, a splinter of the mirror-glass pierced the ring finger of her left hand. Blood, in oval droplets like strung garnets, dripped across the pale rose and saffron carpet as she left off retrieving the fragments to sit in the Morris chair by the window. Outside the antique, leaded-glass, winter's garden of perfect diamonds and brittle crystal dreamt in silence.

"Nothing wakes — nothing dares," she heard the bells, scented the silver. Lucinda sat upright.

The phoenix in lapis lazuli spread its descending wings over a tall mirror framed in opaline moons and carnelian poppies. It hung on the wall opposite Lucinda reflecting her fading color, her heavy lashes. Calmly she stared past the winter window and into the opening door of the phoenix mirror even as the splinter of Silver Psyche worked its way to her heart.

When Lucinda did not appear for dinner, her brother Tove went to her room and knocked. There was no answer so he called her name and opened the door onto darkness.

With reluctance, Selene rose from her bed of clouds and sent frosted moonlight glimmering in from the garden through the open window. Tove shivered in the cold and his heart quickened, with fright or with promise, at a scent fainter than violets, sweeter than narcissus — like silver — sweet silver. At the window, web-fine lace hung like a pall and, as he leant his palms upon the sill, he caught the dream-edge chiming of bells, paper-thin, costly.

There came a sigh, his name upon his sister's lips, and Tove turned suddenly from the window beside the empty chair to the tall phoenix mirror. It was as dull and unreflective as lead. Empty.

Hastily he lit a match and then a candle. Sure his sister must be hidden in the garden and teasing him, he leaned into the frozen night but her name would not come to him. The halo of gold candlelight flickered and grew wan as he held it aloft searching the sculpted, opiate landscape. Again her name rose to his throat and died there. Implacable, unfathomable, lulling — the bells — the sweet silver.

Forcing himself from the sill, Tove ran up against the vanity and mirrored shards of the Silver Psyche spilled and glittered, tinkling discordantly, to the carpet. From the pool of broken silver shimmering at his feet, he followed the garnet drops of blood across the pastel carpet to the carved Morris chair and then to the phoenix mirror. At the leaden surface, the dark trail stopped.

Fear wrenched his heart and stung his eyes.

"Lucinda!" he cried above the clamoring bells, and dropped the candle. It guttered and went out, leaving him in darkness and moonlight as he beat both fists upon the closed door of the phoenix mirror.

In the still before dawn, snow began to fall. It drifted in like stardust, spangling the sill, carpet and the left side of Tove's jacket as he sat in the Morris chair with his face buried in his hands. He had come to his senses some time ago and had stopped pleading with an unresponsive mirror, had stopped combing the house and garden. The answer was here — there: the Silver Psyche should never have been made, much less hung in a young woman's boudoir where she might dream.

"I never believed," he shuddered.

"Tove," came Lucinda's voice, dying.

He jumped to his feet and grasped the edges of the phoenix mirror in his hands. "Dear God, Lucinda!"

"Farewell —"

"Lucinda!" In desperation, he turned, picked up a handful of the mirrored shards and flung them against the dull glass. They jangled loudly and changed to strange black flowers that floated to his feet. Among the petals circling the heart of each was one of blood-red. Tove knelt, picked up a flower and raised it to his face. Blood from his cut hands stained the flower which smelled sweetly like silver. He leaned, spent, against the phoenix mirror and looked into it from the heart of the lotus — the black lotus. The frozen surface of the mirror ran like quicksilver and for a moment it brightened, steadied and gave back his own reflection. Then it wavered, like a pool brushed by trailing willows, and beyond — within — was Lucinda and another with lotus bells upon his damask cloak. Fading swiftly, like a dream-memory, the images vanished and the phoenix mirror closed.

Tove crushed the black lotus in his hands and let it fall. Then he got to his feet and left the room, leaving the door open behind him. He couldn't hope to fight the Dream-King.

They were all his: the clamoring bells, the sweet scent like silver, the secret of the black lotus and the Silver Psyche — as were all mirrors, illusions, dreams — as was now Lucinda. Morpheus. ⋙

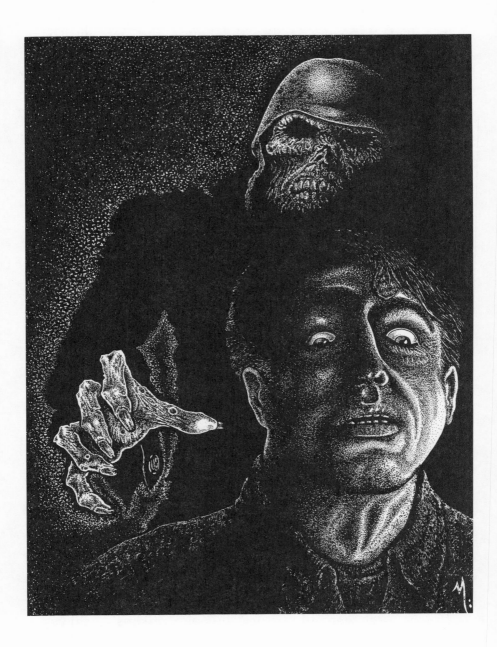

The Grey Smudge

JOSEPH PAYNE BRENNAN

illustration by
MICHAEL D. PARKS

August 25, 1984:

I make these notes for my own personal record. They may be of interest to me when this matter ends. I can't remember exactly when I first noticed it; I guess about six months ago. I'd sit down at the typewriter, as I am sitting now, and as I looked up, or perhaps paused to insert a fresh sheet of paper, I'd imagine I glimpsed a sort of grey smudge — in the corner of my eye or in the corner of the room — I wasn't sure which.

In the beginning I shrugged it off. I was behind schedule with several urgent assignments. I didn't have time to brood about a grey spot which, if it existed at all, might be nothing but the result of eye strain and prolonged overwork.

The annoying thing persisted however, and at length I consulted an optometrist.

After careful tests, he shook his head. "Your vision is fine and I can't find a thing wrong with your eyes. I thought it might be a so-called 'floater,' but there's no evidence of that."

He smiled at me, puzzled and concerned. "You do look a bit pale and tired. Why don't you take a vacation?"

A week later I boarded a jet for Bermuda. After five days of surf and sun, I felt fine. If I noticed anything out of the corner of my eye, it was definitely not a grey smudge.

Nevertheless, I was home and back working for only a

few days when I again noticed the irritating speck. It appeared to cling in the right-hand corner of the room, somewhat behind me. When I turned my head toward the corner, it slowly faded away.

I saw it again the next day and this time it looked larger. It had no discernible resemblance to anything I could name — just a greyish-black blurred shape about as big as a plum.

This brings the record up to date. It is now August 24th and I sincerely hope no further entries will be made — at least not in reference to this annoying business.

August 30, 1984:

I continue to catch glimpses of the damnable grey smudge hovering in the corner of the room as I sit working. It is slowly expanding in size and it does not disappear as quickly as before. I am trying to get more rest and fresh air. Aside from the smudge, my eyesight remains excellent.

September 8, 1984:

I am wondering whether or not I ought to make arrangements for a psychiatric consultation. The smudge not only persists but manifests itself more often than formerly. Also, while small and round at first, it seems to be changing shape — becoming longer and narrower.

September 15, 1984:

I am less and less able to concentrate on my work. The grey smudge has become an obsession with me. I find myself constantly glancing aside to see if it has appeared. I tried turning all the lights on — flooding the room with light — but the thing makes itself visible nevertheless. I find myself imagining that the corner of the room where it appears is still partially in shadow — in spite of the lights!

September 27, 1984:

Early this morning I telephoned for an appointment

with Dr. Renwick, the area's best-known psychiatrist. Last evening, as I was attempting to finish an overdue magazine piece, I glanced aside and once again saw the filthy smudge. This time it was no longer shapeless. It was not only longer and narrower — it now had a discernible shape. It looked like a detached finger, foul and blackened, floating in the air.

September 30, 1984:

Dr. Renwick probed deeply into my past life. He doesn't say so, but I sense that he believes I am withholding something. I became almost angry. In spite of that, I made another appointment. Meanwhile, he advises shorter work hours, long walks and — perhaps most difficult of all — the elimination of my evening martini.

October 9, 1984:

I have followed Dr. Renwick's advice, cutting my work time in half, taking three-mile walks, omitting my before-dinner martini, etc. — but nothing helps. The hideous dead-finger shape continues to hover in one corner of the room. The possibility nearly paralyzes me with dread — but I now believe it is in the process of acquiring accompanying digits. A thumb appears to be forming to the left of it.

October 14, 1984:

I find myself avoiding the typewriter more and more. I keep glancing aside; three times out of four the repellant thing is hanging there, toward the room's corner. It has grown into a full hand — hairy, shrunken, blackened as if by fire. All my adherence to abstemious living, exercise, etc. has come to nothing.

October 20, 1984:

Dr. Renwick is now obviously alarmed. He advises an immediate cessation of all writing projects. In addition, as soon as possible he wants me to embark on a long ocean voyage. I'm afraid I was not very tactful. I told him that by the time I paid his bill, I would be unable to travel to the Berkshires and back. He again delved into my past, without uncovering whatever it is he seems to be searching for. We parted amicably enough but I did not make a definite new appointment — as he suggested I do.

October 28, 1984:

Aside from the few minutes it takes me to make these notes, I have stopped writing. I decided to plunge into several authors I have long avoided: Proust, Henry James, Trollope — but I find it difficult to concentrate. After a page or two, I inevitably look up and glance aside. The hairy hand, as if suspended in space by invisible strings, is nearly always visible. Even though it looks as if it were extending itself into a wrist, I try to remain calm, recalling Dr. Renwick's assurance that it is merely an hallucination.

November 4, 1984:

The repellant appendage has now grown an arm up to the elbow, a full forearm. I picked up the phone to call Renwick and then put it down again. I have decided to forget his advice — which did no good — and resume my former habits.

November 12, 1984:

The damnable thing has grown into a full-length arm. It is covered with a brownish-colored sleeve of some kind, torn, splattered-looking as if it were covered with caked mud. I am trying to ignore it, forcing myself to finish a magazine piece. I will shortly get it into the mail.

November 22, 1984:

The arm has acquired a shoulder and I fear the shoulder will shortly begin burgeoning into — what? A neck and head, a torso? My days are filled with dread, my nights with wild tossings and terrible dreams. I cannot see it in the dark, but I know it's there. (The magazine article came back with an apologetic note pointing out many mistakes. On rereading it, I had to agree. In fact, the piece is almost gibberish.)

November 30, 1984:

I am haggard from loss of sleep. My appetite has vanished. My hands tremble; my face twitches. The monstrous thing has expanded into a half torso and a head. The facial area of the head is so far too blurred and unformed to discern individual features.

December 8, 1984:

In desperation, I now remain away from the house most of the day, in spite of the cold weather. I walk until exhaustion forces me to a park bench. I sit shivering until I am nearly numb. Only then do I return to this accursed house. It's always waiting in a corner of whichever room I occupy. It now has a full torso and a second arm. The facial features remain blurred — dirty looking and indistinct.

December 15, 1984:

I almost collapsed in a park yesterday. I barely made it back to the house. In my weakened, half-starved condition, the intense cold was too much for me to endure. I must stay confined to the house — much as I dread it. My only nourishment is hot tea and an occasional cracker. Dr. Renwick's hallucination — as I think of the ghastly thing — though still shadowy and dim, has finally taken on the complete, full-formed figure of a man. It hovers in a corner, motionless, waiting.

December 20, 1984:

In spite of deepening terror, I find myself gnawed with growing curiosity about the thing's appearance — its features in particular. The face stays strangely blotched and shapeless — almost amorphous. The head is now encased in an odd, rounded sort of hat. I am getting too weak to move from my chair, but I have decided that I will not seek out help. Something convinces me that it would be useless to do so. I shall wait the thing out. I cling to the hope that once it has fully materialized — it will disappear.

December 27, 1984:

I scarcely remember the holiday. The telephone rang a number of times and somebody hammered on the front door, but I did not stir from my chair. The hellish thing waiting in the corner becomes more repulsive by the hour. It appears to be attired in some kind of uniform, or what remains of a uniform, ripped, mud-grimed, splattered with tar — or is it blood? I have decided the face continues indistinct because it has been mauled — or crushed.

January 3, 1985:

The thing rarely leaves at all now — at most for no more than a half hour. When complete exhaustion forces me into a few minutes' sleep, I sense that it is still present. The lights stay on here — I hardly know night from day. The 'hallucination' appears fully formed and solid. It is dressed in an old army uniform — grimy, blood-smeared khaki. What I thought was a rounded hat is a metal helmet. The thing's countenance is still ill-defined because of a terrible wound; part of the face appears to have been ripped off — the rest is a mask of blood. I ask myself why this horror continues to haunt me and I have no answer.

January 7, 1985:

During my last brief interval of feverish sleep, I experienced a vivid and frightening nightmare. I was back with my division in World War II. We were near Aracourt and Lorraince, under intense German artillery fire. Lieutenant Rickson and I, acting as forward observers, were trapped in a barn in advance of Division Artillery Headquarters. A frantic radio call came in from Captain Skaron. At that point I awoke with a pounding heart. The damned thing was there in a corner of the room. I could swear it was staring at me. In spite of the nightmare and my ever-present fear of the hallucination, I got up and advanced on the thing. A kind of rebellious fury seemed to have seized me, a fury more intense than my fear. The thing faded away before I reached it but after I returned to my chair and sat down, it reappeared as before. I cannot stand much more; I shall either go insane or perish of sleeplessness and starvation.

January 9, 1985:

I have finally recalled the true circumstances of forty years ago which triggered my nightmare, and the possible basis of this whole frightful siege has become clear to me.

Captain Skaron called to instruct me to leave the barn and make my way across the adjoining field to a nearby ridge where I could get a good view of the German 88 artillery pieces which were decimating the Headquarters area. I was to radio back the map coordinates so that our own artillery could begin counterfire with some hope of success. I knew that the chances of crossing the field, scaling the ridge and returning alive were almost non-existent. There was no cover in the empty field; I would be under direct observation by German advance elements. And then I remembered that Captain Skaron was due for a transfer that very day. As soon as enemy fire slackened, he would in all likelihood leave Division Artillery Headquarters in a jeep and head for the rear echelon. In any event, I could always say that due to interference, his instructions to me arrived in garbled form.

I told Lieutenant Rickson that Captain Skaron was ordering him across the field to the ridge to report on the German gun positions. Rickson stared at me in momentary disbelief and then grimly shook his head. "That's what I get for having a few months' seniority!" We shook hands and he started across the field.

He was only a third of the way across when 88 shells

began whistling in. He started a zigzag course, dodged and doubled, but it was useless. The Germans could aim the deadly 88 artillery almost with the accuracy of rifles. When Rickson was less than halfway across, a shell struck only feet away. Almost immediately afterward, a shell hit the barn, setting it afire. I left my receiver in the burning building, crawled out and hid in a ditch.

Hours later, after the enemy fire finally slackened, I squirmed, crawled, and darted back to Artillery Headquarters. Captain Skaron had left and no one present seemed to remember exactly what his instructions had been. I reported that Rickson and I fled the burning barn after we spotted German infantry approaching. I said that Rickson was killed by a shell shortly after we left the barn and that a near miss had left me numb and disoriented. The field and ridge were fought over for weeks. Rickson's remains were never identified.

I now understand that my feeling of guilt, festering in my subconscious mind for many years, finally conjured up the monstrous apparition which appears in a corner of the room I occupy. I feel immensely relieved. Now that I understand the source of my haunting, I am confident that I can at last rid myself of it — exorcise it, as it were. After all, Lieutenant Rickson did have seniority over me. He was also more experienced. It was only fair that in spite of Captain Skaron's instructions to me, Rickson should have undertaken the suicide mission. I am sure he would agree. The thing which has driven me to near madness is not Rickson returned. It is only a foul and frightening hallucination incubated in my own subconscious mind — obsessed as it has been with a false sense of guilt.

I am sure that I will sleep better tonight.

January 10, 1985:

I did not sleep well. Fearful nightmares racked me

until I awoke, feverish and exhausted. I kept dreaming that Rickson pursued me round and round that empty field while German artillery shells exploded on all sides. Although Rickson had been mangled by a shell blast, his bloody face stayed only feet behind me no matter how hard I ran.

Nevertheless, in spite of the dream, I still feel that the worst is over. As I write this, I glanced aside, into the corner, and the grisly thing was gone!

I am free at last! Wait — my God! The thing is standing right behind me! I —   ❧

(The writer's account, still on his desk when police broke in, ended abruptly at this point. He had been strangled and his body had been savagely gashed and torn. Detectives do not place much credence in this lurid diary. They are searching for a demented homicidal intruder who may have escaped from an asylum. Their only clue is a brass button found clutched in the hand of the victim. It appears to have been pulled from the jacket of an old army uniform of World War II vintage.)

A Case Study

DONALD M. HASSLER

> . . . what the hurdles of
> self-consciousness can
> mean to a writer.
>   W.J. Bate, SAMUEL JOHNSON

When my student's father died, he lost control
So gradually it took almost a year
Of painful posturing to purge his fear
For death's liturgical and protean role.
In fact, he says he never dreams. But the toll
Must be immense as body tics and queer
Convulsive stammerings like stains appear
To soil the garments of his roiling soul.

But then by grace self-consciousness was gone.
He woke up clean, sweating in the dark
and phoned me with the innocent remark
That he missed his dad but welcomed the dawn.
Such secondhand accounts define the void
For me, and pay my filial debt to Freud.

ŝ

Marine Passage: Two Mothers

JANE YOLEN

"Death was the first mariner" — Cirlot

1. Isabelle

My mother sailed in a leaky boat,
the crab at work upon her throat,
and that awful smell, now sweet, now salt.
I blamed her for leaving
                              (as if dying were a fault).
It is years now since she's been gone,
but the beat of the waves on that beach goes on.

2. Betty

The crab that gnawed my mother to death,
not my mother, but mother nonetheless,
scuttled sidewise and exceedingly slow
up the spine's thin coast
                              and would not let her go.
She ranged five years on that dark shore
till Death came at last to row her over.

3. L'envoi

I wished it then, I wish it now:
That I had been in that boat's bow
to take their pain as if my own.
But we choose to bargain
                    when we know there's none,
excusing our relief that we're upon the strand
and the mariner has not come — yet — to take us
                              by the hand.

Skeleton Key

SCOTT H. URBAN

Oh Lord, how skillfully
   you wrought this

ivory cage. It holds us
   to treadmill reality

and focuses our eyes
   on that which

will eventually envelop
   us. Divine Warden,

your craft is such
   that we do not

realize we are behind
   bars until we

have slipped them
   forever.

२९

The Pursuit of Happiness

MICHAEL N. LANGFORD
illustration by
MARK MAXWELL

It was warm that day. I remember that so clearly. It would have blinded you to look straight up. I only know I was blinded by glimpses of a heaven populated with immaculate masses of clouds, performing their day-long, slow-motion square dances to golden sunlight songs. Trees gently embraced our lake, and they weren't pines or maples but only the most towering oaks, vast lives forever rooted yet ever reaching toward one another in the speechless breezes that played across those glowing emerald hills beyond the still waters of the lake.

Lisa casually reclined on the lounge mounted at the stern of our rowboat. Methodically pushing and pulling the oars, I paused now and then to fill my lungs with the clean, fragrant air and eventually propelled the small, smooth-gliding craft into a patch of shade, created beneath some ancient, looming, oaken arms.

And in that sudden coolness, as Lisa slowly turned her head, sending strands of dark, shining hair tumbling down her shoulder, she seemed to be taking in every sight, every sound, every piece of Paradise that was present.

Turning again to me, she spoke slowly, softly, breathlessly. She spoke of the beauty then bathing our senses round about with such care and of the wonder baptizing our hearts at that moment with nothing less than purest joy.

Then awakening from her trance for a strange, lucid instant, she begged me. Swear, she said. Swear we would return there someday.

I could only smile and nod. Satisfied then, my Lisa fell backward into a far-away grin, gazing into treetops as we paraded below them.

But soon she went into a monologue about the terribly boring duties and responsibilities of an Egyptian princess and, amid occasional giggles, continued to explain that her only respites from perching atop pyramids were these barge excursions up the Nile. I laughed along with her, but not so much at her ridiculous exhibition as toward the simple beauty of that moment.

We were intoxicated with happiness.

Later, while we floated steadily toward the picnic lunch waiting on shore, Lisa jumped straight up, pointing in that direction and proclaiming she had discovered America. Laughing, she lost her balance. I lunged for her, and we flung each other into the waist-deep drink. Still laughing, she found her footing and came up, splashing me like crazy. Then she launched out for land — half swimming, half wading — with me in soggy but hot pursuit. And in the gentle grip of ecstatic hysterics, we staggered ashore in each other's arms and fell, rolling into a patch of clover.

My eyes looked long and deep into the honey-brown mirrors that were hers. She grew quite still and quiet, though still grinning, and her eyes bloomed even wider, glistening. Opening her mouth slightly, she leaned my way as my own lips leaped forward, landing on hers, lingering in the moistness, then bounding slowly, tenderly across her jaw and down her neck.

I had known Lisa only two weeks, but all things before seemed incredibly empty by comparison.

Almost too good, I thought. Too good to be true. All of this. So wondrous, so gloriously strange. I wondered. I really wondered. I looked at Lisa. And she found my doubts, confidently bringing forth each of them into the dazzling sunlight and gently dispelling all of them forever with a kiss that could only be likened to the alighting of the first of all butterflies upon that trusting primeval blossom.

Then, as I lay beside her, staring up into the calmly stirring leaves, the pain pierced me. Intense, insistent needles drove again and again into my forehead, temples, eyes. I know she called my name. I know she did. And in that endless half-minute, fuzzy, phantasms of Lisa danced before me, leaning close with growing, amazed concern.

Again she called my name. But what was it? Blackness swallowed it.

Somewhere, in a meaningless later — which seemed not so much later as just beside or surrounding all that I knew — the black became gray. I was stretched out flat with my head thrown back. The cool air flowing through my nose and throat began bringing me back from a long lethargy. I only knew that each breath returned more of that clarity, that intoxicating sharpness I had missed for so long. Moving my fingers, I found cold steel beneath me and close around me.

The sound of a small motor preceded a flood of light at my feet. A door had opened. The slab on which I lay slid forward into the flood. I was blinded by white lights, white walls, and the stiff, baggy white suits completely encasing the silent pair who yanked me to my feet and began half dragging, half pushing me down a long, narrow, winding corridor. Our footsteps echoed as my head flew off into a whirling blur, falling finally again into that familiar black.

My eyes slowly brought focus to a white-on-white grid, an office ceiling. I was lying on an over-stuffed couch of some rough, gray material. Across the small room in a plastic eggshell of a chair sat my interrogator.

Who was he? A film star, a president, my god, my father? His wrinkled face quivered as he pronounced lilting phrases in a language that stirred my deepest sense of self. I became lost. So evocative were his words! So many forgotten faces came beckoning into the edges of my awareness! I wondered. Were these memories of my earliest thoughts? His rasping speech droned on, sprinkled with long, smiling pauses I soon realized were carefully designed to regulate the rush of unspoken emotions that these barely unremembered words thrust into my heart from the frontiers of my farthest and most ancient past. Yet even by realizing my interrogator's plan, I could do nothing at all to contain the rivers of long ago, tender reverie his undefinable utterances unleashed from my depths.

Then a few words lapsed into my conscious knowing like a suddenly remembered childhood game. The old man was asking for my name. I had no answer and could hardly believe it.

Neither could I grasp the starkness of this bleak, light-gray cubicle. And at that moment I found myself floating just above the space where the couch had been. My interrogator fluttered an eyelid as the couch again coalesced beneath me. They had removed it too soon. I was not quite lost.

Immediately, they abandoned the sentimental approach. All artifice would be stripped away, they claimed. There is no name, they mocked. At least no one name, they laughed in a variety of convincing tones and tongues from the speaker where the old man had been. No interrogator either, they sneered.

Then they told me I was lazy. Been on vacation too long. Time to get back to it. Seems like twenty-three years with only void before it, they mumbled. Always seems just like a lifetime. Good chemicals with the wires attached just right always do. But you can't live your life that way, they screeched.

And again the borders of memory attacked me. But this time it was a musty wardrobe filled with past vacations, all those things I had been for two weeks a year, once each year, to escape all that I was. I reached in, thumbing through the moth-eaten threads, then glimpsed in the murky depths of the wardrobe, something lurking uncomfortably close to the core of me. The carbon-steel shovel that was most of what I was.

Shore up the tunnel, they screamed. Maintain quota and ore quality.

I wouldn't accept it. I could not.

But then I saw them. And I knew I was seeing them. And they knew I understood. The tangled interlacing of routines and subroutines crowded onto ten-thousand cosmic strings stretched around all eighteen dimensions. And the datum that was I, waiting only for the next run, the next, hollow, number-crunching run, truly had no name.

You're only one or zero, which are the same, they yawned, turning away.

Or maybe One, I thought. And maybe The One, I said, leaping to the feet I knew I had had on the shores of a lake.

At the threshold of the light-gray cubicle, a door slid open abruptly just before I reached it. In mad flight I ranged for hours or days across the mazes of bright, winding corridors. At first I ran with hope, thinking I was surely being pursued. Then, upon realizing that I had no pursuers, that perhaps escape had no meaning, that maybe I had no meaning, I slowed. I stopped.

Crying, wailing, I beat my fists bloody against the morgue-like drawers lining every inch of every wall. I bounced off of wall after wall within the echoes of my screams until I noticed a name plate with writing so haunting. It was English.

I ran down hall after hall, faster and faster, scanning every name. After thousands of appellations, empty of any meanings, had flown past my weary face, I ran a finger finally across "Lisa." I pried open the drawer.

Somewhere those who might have pursued me awakened at last with astonishment and began their investigation. They spoke of security procedures, of unauthorized entry and activation, and of reprimands of improprieties, all for the sake of maintaining the appearances needed to mask their various cynicisms and apathies. Then they spoke of permits and the disposal of bodies. I could feel their voices, dissolving at the edges of what they had expected of me.

A rising full moon splashed silver into the treetops and across the water. I pulled back on the oars and drew a deep breath. Lisa smiled. ❧

Siren Strains

JAME A. RILEY

While abed in my cabin, it commences.
Slowly working its way between the
Night-birds and the distant, lakeside frogs.
Jumbled dissonance of eerie sounds
Assault my ears in a rising fugue.
Violent notes of an unknown player
Chip at my nerves like cold steel pick
On a colder block of ice.
Horrid resonance claws at me,
It seems,
From the fathomless forest dusk.
Pandemonium in icicle blades;
Red-hot needles sear my mind.
The din drives me mad
And I am dragged into the dreamland
of insanity by a
Horned musician's hands.

෮

Assassination Festival 11/22/63

MARVIN KAYE

The world is whining in the wind today
   The childhood baubles and their crystal-sweet delight
      Are ash crisping beneath the grate

The earth has slid its somber course again
   The glinting promises of polished-steel delight
      Are crumpled in the snow

The heart is chill with pain that will not cry
   The savages are posturing in benedictions bright
      And blood is flowing on the pyx

      GLASSY EYES SEARCH CLOUDDRIFTS
      Wormy fingers find a text
      CALLOUSED KNEES BRUISE THE EARTH
      FESTERED TONGUES CROAK IN SOLACE

      Where do the echoes of a carol die?
      In which mirror are sunsets etched?
      What book records our dead delight?

A woman is mute upon an agate shore

      What peace resounds among the drums?
      How many rainbows blast the twilight?
      Who choirs in the shattered air?

A child is stumbling on the calcium steps

> How many sorrows shall we strangle in the crib?
> Which lethean waters must we swizzle quick?
> What cineramic sunbursts should we view?

A woman grieves, but we must teach the child

> A bird twits in the thorn-brake
> Still upon a branch he sits
> Drinking of the droplets
> Running on the wooden leaves
> His song foretells his flight
> Among the thorns

ε

Door Closing

WENDY WEBB
photo by
ERIC TURNMIRE

They were like cats, teeth bared, clawing their way out.

He could feel the hair on his neck bristle in defense. It was too late. Soon they would be all around him. Crowding. Pushing. His hands started to shake. Beads of sweat popped out on his forehead.

They became piranha in a feeding frenzy.

He stood frozen in place, helpless to stop the flood of humanity pulsing towards him. Another door to the grand ballroom swung open releasing its occupants. The business meeting was over and he had left too late. They would surround him, violate his fears. Suffocate him.

He took a deep breath and felt his chest tighten. He pushed, forcing the air out and heard the shrill crowing of a wheeze. He knew that the veins in his neck would be bulging.

They were around him, swallowing him whole into the gaping maw. He closed his eyes against a surge of nausea and wondered how much longer he could stay standing.

"Get out of the way." The voice was hostile, menacing.

"Hurry," another voice said, "I want to beat the traffic home."

He felt a briefcase hit the back of his thigh and shuddered at the touch. A rolled up newspaper raked across his sleeve. A kaleidoscope of smells burned his nostrils: perfume, sweat, cigars. He felt the pitch and yaw of the crowd and knew that he was moving with it. The only thing worse than his fear of crowds was his fear of heights.

But he was better now, he told himself. Better than he used to be. Therapy had been of some help. At least for a while. So he had avoided elevators, escalators, airplanes, and until now, crowds.

The mob reached a bottle-neck and slowed to a shuffle. If he could just reach the door, breathe a little fresh air.

"Are you okay?" The tall, slender, red-haired woman, only inches from his nose, peered closely at him. "You look kinda sick."

"I'm . . . okay. Just . . . need . . . air."

"Maybe I can help." The red-head took in a deep breath and bellowed, "Move on. Sick man," then faced him with a wry smile. "Cheerleading paid off." The smile turned to a grimace as a handbag hit her in the shoulder. He heard her mumble "Animals" as she was enveloped by the throng and ushered off unwillingly to another part of the building.

The bottle-neck loosened, and people swarmed to take up the space. The crush intensified throwing him against a wall. Propelled by the mass, he slid sideways across the face of the wall. He could feel the velvet roses of the gaudy wallpaper scrape against his clenched fists. Then suddenly it was metallic cool, hard and unyielding. He tried to turn but felt a "give" and stepped back so as not to fall.

The voice was prerecorded. Inhuman. "Door closing."

He stood transfixed as the door to the elevator slid shut on quiet tracks and began its ascent.

"Level two," it announced.

He jabbed the buttons and saw them light at his touch. "Level three."

Adrenaline surged through his body. His knees began to shake. He lifted a trembling hand and punched the red disk marked "Emergency."

There was no response.

"Level six." The glass, cylindrical prison rose silently on its cables.

Sweat poured from him, through his shirt, his jacket. It didn't matter. The only thing that mattered now was to stop this thing. To get off. He would take the stairs down. The narrow tube of an inside stairwell resonating with his every footstep, would be a joy right now. If only he could get to the steps. If only . . .

The phone.

Of course. There was always a phone on elevators. And a voice waiting to help on the opposite end. He would call and explain his awkward situation. He hoped his voice wouldn't crack when he spoke.

"Level ten."

He wiped a sweaty palm on his trouser leg and reached for the small metallic door marked "Phone. For emergency use only." He tugged and felt the spring loosen throwing the door open. He picked up the blood-red receiver and held it to his ear. His eyes scanned the instructions and stopped when he saw the small hand-scrawled notice attached to the dial. His mouth dried to dust as he read and reread the message: TEMPORARILY OUT OF ORDER.

"Level sixteen."

He closed his eyes against the flood of panic, and felt himself slide to a sitting position on the floor. He took a deep breath and forced a look onto the lobby area. The people had become small insects, becoming yet smaller. Tiny, tinier, tiniest. He had considered entomology as a major one time, but was forced into something more practical. Forced?

"I'm telling you, son, don't waste your time with

bugs. Let the Raid men handle them. They've got the experts. They don't need you." His father had paused for a deep breath in yet another one of his tirades. "Business. Now that's the thing to get into. It's practical." A frown crossed the old man's face. "For God's sake don't slump. Sit up. And whatever you do, don't let your voice crack when you open your mouth."

Tiny, tinier, tiniest. He could barely see the lobby now. Soon they would be in the jam of traffic fighting to get home. And he? He would be riding the elevator to whatever destination it had decided on.

"Level forty-two."

Forty-two. Do I hear forty-three?

"Level forty-three."

He would have laughed out loud if it had been some TV sit-com character entombed in a run-away elevator. But it wasn't. It was himself locked in a glass cage forced to face his fears. He looked out through the glass. The people had become specks of dust. They were barely moving now. He putted a breath on the glass and wrote his initials in the moisture, then sat up suddenly. He blinked with the realization and felt a smile starting.

He was going to be okay. He was going to be okay. He'd weathered the crowds of the lobby; looked out the glass of the moving elevator and saw the safety of the ground fall away; even had the nerve to initial the wall with his own breath. The elevator was going to have to stop eventually. He would simply and casually — get off. It was all so simple now. He wondered why he never realized it before. He could hardly wait for his next therapy session. There would be so much to talk about.

"Level seventy-six. Door opening."

Seventy-six. It was a long walk, but he could do it. It had been worth the wait. He scooted through the door before it could close on his courage, and felt a stiff wind cut through his jacket. A button popped off and fell silently away.

The muffled voice came through metal sliding together on its tracks: "Door closed."

He inched a foot forward and felt the concrete come to an end. He didn't have to look to know that an elevator call button wasn't there. Would never be there.

The only way down to safety and a next therapy session was gone.

The high-pitched scream of the elevator cables merged with his own. ❧

Midnight Visit

CARLETON GRINDLE

Greatly changed from what I remembered, but recognizable, he walked into the room. I rose from the chair but did not offer him my hand. A clot of dirt fell from his bony arm and shattered dryly on the linoleum. He stood watching me, I don't know how or how long. After a time, I sat back down again.

There was nothing I could say, nothing I wanted to say at that exact moment. Nothing that would help.

Much that would hurt.

"I said I'd be back." His voice seemed sad.

"Tom," I told him. "I'm sorry."

His sockets gazed at where my head had been when I was standing. He stood still. Had he not really seen me? Had my feeling he was looking at me been only an illusion?

His voice was dry and distant. Death was his ventriloquist, I thought. "I'm sorry, too."

"I deserve this," I said. "For what I did, I know I deserve this. Only — Tom, I'm scared. You really got me scared."

Tom stepped closer. He came up to where I sat and stood there, arms swinging at his sides, fleshless fingers flexing. The dark, deep sockets still refused to consider me.

The tears streaming down my face weren't scalding; they were icy cold. "I deserve what you came here to do to me, Tom. But, oh, God — "

"You didn't mean to kill me. Is that it? You didn't mean it?"

"I won't lie to you. I did mean it, at the time. Oh, God, I did mean it. But ever since —. All these months, Tom, all these months. I've regretted it. I've felt so much guilt. I'm so damned sorry for what I did."

"I know."

"You know? How? You can't know."

"Yes I can. The dead dream. They can't help what they dream. I dream about you. Even your thoughts."

Jerking, his hands moved toward my throat. They paused. I felt his fingertips brush against my skin.

I said, "Please don't."

His hands stopped shaking. "I wish I could." They moved again. "The dead can't help what they do, either."

The Lon Chaney Factory

BRAD LINAWEAVER

illustration by
JAME A. RILEY

The darkness was not complete. A green shape moved within. A hand. It sidled across an unseen floor, spider-like. The merest sound of scratching could be heard in that Stygian womb. Then the hand rose into the air, pointing a luminescent finger at a sliver of white light that had just come into existence, growing as a door opened — flooding the room with scenery.

A gruff voice spoke: "I've seen that before. What else have you got?"

A quiet voice answered: "Nothing special, I'm afraid."

Screaming, an old crone on a broomstick swept down from bat-clustered rafters to glare at guests on the floor far below. She flew right through the fat producer who was the owner of the gruff voice, and who almost lost his unlit cigar as he yawned at her mad face. "Halloween again?" he asked of nobody in particular.

Through an octagonal window at the producer's left, the full moon turned into a blood-shot eye. A skeleton hand groped its way out of the floor in front of him. Wolves howled way down in the machinery beneath. "Let's see the rest of it," said the producer, and the two men walked farther into the gloom.

Out of a circle of darkness strode Count Dracula, fangs gleaming from no discernable light source. At his right loped a werewolf. A gauze-covered hand reached out just behind the producer and . . .

63

"Turn it off!" said the gruff voice.

"Yes, Mr. Cordone," said his companion, removing a small card from his vest pocket, and touching a button on its clean, plastic surface. The monsters were gone. The light was on. Two men stood alone amidst a few props in what appeared to be an abandoned factory.

"Look here, Fossett," said Cordone, mouthing his unlit cigar, "we've got more vampires than we can shake a stick at and mummies coming out the kazoo. I wanted something different this time."

The younger man paused before asking, "What about my suggestion to get away from horror for a while? We could try a musical revue, say."

Cordone turned so that his cigar — which seemed a natural extension of his face — was pointing at Fossett's chin. "Doctor, I hired you for your technical skills, and you're not a half-bad scenarist. But basic showmanship is *my* job! I like your test holograms for a thirties musical program. If the market ever wants 'em, we'll provide. But now we're in the biggest horror boom since the holo shows caught on. And I want something that will swamp the competition."

Fossett wished he hadn't used that word — it reminded him of his failed swamp monster proposal from the previous month.

Cordone kept on: "Where the hell are the smells? I didn't get one whiff from the decay of rotting corpses or any of that stuff."

"Trouble with the software. We'll have it all together by the end of the week: sounds, smells, colors . . ."

It was as if Cordone hadn't even heard him. "What you were just showing me was going to run the full gamut, right? Frankenstein's Monster was next, I suppose, complete with thunder and lightning."

Ted Fossett brushed his black hair back on his head, and took a deep breath. Now was as good a time as any. "Mr. Cordone, I've been giving this matter a lot of thought. There is really nothing wrong with the concept of our current show. The audience feels at home with the traditional elements, as if they were long lost relatives. The trouble is in the faces."

"Yeah?"

"There aren't any."

The producer removed his cigar from a suddenly pensive mouth. "You trying to be cryptic with me? Never mind. You can explain what you mean over lunch. I've gotta be outside for a minute. If I don't light this weed and smoke it pronto, I'm gonna die."

On the ride over to the restaurant, Fossett spent his time trying to avoid the acrid cigar smoke and thinking up a proposal for his next holo-show that would be Cordone-proof. With the finality of a dungeon door slamming shut, he'd settled on his course of action by the first course of their meal at The Oyster's Shell.

"Now, what did you mean about faces?" asked the producer, mouth finally sans cigar and about to go to work on a martini.

"You're not really bored by the subject matter of your horror house: it's not familiarity with the material that's the trouble. Our monsters don't have faces. Our Dracula isn't Lugosi or Lee or Jourdan or Langella or Tomikin. He's a vague approximation of a childhood memory, a painted mask. That's the trouble with all the characters."

"You propose to redo the monsters based on famous actors in the roles?"

"I would, except that you were also right about having saturated the public with these particular images already. They are so used to seeing the figures as they stand, they wouldn't even notice improvement in detail. No, we need something different."

The producer was smiling now. He started on his second martini. It did his heart good to see creative employees being creative. "Something new?" he asked.

"Something old. Something with terror, yet also a memory. A program built around the portrayals of one great horror star."

"I like it! How about Boris Karloff?"

"A wonderful suggestion, but many of his famous roles are already part of the package we're selling. Oddly enough, we do not have a single characterization from the first movie star to be associated with macabre roles."

"Who's that?"

"Boss, I give you Lon Chaney, the man of a thousand faces. And what a face!"

A hundred photographs covered the walls of his office. Fossett had a good research team at Doppelgänger, Incorporated. Some of the old boys went back to the period of animatronics and robot mockups. They'd made the transition to the holograms readily. Looking at the photos that they had managed to gather, he figured they'd make good librarians as well.

He saw that most of the material was on loan from The Ackerman Museum. A booklet on the Chaney section of the collection was on his desk. Other photographs would be forthcoming. And holos would be made from them as well as the films.

Fossett had insisted on seeing the classics. His grandfather had been, what they called, "heavily into nostalgia." That's how, as a boy, Ted Fossett had seen the original version of *The Phantom of the Opera*. Old flickering melodrama that it was, the picture had exerted a strange hold on its young viewer . . . as it had for generations before him. For the first time, Ted Fossett had beheld the face of living death. He could not forget.

The first photograph he went over to examine was of the phantom. It was the only one in a frame. Yes, it was as he remembered, and yet there was something more. He turned away, waited, looked again.

Had there been a subtle change? Those high cheekbones, protruding to such an extent that they almost seemed to be eggs pushing their way out of the side of his head, had shifted, perhaps. Or the way in which light moved across the skull face, forming a spiderweb of shadow lace, above which the black eyes stared . . . was there movement? The phantom seemed alive in that frame, under the nonreflective glass. The eyes seemed to follow the viewer around the room.

He took the picture off the wall and held it close. *Memory comes on little cat's feet.* He was holding his first nightmare. He'd forgotten just how effective that old movie had really been. It had taken a second bow in his dreams.

Doppelgänger, Inc., wasn't in the business of dreams. It was in the business of convincing people that they remembered what they had really forgotten. The more superficial, the better! The movies for which they provided holographic effects were simple minded trips, offering the audience one easy-to-digest emotion per film. He couldn't bear to watch them. At least these souped up haunted houses had the merit of lacking pretension.

Until now. Wasn't he biting off more than Mr. Cordone could chew? He looked at the phantom in his hand. He looked at the picture's frame. Until now, the holo-shows had been nothing but frames. Now he was proposing to put a picture in that frame.

It had better be the right picture. With the amount of money he would be spending in the next three months, he couldn't afford to be wrong.

Trouble comes in threes. That's what he was telling himself, over and over. First, he had overslept. Dogs barking in the night had awakened a mockingbird that began to sing. Perhaps the all-night illumination in the street by his house had confused the demented bird into thinking it was daytime, but whatever the reason, its distracted chirping had gone on until dawn.

Oversleeping wasn't so bad, he insisted. One of the reasons to be an executive was to occasionally slip back into patterns of freedom from the good old days of unemployment. Just so that it wasn't frequent. He had no desire to return to the good old days of starvation.

That's what made the second problem so intolerable, the thought that he wouldn't just be late for his appointment, but might miss it altogether. Of all the times to run low on a charge! The blue beetle shape of his car was already the size of a coin in the distance behind him. He was near enough the research plant that it made more sense to finish the trek on foot than to go to a supply station. He could send someone for the car.

Naturally it had to be a hot day. Mouth half open and his eyes stinging, he noticed that beads of perspiration were even showing through his watch that he had taped to his wrist, as he did every morning right after his shower. He wiped off the face on the thin film of poroplast so that he could once more masochistically take note of the lateness of the hour.

Every step kicked up small dust clouds that made straight for his eyes. *My kingdom for a handkerchief,* he thought. The blue sky, the flat horizon, the sun baking his neck to a wattled brown — it all put him in the mood for the air-conditioned dark of one of his holo-shows. It was still a long walk before that.

One minute he was trudging down an isolated country road, wondering what his third stroke of bad luck might be; the next, he changed his mind about the fates. A car pulled up beside him, an old gasoline burner. "Need a lift?" asked the man inside.

The top was down on this old convertible. Fossett had a good look at the man behind the wheel. He was a nondescript sort, his long brown face relaxed under an old fashioned touring cap. "Don't see many of those anymore," said Fossett.

The man's eyes gave him the once over. "What, my cap?"

"Oh no," answered Fossett, laughing. "I mean the antique."

"She runs just fine. You getting in?"

Fossett needed no further inducement. The worn leather seat was especially comfortable after the mile he'd walked on foot. From a recent cleaning, the covers had a fresh smell that was new to him.

"Where you headed?" asked the driver.

"Not far. There's a new research and development lab of Doppelgänger, Incorporated, at the end of this road and, say, it dead ends there. Where are *you* headed?"

The driver allowed himself a thin smile. "Same place. I work there."

Fossett had not been to the plant before. A recent addition to his holdings, with new equipment — and ideas — that industrial spies would happily sell to the competition, Cordone had seen to it that it was in an out of the way place. The regular staff had a barracks behind the plant where they would feel that they were living the austere life

of boot camp privates except that they knew they were DI
employees receiving triple overtime for shifts lasting no
more than a month at a time. The executive staff was flown
in. That's how Fossett was supposed to have arrived,
except that he missed the shuttle.

Somber thoughts of uncharged private vehicles were
sneaking around in his mind when he noticed that the fuel
gauge on the old coupe read near the top. Wondering
where his benefactor had found so much gasoline, Fossett
opted for a different question: "What department are you
with?"

"I'm the janitor." The man straightened his arms on
the wheel and brought his head back on his shoulders until
there was a popping sound. "Not as limber as I used to
be," he said.

"Oh," Fossett replied. "I'm with the holo development
team. My first time out here, though. I normally work closer to town. Anyway, it was fortunate you passed by. I
appreciate the lift."

"Sure." This response seemed to satisfy the man. It
didn't satisfy Fossett, but he was through talking. It was so
damned hot. He was thirsty and tired. Now the old fashioned nature of the transportation seemed more irksome
than welcome. How could anyone stand to drive around
without air conditioning?

Fortunately, the trip was nearly over. As the mush-
room-shaped building came into view — its whiteness
almost blinding in the afternoon sun — Fossett spoke to
the driver once more. "I'm Dr. Fossett. You'll have to let me
buy you lunch sometime."

"I'd like that. Maybe I can do something for you."

Fossett waited for the man to give his name. He didn't
The long silences were becoming annoying. He felt a need
to make conversation, no matter how inane. Unprompted,

a question slipped out: "How did you ever wind up a janitor?" Instantly he regretted the phrasing.

There was no hesitation in the man's answer: "I've
always looked for jobs nobody else would do — or could
do. Here we are." The car pulled into a slot marked MAIN-
TENANCE. "I'll see you later," finished the driver. There
was something languid about the manner in which the
man unwound himself onto the ground. Walking with a
cat-like grace, he went into the building, while his passenger continued to sit in the hot car in the hot afternoon. At
length, Fossett seemed to wake up, wiped the sweat from
his forehead, and followed the man into the coolness of the
building.

It was a side door through which he entered. If the
other installations of the company had struck Fossett as
unbearably antiseptic, they were nothing compared to the
hospital sterility of this place. The odor was of every disin-
fectant known to the nose of man. A dull hum emanated
from the walls and was so annoying to Fossett that he forgot his thirst. Taking a few steps down the hall, the echoes
sounded as the beating of gongs in the palace of an Asiatic
despot.

"You're not supposed to be here!" A woman's voice
reached him from behind. He turned. The same voice
spoke in an entirely different tone: "Oh, Ted. Excuse me."
She walked over to him, wearing sane sneakers that did
not bellow at his dust-laden ears. "We were worried that
something had happened to you."

"Blossom!" he replied cheerfully. That was one good
thing about the hallway. There was plenty of light. Once
again he admired the fine doll features of Dr. Tajima, a very
talented Japanese woman who, among other things, had
introduced him to the pleasures of sushi the night he had
wanted to taste everything. Now they exchanged a brief

kiss.

"Plenty happened to me. Don't ask! Am I too late for the demonstration?"

"The Lon Chaney Factory cannot begin without you."

"How in God's name did you become involved with this project? I thought you were still in Fuji."

"Cordone brought me over as a surprise for you. Besides, some of the work was farmed out to the Japanese branch."

They were walking down the hall as they talked. She punched for an elevator as he said, "But I didn't know about that. I should have been informed."

"You know how Cordone loves surprises."

"Yes," he answered ruefully. "I hope there aren't any more. At any rate, I shouldn't be complaining. If the janitor hadn't picked me up, I'd still be walking that damned road to get here."

"Janitor?" Tajima asked as the elevator door sighed open.

"Yeah," he answered as they stepped inside. "He gave me a ride."

She looked at him closely, then said, "There isn't any janitor here, Ted. The building is fully automated."

The doors closed.

>   *. . . the tintinabulation that so musically wells*
>   *. . . from the bells, bells, bells, bells . . .*

The Hunchback of Notre Dame ushered them into the bell chamber of the cathedral, where he threw his twisted body with unexpected grace upon the heavy ropes. The clanging was almost loud enough to hurt the ears of the hunchback's visitors. Almost, but not quite. The customer was always right.

It seemed to be Chaney's hunchback: God knows that

Fossett wanted it to be. With microscopic attention, he watched the performance of the hologram. Its body movements were copied from Chaney — the athletic gyrations under the heavy rubber padding accenting the suffering of the gnarled face under the chaos of scraggly hair that would be forever famous as a visage of noble torment. They had taken the movements right out of the film and transported them here. Through computer overlays, they had extrapolated what different movements would be, and the final result worked.

Except that something was missing. Fossett was about to comment, but Tajima was already several steps ahead, gesturing for him to follow. Reluctantly, he left the cathedral set . . . and entered a circus ring.

He Who Gets Slapped bounded up close to Dr. Fossett, the smile on the white clown's face not covering the frown underneath. For three full seconds, Fossett stared into that face, as closely as he would peer at his own reflection in the shaving mirror. The pathos was there, as he had remembered it. Yet something was wrong, as there had been with the hunchback. He was about to tell this to Tajima when the lights went out around him.

The moaning of wind through junkyards. The faraway call of a lost train whistle. When the light came back on, the circus was gone. But the clown was still there, only a few feet away, standing with a slightly stooped posture. The white of the face and the suit was brightly outlined in the moonlight. Cold orb above; sad clown below.

When Fossett had written the script for the Chaney holo-show, this had been his favorite scene. It was inspired by an old article by Robert Bloch with the unforgettable Chaney quote: "A clown is funny in the circus ring but what would be the normal reaction to opening a door at midnight and finding the same clown standing there in the moonlight?"

"It works," said Tajima in his ear, taking him by the arm.

"It *should* have . . ." he started to say, but broke off.

She either didn't hear him, or pretended not to. Already she was walking ahead again, saying, "Wait until you see this!"

This was a collage. First, they stepped into a set for a laboratory. Dr. Ziska bowed in welcome. The white lab coat did nothing to put the mind at ease when noticing the countenance above it, Chaney's 1925 performance as a mad scientist from *The Monster*, truly a film that foreshadowed much. The Ziska hologram pointed to a sliding panel that was opening in the stone wall, that perennial device of the silent melodrama. A procession of characters entered the room, to surround Fossett and Tajima, all of them Chaney, all of them menacing.

The ape man of *A Blind Bargain* shambled off to one side as the ghoulish vampire of *London After Midnight* took up a position directly in front of Fossett. He bowed to the lady, this pale fiend, making a motion to tip his stove-pipe hat, but thankfully not removing it, as one feared it was an essential portion of his head . . . and removing it would reveal the gray matter of an evil brain. The razor-sharp teeth were visible in the partly open mouth, a nasty slash that bisected his pallid face. Fossett thought this to be the most effective holo thus far, even though it left something to be desired.

He was just about to see the truth lurking behind those popping eyes when his attention was drawn elsewhere.

Tajima was approached by The Red Death, that disguise worn by the phantom in one of the more ironic moments of Chaney's career. The skull mask remained in place. There was to be no unmasking here. Yet whatever was bothering Fossett about the other figures did not disturb him about The Red Death at all. Why? He had to know!

Others came: the armless man with the magic feet from *The Unknown,* a character of many facets, but here displaying only a scowl. He was followed by the legless man of *The Penalty,* and his frown seemed burned on — that was a feature of his character that Fossett remembered. Together, these two seemed to make a whole person.

There was more, such as the Fu Manchu appearance of Mr. Wu, complete with Mandarin's robes, but also wearing a loathsome grin that Fossett had never seen in any of the research material. Then came Singapore Joe from *The Road to Mandalay* — there was nothing monstrous about this character but for his all-too-human cruelty. Fossett didn't remember the scars on the man's face being quite so pronounced as they now appeared. As for the film-covered eyeball, that white egg orb . . . had it been as large as was evident on the holo?

So it went. Figure after figure, sneer after sneer, the varieties of character had all been covered over by a smooth sheet of malice. Terribly different expressions had somehow been made to appear identical.

"I think I've seen enough," he told Tajima. "We still have a lot of work before us."

"All right," she answered, raising her clipboard and touching a button on the attached communications card. The show was over. From where they were standing, they could see all the sets, including the largest one just ahead of them: the phantom's chamber.

"What's wrong?" she asked, as they headed back the way they'd come.

"Two things. One, I don't like the changes in my script. I'd stressed the multitude of Chaney's portrayals, each one special."

"They kept the hunchback and clown segments exactly as you wrote them, according to my notes."

"I can see that. However, this last bit in the lab scene had all these different personalities treated in the same unimaginative fashion."

"Those changes came from Cordone. He left your grand finale with the phantom untouched." The smile she offered was less for him than for her; she didn't enjoy being the bearer of unwanted news.

"How obliging of him," said Fossett almost under his breath.

"He'll be here shortly. He wanted to watch the finale with you so you're not really missing anything. Ted, you said there were *two* things that bothered you. What was the other?"

His left eye had started twitching. *Damn tension comes with the job,* was the message of the ragged nerve. "I'm not sure," he admitted, "but whatever it is, it's the real problem."

As they left the demonstration area, the first person they ran into was Cordone. The way he was standing in front of the doors made Fossett think of holograms. He'd always felt there was a basic unreality about the man, even though the checks were tangible enough.

"What's this about a janitor?" asked the producer without preamble.

Tajima took the lead. "There was an intruder whom Ted noticed. We've had staff looking for him but there is no sign of either him or his vehicle."

Cordone was in his element: "Well, dammit, that probably means he got away! We're too near our next release date for a spy to steal our thunder."

"I don't think he was a spy," said Fossett.

Cordone turned on the sarcasm: "Besides being late today, you're also playing detective? How do you know?"

"There was something odd about him. A spy wouldn't draw attention to himself by driving an antique. He wouldn't try slipping in under cover of a job that doesn't even exist. Although I was convinced there was a janitor when I saw the maintenance parking space."

"That's for robot supplies," said Tajima.

"Well, I've turned it over to our best security people," said Cordone. "All I need is a description from you since you're supposed to be so hot with faces."

"Faces!" exclaimed Fossett. "That's the problem in there. What have you done with Chaney's faces?"

The change of subject was accepted easily enough by Cordone. He'd been waiting for Fossett to make the complaint. "Sit down, doctor." he said, then noticing Tajima, amended that to the plural. Joining them in the most comfortable chair — which unconsciously the other two had left for him — Cordone took out one of his hyperthyroid cigars.

"Excuse me, sir, but smoking is . . ." began Tajima.

"Perfectly safe this far from the equipment," he finished for her. "I'm not interested in your convenience. I do worry about machinery that costs a small fortune. And I worry when my people lose sight of the priorities, eh, Fossett? Now, what's the trouble?"

There was something cold inside Fossett's stomach. "You've changed my design. I wasn't told."

"*Your* design? Oh, you mean what you designed for me. The minor alterations were done for purely monetary reasons. Nothing to concern yourself over."

Tajima did not hide the concern in her voice: "The

script changes were for dramatic reasons, Mr. Cordone. That's what my memo indicates."

"Honey," he said, and there was nothing of sweetness in his voice, "Fossett and I aren't talking about *that*. We're talking about a much bigger change, but one I *had* to make. And I remind you that positions in the entertainment field are not protected by the World State. If you want to keep your job, just shut your pretty oriental trap."

She was too surprised by the crudeness of his remarks to say or do anything. If anything registered in her expression, it was fascination that she finally realized the sort of man who was her boss.

"I liked your Lon Chaney idea from the start," said Cordone to Fossett, "but we couldn't afford the detail. That part was out."

The detail. The lines in the face. The subtle ones underneath the smiles and the frowns. The remarkable skull of the man they called Lon Chaney. Fossett had dreamed about those contours of flesh and bone. More than that, he had seen the pain that the silent cinema star had inflicted on himself to achieve his difficult results.

As far back as the 1930's and the first decade of sound movies, technique had been standardized and union makeup artists took over the job. It was the same as every other area. The Twentieth Century was the age of unions — before increasing centralization rendered such organizations superfluous.

Lon Chaney had been the last great cinema artist of an earlier period reaching its full flower in the twenties. It was the hard, rough world of the self-contained showman. He was actor, mime, story consultant, and designer of a thousand faces. And he knew the ropes.

"When I realized what you wanted," said Cordone, blowing a cloud of cigar smoke that to Fossett was taking on the features of a gravestone, "I almost laughed myself sick. Capture every line of every face! Bring out every nuance. Run a program to anticipate what new postures, new lighting, would mean to those roles. Fossett, who's gonna spend that kind of money? As the rest of your package was good, we went ahead with it, minus the absurd details. You were too busy to keep track of it anyway."

"Then it's just the same," said Fossett to the floor, "as all your other holo-shows. You've taken the soul out, and left nothing but masks."

"I give the public what I want. Nine times out of ten, it's what they want, too. They're lookin' for a show, that's all."

Apparently Tajima had decided that her position with the company was not the end-all and be-all of existence. She spoke again: "You also removed certain characters, Mr. Cordone. That had nothing to do with the budget."

To her surprise, Cordone sighed. "There was no way we were putting the Christ exhibit in. Besides, I don't believe that was Lon Chaney."

Fossett exploded: "The photograph was recently unearthed! Experts have verified it! It is a long lost studio portrait of Chaney as Christ. I'd stake my career on its being authentic." This torrent of explanation and defense had no effect worth noting.

"It doesn't matter," said Cordone flatly. "That wouldn't fit the program even if it was legit. Just forget it! Now we have one last piece of business to conduct, then I have to get out of here. Christ, er . . . I don't have all day to waste." Cordone went inside the bowels of dreams. After exchanging brief glances of common distress, the other two followed.

Tajima lowered her head and spoke in the direction of the card affixed to her blouse, just above her left breast: "We're going to need the phantom." Somewhere in the dark, a head nodded.

"I don't think you'll have any complaints about this one," said Cordone. "Your script was fine. The material grabs!"

Fossett wasn't listening. He was worrying. Of all the faces, the phantom's was the most important to him. He couldn't bear to see what Cordone had done with it.

Not a mask, a mere mask. The man would not be there. The self-inflicted agonies of wire and hook, a life-time's knowledge of what it meant to be different — the memories of deaf and dumb parents — and the reality of loneliness, all there in the pulled back mouth, flaring nostrils, and unbelievable eyes. It wasn't some cheap fun-house fright. He couldn't let Cordone get away with it.

The little voice that spoke in his head was as unbidden as it was difficult to ignore: "What sort of job will you look for next?" The twitching in his eye returned as he realized he would do nothing. *I'm sorry*, he said to himself — *sorry I've betrayed you, Lon Chaney.*

"Damn it!" came Cordone's voice, gruffer than ever. With a clattering as if an empty bucket were rolling down-stairs, he'd stumbled over something. "Get some more light in here!" Tajima did.

Several empty cylinders marked CLEANING FOAM were slowly turning on the floor, coming to a stop like hands of a watch winding down. "What are these doing here?" asked Cordone in a voice so low that it didn't sound like him.

"The maintenance robots use them," said Tajima. "I don't know how they got here. Ted, uh, I mean, Dr. Fossett, didn't we just return this way?"

"The janitor," said Fossett.

"That does it!" shouted Cordone. "I asked you before if you could describe the guy to one of our identi-artists."

He walked over, limping slightly from the wrench he'd given his foot. "What does the man look like?"

Fossett had been trying to remember the face in terms of its most distinctive features. Cordone had unknowingly given him the key word, "like." Of course, he had known all along, but couldn't allow himself to believe it.

"He looks like Lon Chaney," said Fossett.

For a moment, neither Tajima nor Cordone did anything but stare. They could hear each other's breathing. When the silence became too loud to bear, he continued: "Without makeup, I mean. I was so busy admiring the numerous portrayals that I almost forgot his appearance when he wasn't in a role. He was a rather plain-looking man. You'd pass him on the street without giving him special notice. A long American face is what he had — you'd see it on the great plains, sweating behind a tractor, you . . ." His voice trailed off as the weight of the silence returned. He had become obsessed with faces in the last few months. He could tell the one that Cordone was wearing: someone observing a body after a terrible accident. And Fossett didn't enjoy the pity on Tajima's face much more.

"Is this your idea of revenge just because you don't like the way I fixed a fucking holo-show?" asked Cordone, veins standing out on his neck as exclamation.

"No sir, I didn't even know what you'd done until you told me. But the man really looked like Lon Chaney!"

Nobody could switch tracks faster than Cordone. He'd removed one of the verboten cigars and was pointing it at Fossett as if it were a surgical instrument poised over tonight's surprise cadaver: "If this is your idea of faking insanity just so you can collect on the DI medical retirement, I swear that I'll fry you!"

That's when the lights went out. "Tajima!" shrieked

Cordone. "I didn't do anything!" she yelled back. "Listen," said Fossett . . . and they did.

Laughing in the dark.

"Who's that?" asked Cordone. "Listen, you bastard, whoever you are, Doppelgänger, Incorporated, has a policy on trespassing that's gonna put you so far behind bars that by the time they rehabilitate you . . ."

The lights came back on. At the far end of the building they could see the exhibit for The Phantom of the Opera. The organ room was bathed in a light so purple that it looked like burgundy wine, and next to it was a section of opera seats with the great chandelier above set out in aquarium blue. A silhouette moved near the keyboard.

"There he is!" shouted Cordone, as he hobbled off in that direction.

"That's the holo-show," whispered Tajima.

"Is it?" asked Fossett, grabbing her arm. "Have you seen it all the way through? Is anything different?"

"It's just the program," she insisted, as they watched the producer. "The keyboard part of the Wurlitzer organ is the set, but the big section above is a hologram matted in. Over there, the seats are real, but the chandelier is a projection. And the phantom, of course, is like all the other Chaneys in here."

"Gotcha!" Cordone had reached the phantom. His hands grabbed air. Turning toward the others, he had the aspect of a small boy whose toy had broken in his hands, as the wraith of the caped enigma hovered about him. A shadow.

Fossett was the first to reach him. Without saying a word, he took the producer's arm and started to lead him away, when he caught sight of the death's-head monster. It was bland. It was blank. It was just a green putty face, with painted eyes and jack-o'-lantern grin.

Fossett's arm dropped away and hung limp as a thing dead. He felt like crying.

"I . . ." Cordone began, catching a glimpse of Fossett's face contorting in inner agony. He didn't go on, but turned back to confront his handiwork.

"You're an amusement," he told the hologram. "Nothing more." He began circling the exhibit. "You're not art. You were never anything but mass entertainment. And when mass taste changed, you didn't change with it." He was in the seats now, and talking to the hologram as it went through its paces — it pointed at the organ before sitting there with a flourish.

"What's Cordone doing?" asked Tajima in Fossett's ear.

"I'm not sure," he said. "It isn't like him. Maybe he's only talking to me."

"Spook shows! Horror man! It's all crap," Cordone went on, as the swelling notes of organ music rose to drown his voice. But he would not be silenced, raising his voice to be heard again. "I've never liked you, never liked these fantasies. I don't let my kids watch this stuff. Too many dreams, too many nightmares. It's bad, I tell you! People who spend a lot of time with this stuff aren't healthy. They're not any good at business, I'll tell you that!" He was shaking. "I hate you. I hate you!"

There was a flicker in the light, a gasp of whispery sound. A man in a cape glided over by the seated figure at the organ. The black phantom sitting, sitting, playing an imaginary organ, grew fuzzy around the edges, slipped out of sight . . . but The Phantom of the Opera was there. He bent down, brushing his fingers over keys connected to nothing, making hollow clicking sounds that could be heard, just barely, in the din of the musical recording. The deep notes of Bach throbbed against the walls but he straightened up and shook his fist at the keyboard — an island of fact in a chimera. The phantom turned his back on this illusion. The phantom strode over to a point where the two sets were joined.

"Oh my God," said Fossett. He could see the phantom standing there, half in purple light, half in blue — could see that the phantom had a face.

He knew that face of night, of pain, of truth.

"What's going on?" Cordone's voice sounded very far away, but he was only standing among the seats. From under a velvet cape of bloody red, a black-gloved hand spidered its way to a lever on the wall, a lever that Tajima had never seen. With a tinkling of glass, the chandelier moved. The phantom's arm fell away from the wall. The chandelier fell from the ceiling. "Turn it off," said Cordone, his voice pleading, arm involuntarily covering his head from what he knew to be unreal. Tajima's finger had already brushed all the OFF buttons on her card before Cordone gave his command. The show was over. The phantom was gone.

There was a crash just the same. ❧

Dedicated to Forrest J Ackerman

The Ballad of the Faithful Wife

MILLEA KENIN

"Till Death do us part,"
that's a coward's oath;
let Death wed us anew,
her frostfire kiss us both.

When all I love must die,
shall I prove false at last?
No, rigor stiffens will,
and my hand still holds fast.

I'll travel at your side
wherever you must go —
past the cold dolmen's gate,
into the shades below,

Across the frozen waste
where stars unmoving shine.
You pay no heed to me;
your hand's like stone in mine.

Rib's arches crack like ice
beneath the shroud you wear,
crumble at my embrace —
and you — you are not there —

ॐ

Marker

JOSEPH PAYNE BRENNAN

Stepping out of brush
up a pasture slope,
it loomed suddenly:
a skeleton oak,
on one branch a rope.

The trailing end,
frayed and grey,
swung in the wind
much as it might have
on another day.

I had heard stories:
foreclosure, despair,
disappearance, discovery
(after a month, they say)
of a thing treading air.

The old dead oak
where a crow disports
still held the remnant rope.
I left it dangling —
a marker of sorts.

❧

The Dancer In The Dark: Interlude Three

THOMAS E. FULLER

an excerpt from a forthcoming novel

The man woke with a start, his heart pounding with such a frenzied urgency that he could almost feel it crash against his ribs. He gulped down the moist hot air until it seemed as if he would saturate his lungs with its steam and drown from the inside out. He flinched from the irrational horror that his eyes were somehow blinking without the use of his eyelids, producing monochromatic visions that vanished as fast as they appeared. He was disoriented and for one endless moment tottered on the edge of panic as he desperately fought for some mental equilibrium. With agonizing slowness, it finally came.

First, he fought down the hysterical gulping, forced himself to regulate his breathing until it normalized. Slowly his need for the saturated air abated and his breaths came slower and slower. As that happened, he could feel the adrenaline-powered fury of his heart also subside. The irrational fever fear that had awoken him was being willed back into submission. Gradually, he regained control of himself and began to bring his current environment back into focus.

First came the immediate sensations. He was leaning against something rough and bluntly irregular. Pine tree. It was a large and particularly ancient conifer, one he had chosen for its great drooping branches of close-packed needles so he would have some protection in case of rain. He pushed himself back against it, deriving comfort from the grating pressure of the jagged bark through his shirt. Yes, this would help, this was familiar, almost prosaic. There is nothing threatening about pine trees.

Then came the sound. Just one — for some reason the night, it was night he now realized — was singularly devoid of sounds. But there was one, a thick, gurgling noise, almost as if honey were trying to transform itself into a cascade and being reasonably successful at it. It was close, no more than five feet away. He strained to hear it and as he did the monochromatic flash flickered again and he saw the creek bank for a blinding instant and for seconds afterwards as the afterimage etched itself into his eyes. The sound was water, a broad shallow creek that couldn't have been more than fifteen feet wide. Yes, that's what it was. That left only the flashes.

That's the easy part, you damn fool, muttered a previously paralyzed part of his mind. The flicker exploded again and he knew it this time. Heat lightning. Just heat lightning. He forced a nervous laugh through his sleep-dried mouth. Grown man scared out of his wits by goddamn heat lightning. As the man laughed, he pushed one trembling hand through his lank black hair. It came away soaked, almost as if he had been washing it when he fell asleep. Goddamn heat lightning.

Now his eyes were becoming adjusted to the dark and he could see between the momentary flares of lightning. He had set up camp by the creek, chosen it with the cautious care of his kind. His bedroll lay on the ground next to him, he hadn't even unrolled it. It had been too hot for that. Instead he had fallen asleep leaning against the tree, watching the coals of his little fire slowly bank and die. The ashes were still there, still surrounded by the rocks he had carefully arranged and the empty cans of beans he had for his dinner.

The man liked to think of himself as a free spirit, an unencumbered rambler, independent and self-reliant. To the housewives and storekeepers he met, however, he was a bum, a tramp, a hobo. Well, he certainly wasn't a bum, bums begged. The man didn't beg, not even for a cup of coffee or a cigarette. Bums did that. The man specialized in odd jobs — he was particularly good at yard work. Cutting firewood, mowing lawns, weeding gardens, raking, you name it, the man did it. Housewives were a good touch for a quarter or fifty cents or even a dollar if it was a real nice yard and you did a real nice job. And they were usually good for a sandwich and some lemonade while you worked and a piece of pie when you left. A very satisfactory arrangement all around.

Storekeepers were another matter. To begin with, they were harder to convince and they spent so much time watching you that they didn't get their own work done. But once they caught on that you weren't a bum, they settled down and things got pretty good. Storekeepers paid good for sweeping and heavy lifting and such and sometimes they came across with a storeroom corner where the man could lay down his bedroll. But then they'd start talking about what a good worker the man was and trying to get him to settle down and make something of himself and the man would know it was time to move along. Folks just didn't understand rambling.

The man had spent the summer in the mountains, up near Asheville and Boone way. Lots of summer hotels up there and they always needed some kind of work done. But they were closed for the season and the man was heading south, going down to Florida. Much as he liked the mountains personally, the winters were a little rough on people who seemed to spend most of their time sleeping outside. So he was heading south. Ordinarily, he would be hitchhiking, having invested in a cheap pair of new pants and a shirt, or at least clean ones. Folks were more likely to pick you up if you looked clean. But this was an election year and drivers always want to talk politics in election years and it was just too much trouble trying to guess who they were for. So the man was on the tramp, heading south.

He wiped the sweat off his forehead again. It clung to his hand, gelatinous and greasy, and he marvelled at it. Heat sweat, in the middle of October, sticky, clammy heat sweat. It had been cool — hell, it had been downright cold — when he had left the mountains, but here he was, covered with sweat. And it wasn't even daylight. He squinted up at the sky. Clouds covered it but he figured it had to be at least four o'clock. It should be cool. Even in the summer, four o'clock in the morning should be cool. He'd seen some strange weather in his twenty years on the road but nothing like this. That settled it, no more tramping. Soon as it got daylight he'd find himself a nice slow-moving freight and ride the rails to Florida. He hated having to dodge the yard bulls but a man could wear himself down to the bone walking in this weather.

Now that he had made a decision, he found himself relaxing, settling back further against his tree. But one thing kept nagging at him — what had woken him up in the first place? The man didn't like to admit it but he had been terrified. He hadn't felt fear like that since he had been on the run from that bunch of Klansmen up in Indiana four years ago. They'd gotten it into their pointy heads that people like the man were undesirables, like blacks or Catholics or Jews or something. They had sicced dogs on him, very big dogs, and chased him for miles. It had been that same fear that had ripped him from his sleep. A dream? Had to have been a dream — nothing threatening in these humid woods. Was there?

The man took a deep breath to clear his head and noticed the smell. It was a heavy thick smell, almost a perfume. It reminded him of the time he had done some fruit picking on the peninsula. It had been late in the season and a lot of the fruit had started to rot. That was the smell, the cloying sweet smell of over-ripe oranges and lemons with a faint hint of orchids. Orchids in Georgia? He shook his head and the odor faded a bit but it was still there, floating around him like a scented fog. He wished the stupid heat lightning would stop, it was making it hard to concentrate. Funny, heat lightning had never bothered him before. He was feeling very strange, almost drunk — or drugged. His thoughts were becoming sluggish, like bubbles rising through oil. He shook his head again. It didn't help much.

What had woken him? It couldn't have been the smell, when you'd slept in some of the places the man had slept, smells didn't bother you much. Besides, it wasn't that kind of smell. It had been something else, something . . . disturbing.

The listless narcotic feeling still clung to him and the sweat still poured from his body like a miniature flood. It was getting into his eyes, making them play tricks on him. In his lethargic state, he could have sworn the heat lightning had left its clouds and was now flashing about at ground level, twisting in and out of the trees as if it hunted for something. Once again he tried to concentrate. On the other bank, there was something on the other bank of the creek.

It floated there, a pale, perfect image among the dark pines and the crawling light. The man stared harder. No, floated was the wrong word. It danced, yes, that was it, it danced, a flowing, sensuous dance. The man's throat became even drier and the thick scent of citrus and rot filled his nostrils to smothering. He felt his heart begin to pound again and knew that this time he wouldn't be able to slow it down. He stared at the pale thing on the other bank.

The heat lightning groveled and slithered around it as it danced, twisting and swaying itself into shapes and postures that ripped deep into the man's fevered body. A flood of pure blackness poured from the figure's head, alternately revealing and concealing it. The man found himself staggering up to his feet. The creek was shallow, he could cross it. The thing on the other side wanted him to cross it. The next thing he knew, he was stumbling down the bank and into the water.

It oozed rather than flowed around him, with the texture of wet honey instead of water. It was blood warm in spite of its sluggishness and he found himself slogging forward, the thick fluid rising first to his knees, then to his waist. He didn't really notice, all his senses were locked on the pallid beckoning figure and its flickering attendants. It wanted him to cross.

The man was approximately halfway across the creek when some buried part of his mind noticed that something had happened. He slowed, something was different, something had changed. He found himself listening, listening as if it was the most important thing in the world. Then he realized that it hadn't been a noise that had startled him. It had been silence. There had been a sound, since he had woken up, there had been a sound. . . .

The Watcher fell on him from above without warning and specifically without sound. It slammed into the man's body and wrapped its strong wiry arms and legs about him. The impact of its falling drove them both under the blood-thick water. For an instant the water in his face revived the man and he surged back to the surface, clawing back over his shoulder at the thing clinging to him. But he was still so sluggish and the Watcher was so very prepared. Something flashed dully in the heat light and the man felt a smooth sliding across his throat, then another across his belly, then another. It was so very fast. And then something much thicker than creek water gushed down him and he felt the night breeze touch parts of his body that breezes, or anything else, had never touched before. He slumped back into the clinging arms of the Watcher who released him. The man's head slid under the water. He didn't notice.

The Watcher dragged the heavy body back up the bank to the camp site. For a moment, its eyes watched the pale figure on the other side of the creek as it swayed and turned. Then it carefully and methodically set about its business.

Several hours later, after Watcher and figure and heat lightning had all gone, a pack of wild dogs found the man. While they fought over certain other things that lay around him, their struggles caused him to slide quietly into the stream. The languid water enfolded him gently and took him on his last ramble. Six months and twenty miles later, his handsome white bones were found by some reasonably astonished fishermen. Considering what was left of him, the coroner justifiably ruled cause of death unknown. 🙒

The Strange High Armadillo In The Mist

GERALD W. PAGE

illustration by
CHARLES SCOGINS

West of the river the slums rise high and there are streets no honest foot can safely tread. The gutters of the potholed thoroughfares run as thick with refuse as with rain and the grim, squalid bricks are covered o'er with compositions of chalk and spray paint whose whole objective is an assault upon the esthesia of more sensitive minds. Here, the gentleman of erudition and culture may not venture without reminder of the tenuous nature of life and security, of the cloaked horror hidden seemingly behind each door. Here also is located the small but superb ice cream parlour of Elfego Bachrach, rumoured to be the finest in the city. From even the greatest of horrors, irony is seldom absent.

It was while partaking of the butter pecan and caramel parfait of Mr. Bachrach that I noticed a strange man with his slouch hat drawn low so that it shadowed a curiously malformed face. He was standing on the street, peering cautiously through the grease-washed, flyspecked window of the parlour, giving no indication what his business in the vicinity might be. There was about him that which drew me strangely, compelling my curiosity, poorly suppressed at the best of times, to assess him with several sorts of fevered imaginings. He glanced once my way, then his gaze passed on to consider others of Mr. Bachrach's customers, as if my blatantly inquisitive staring neither bothered him nor mattered. A chill, not altogether born of the cold, delicious ice cream, traveled the distance of my spine.

As I tilted my dessert to allow the spoon to excavate from the dish's troublesome lowest hollow the last of that concoction which had drawn me to this most unsavoury part of town, I saw him turn away and move off down the uninvitingly grimy boulevard. Whether it was the slump of his shoulders or his obvious predilection for the darkest of the street's vast array of grim and menacing shadows, I cannot say; but something made me rise and, putting on my hat and leaving with scarcely a tip of it to the squinty-eyed Mr. Bachrach, I trudged off down the street to follow him.

Now, I hold that the most merciful thing in this whole universe is the inability of the city dweller to know what goes on behind the doors of the minds and hearts of his fellow megalopolitans. It was the fading dusk of an autumn day and the shadows had lengthened across the narrow, oppressive streets, forming tenuous bridges to join the pools of shadow perpetually lodged within and between the recesses of the tenements themselves. Ordinarily, I would not have permitted myself to be caught in this portion of town so long past the ending of the sun-drenched hours of afternoon, but Mr. Bachrach had but recently introduced three new flavours into his bill of fare. Unable to reach a decision, even after hours of contemplation, I had done what I should have done at the outset and ordered all three, raisin-raspberry cream, boysenberry sundae and the aforementioned parfait, and relished each in turn, with no heed to the waning day. Now, my curiosity piqued and my courage bolstered by the sucrose, I threw caution to the wind and pursued the mysterious gentleman of the shadows.

Night falls quickly and dangerously in the slums. I soon found myself pursuing the subject of my strange fascination — all unbeknownst to him — into a neighborhood less reassuring than any I had yet traveled through; and all the while the lowering dusk impeded my visual contact with this compellingly mysterious figure, until that time when he turned the corner some fifty feet ahead of me and I did likewise only to find myself, so well as I could tell in that inky and un-streetlamp lighted precinct, facing an entirely deserted avenue.

So startled was I that it was impossible for me for several unmeasurable moments to consider those options open to me with more than cursory intellectualization. But presently I decided there was nothing for me to do but turn and retrace my steps until I had returned to more civilized environs. But I had traced less than a block when I realized I had no idea from which direction I had come.

There is, I hold, no more frightening thing than for a gentleman of culture and discernment to find himself at large upon a strange and unlighted street in a portion of the city known only for the sinister quality of its denizens. My imagination, at the calmest of times alive with the most outré and elaborate of phantasms, was now churning with the direst and most dreadful of chimera. My fragile nerves quavered with the turmoil of my emotions. Each sound — the clatter of a garbage can lid, a slamming door, the distant rumble of traffic I prayed to see — stirred my mind to incredible images.

So impressionable are my sensibilities that before long I saw in every shadow a lurking robber or worse. Thus, when I perceived behind me the sound of light treading footfalls, I turned and greeted with a small shriek the unexpectedly welcome sight of a cat.

Now I hold that there is no creature more noble than those of the feline species. This particular individual of the genus was a large and rather scraggly example of the common alley cat, a species one would expect to be found on every step in this quarter of town, though I had seen no cats at all before this veteran Tom. So pleased was I to see this furred creature that I began to call him in a high lilting voice. He watched me with yellow, suspicion-glutted eyes and no intent whatsoever to heed my call; thus frequently do these animals respond to the self-important importunings of their vainglorious cousins of the human genera. Then it turned and walked off, not with the speed of one in fear, but with that insouciant nonchalance by which one may know the complete and inevitable (to say nothing of proper) sense of superiority with which cats are gifted. But sensing the majesty of this animal despite the sparseness of its pelt, obviously due to the vicissitudes of its surroundings, I followed the creature back the way I had just come and into an alley I would not have normally approached in broad daylight.

Abruptly, I could no longer see the animal. Had I lost this creature as I had earlier lost the human I had followed? But no — in the stygian gloom there came to my ear the welcome and familiar sound of purring. Unmindful of the clutter strewn about the dank pavement that floored this alley, I hurried toward it.

And then, as abruptly as my visual contact with the creature had escaped me, so did the audible. The purring ceased as I stood not three feet from the place from which it had originated.

It struck me then, in one of those passing moments of mental clarity which can occur to one in the midst of the most foolish and irredeemable of actions, that even a cat may be possessed of motives that run counter to one's well-being. I toyed for the moment with thoughts of fleeing. But it was already too late.

I heard strange laughter. Something rose up in the shadowy space directly in front of me, the very spot where moments before the alley cat had lured me with its purrings, there stood now the figure of a man. He was taller than I and more gaunt. At the very moment he appeared something of a miracle occurred. The moon came out and in the glow of its light he seemed as pale as death. He smiled. I have never seen such incisors. Nor eyes that yellow in a human being, or ones that glowed quite that way. I found myself mesmerized and immobile, and the strange man who faced me reached with his hand for my throat.

Suddenly, another sound reached my ears, laughter as before, but of an entirely different nature. The strange person before me started and pulled away his hand before my skin could feel its unwelcome and no doubt clammy touch. And as suddenly as he appeared the man with the yellow eyes vanished.

I was suddenly freed of that hypnotic vise which held me. Turning I saw, in the direction from which I came, another figure. Despite the shadows that shrouded it, I recognized at once by the dark shape of the slouch hat pulled low over the protuberance of his face the strange and disconcerting figure I had been compelled to follow from the ice cream parlour. As the beating of my heart sped with fear, this intruder stepped into the moonlight.

At once the question of his strange appearance was answered. In the pallid moonlight I saw at once that the exotic configuration of his face was explainable by the most obvious and prosaic of reasons: it was due to the steel mask made in the likeness of an armored burrowing animal which he wore settled over his head and resting on his shoulder on the manner of those goldfish bowls worn by spacefarers in the lurid covers of the interplanetary pulpwood magazines. But, as if to allay my disappointment at the ordinariness of his headpiece, the newcomer laughed.

Never have I heard such laughter! It combined the inspired thespian reaches of a Christopher Lee with the manic cadence of a cartoon woodpecker. Bizarre and fantastical chills ran up and down my spine at the sound of that laughter as the newcomer leaped the distance between where he and I stood (forcing me to step deftly to one side as he braked himself with the forepiece of his steel mask on the brick edifice behind me).

Foreign as I might be to this distasteful district, I recognized now the identity of my fortuitous benefactor. I stood in the presence — indeed, I trod the edge of the cape of — the Armadillo!

How I escaped joining him on the pavement as he jerked that corner from under my shoe, I cannot say, but somehow I maintained my balance so that I was still standing as he hastily joined me in that posture. Then, for the first time I heard the resonant tones of the Armadillo's voice as he said, "Shouldn't you answer the phone?"

"Phone?" I echoed. "I hear no phone."

"Never mind," the Armadillo said, clutching my arm and looking up and down the alley. "Where is he? Arrggh! Escaped again! Curses!" The beady eyeslits of his mask burned at me. "Come with me," he said. "And be quick about it. Your life isn't worth a plugged nickel if Harold the Werecat returns."

"Werecat?" said I, all intrigued, as the Armadillo hastily dragged me to the alley's mouth. I protested, "But I fail to understand. How could a being in the shape of one of the most noble of all the creatures that populate this repulsive globe, be a threat to a gentleman of learning and erudition?"

The Armadillo reached the mouth of the alleyway and promptly tripped over the abandoned skateboard of some slum-dwelling waif. As he picked himself up, I asked, "For that matter, what is the most famous steel-masked crime fighter on the face of the earth doing in this forsaken tract of city?"

"It had to do with wiping out the Black Bart Gang, dratnabit." He started off down the street and waving his hands in wild gesticulation continued his explanation. "Sixty-three members of that gang. And eight months ago, the McSneary mob. Forty-three members."

"I recall the stories in the yellow press," I said. "You met the McSneary mob in fierce battle replete with automatic gunfire on the Walabaga River Bridge. And as I recall the downfall of the Black Bart Gang involved a high-speed automobile chase — also with automatic gunfire — But how could that inconvenience you? As I recall neither gang could boast a survivor afterwards. . . ."

"Yeah, yeah, I know. But have you ever figured up the cost of those battles? I used 8,347 rounds in the McSneary battle alone. And ammunition costs, believe you me. Oh, sure, people never think of that. They always tell me, so you use tommyguns. Big deal, they say. Those things can use .45 calibre slugs. But a box of fifty goes for about $25.00. And I wrecked three of my own limousines in that car chase. Protecting this city is expensive, and I'm a private corporation. I don't get any grants, I don't get any tax money, I don't have the time or resources to do handloads to bring down my costs. And hey, I can't accept rewards, because I want to be an inspiration to little kids."

"But I thought —"

"Yeah, you thought. Everybody thinks! In his civilian identity the Armadillo must be some international playboy, living in a penthouse atop one of the most exclusive buildings in this burg. Well, part of the time I am. But every now and then, I have to economize too. I have to move to the low rent district. I gotta lay off loyal employees and do my own driving. Do people appreciate all this? Hell, no. I tell ya, buddy, I don't get no respect —"

The Armadillo's litany of grievances was suddenly interrupted by a prodigious clatter. From the roof of the slum above us there issued such a noise that I nearly jerked my neck out of joint so quickly did I respond to it. Something hurtled downward at us!

I leaped aside in the nick of time. The Armadillo was not so lucky, perhaps because he was restricted by the ornamental headpiece upon his pate, and did not see the plummeting garbage receptacle until it bounced ringingly from his mask. Into the gutter flew the famous fedora of the crimefighter, while its wearer skidded into and through the plate glass front of a neighbourhood liquor store.

I would have immediately rushed to his rescue, but something else was falling from the building. I screamed in terror at the sight of a man. A suicide? Some poor victim hurtled to his death by some unseen murderer?

But no! I knew that man. It was the same one I had seen in the alleyway when the Armadillo had shown up to effect my deliverance from his hypnotic spell: Harold the Werecat. And though the roof of the building from which it dropped was four storeys above the sidewalk, this supernatural creature landed on its feet, his legs bending like springs to lessen the impact. And without losing its balance in the slightest way, it crouched and turned and came toward me.

"Armadillo!" I cried. "Save me."

The famous crime fighter was extricating himself from the liquor. He said, "How?"

"Shoot him. I know you carry weapons in your cloak! Shoot him with a silver bullet."

"The cost of bullets what it is and you want I should

have them made in silver? Weren't you listening?"

"Oh my God," I croaked as the menacing creature moved toward me. "Well, do something!"

"Forget it," said the werecat. "That fool's been dogging me ever since he moved into the neighbourhood twelve weeks ago. He's yet to prevent me once from acquiring my chosen victim!"

I could feel volition draining from my muscles. "I really didn't have to hear that," I said, feebly.

"Sheesh!" said the Armadillo. "Look, it's just propaganda. The odds are with me. Sooner or later, I got to win. The Mill Street Decapitator claimed sixty-seven victims in a three-week period and I finally got him!"

"Oh?" said the werecat. "And how did you do that?"

"Well, actually, he called me up on my hotline and confessed."

The werecat laughed. "Hear that? And do you notice that he doesn't come any closer to me than he has to? It's because he's weaponless. He can't afford weapons. Look at his cloak. It doesn't billow in the classic style of the Armadillo's cloak, because its secret pockets are empty of even the famous crime lab. To say nothing of all the various guns, the drums of ammunition and so forth. Ha! It's enough to make a werecat laugh, to see the famed and fearless Armadillo cowed like this."

"Just hold on," the Armadillo said, rummaging in a pocket of his cape. Meanwhile, sweat beaded my poor brow and broke into rivulets and streams that poured into my eyes, threatening to blind me temporarily. But then, I only had temporarily.

"You're mine!" the werecat gloated, approaching.

"Ah ha!" screeched the Armadillo simultaneously. He pulled a baseball bat from his cloak.

The werecat whirled to face him. At that very moment

and with a movement so smooth, it seemed rehearsed, the Armadillo swung and connected solidly. Had that creature's head been a baseball, the Armadillo would have scored a home run. As it was, the creature's head was a creature's head; the Armadillo's swing scored a grounder.

The werecat fell back, stretched out upon the slime-covered street and slid clear to the other curb. The Armadillo, swinging his baseball bat like an Indian's war club above his mask, pursued the werecat. The dazzled creature staggered to its feet only to be met soundly by a rap alongside its head. It rocked back. The Armadillo swung again, repeating his strike from the other side. He kept this up for several seconds as the werecat rocked prodigiously back and forth and then the Armadillo changed his tactic, raising the bat and bringing it down rapidly toward the creature's skull.

The creature, however, was stronger than it seemed, and more agile; even the Armadillo, I think, had forgotten it was a cat. It stepped aside, grabbed at the bat, and before we realized what it was about, it snatched the athletic instrument from the Armadillo's gloved hand. With more speed than even the Armadillo had managed, it swung at the crime-fighter's head.

I have heard clock-tower bells that did not ring with such rounded tones as that. Immediately the bat transferred vibration into the steel-headed figure of the crime-fighter. But he did not fall.

What did happen was that the bat splintered. And more, the were-creature shook as ferociously as the Armadillo. They both stood vibrating in front of one another like sympathetic tuning forks and the bat fell from the werecat's hands. I watched in horrid fascination.

Then, after what seemed like hours, the Armadillo quickly ceased to vibrate. He shook his famous head as if to clear it, and spied the splintered bat upon the ground. In a sudden inspiration he snatched up the baseball bat's broken haft and drove it into the creature's chest in the vicinity of its heart!

Never have I seen such a thing. The creature, the stake stabbing clear through so that it was visible both in front and back, rocked back and screamed horribly! The Armadillo leaped back to escape its clutching hands. But he need not have bothered for the werecat suddenly vanished in a burst of blue light and was gone.

Sensibility returned to my muscles. I stared at the place where there should have been the body of the monster that had threatened to destroy me, and saw nothing. I did not tear my eyes from that spot until the Armadillo's hand touched my shoulder.

He brought me to the phone booth in this perfectly respectable part of town and bid me call the police and wait for them. It was almost dawn, but already a traffic of perfectly respectable and well-kept cars and taxis plied the clean-swept thoroughfares. The Armadillo said that he must go.

"And you must be safely away before the rising of the sun?" I said. "I have often wondered, Armadillo. Could it be? Could it be that you are also a supernatural creature?"

"No, but I'm bushed as hell," said the Armadillo, and was gone.

I dialed the number he had left me and requested that I be met by detectives for I had an incredible story to tell them. Presently, a recent model automobile parked at the curb and two men got out. So well-dressed were they that save for a slightly batrachian cast to their features, I might have taken them for bankers or minor executives of some up and coming investment firm.

And that, officer, is how I came to be mugged. ɞ

Dream

BOBBY G. WARNER
illustration by
CLAY CROKER

"**F**ranklin, come inside!" His mother's voice is a muffled growl from within the house. "And don't track mud on the carpet!" He looks up at the purple sky, then down at his shoes, which are covered with oozing mud. He tries to shift his right foot, but the mire is like glue and his shoe is stuck.

"Franklin!" his mother calls again as thunder grumbles through the purple sky. Clouds scuttle overhead and large drops of crimson rain splat against his face. He trembles in fear but cannot move.

The day grows even darker. A chilling wind tugs at him as heavy footsteps within the house thud down the hallway and stop just beyond the massive, brass-knockered door. His mother will be angry with him for not coming when she calls.

The door groans open and his mother stands grotesquely silhouetted in the flickering orange glow from within the house. Her hair is a mass of wriggling snakes. Despite his fear he begins to giggle and points at the large, blue-black wart on her nose. It is a funny sight — the funniest sight he has ever seen.

She raises her knobby mahogany-colored cane and shakes it at him.

Crimson fluid swirls around his knees and the wind, a howling fury, jerks him this way and that. He pulls free of his shoes and tries to run. His mother's arm reaches after him, telescoping as though it were made of plastic, and

107

steel fingers clutch his collar. He chokes with fear as she opens her mouth. Her voice echoes in his ears, rings. . . .

He knocks over the lamp getting out of bed to silence the telephone. The bulb shatters on the cold floor and he fumbles in darkness, feeling for his slippers.

"I've got to wake up!" he tells himself as he gropes his way down the dark stairs. The jangling noise grows impatient, urgent. God, will the stairs never end?

His foot snags on worn carpeting and he pitches forward. There is nothing to stop his fall; nothing but empty dark. . . .

The bottom of the well is covered with a thick layer of slime. The stink rises to his nostrils, and he tries to crawl away, whimpering in fear and revulsion. Something flaps against his face. Angry, shrill noises fill the well. Bats! He flails his arms, striking several of the creatures.

He falls in the slime and struggles to get up. The bats have gone. Far above he sees a tiny circle of dim light. A small, luminous face peers down from the edge of the wall. Leaping up, he shouts, "Help me! Please get me out of here!"

The face disappears and the circle of light begins to eclipse. "No!" he cries, realizing what is happening. "NO!"

The covering slides into place, leaving him in total darkness.

Something moves in the darkness behind him, and he whirls, throwing out his hands to ward off the unseen threat. Rough fingers grope for his neck. "You've been such a naughty boy, Franklin," says his mother as her fingers caress his neck. "Time for your punishment. Naughty, naughty. . . ."

He stands in the living room beside the ringing phone. He picks up the receiver and says "Hello?" The wan light from a quarter moon falls through the window.

"Hello!" he says again. The phone is dead. He feels something move across his foot and the cord begins to writhe like a serpent. The receiver emits a hideous growling hiss. He drops the instrument and it snakes across the room, vanishing into the shadows.

His mind works furiously. He must still be asleep, must still be dreaming. But it seems real enough — except for the telephone that acts like an angry viper. Pinching his cheek, he feels a sharp pain. He is awake!

He fumbles in a drawer, finds an old pack of matches. He strikes one and —

A brilliantly lit hall surrounds him, its walls covered with precious art. He notices a door at the far end of the corridor. Slowly, he walks toward it.

He pauses to study the painting of a beautiful young woman. She seems to be familiar. There is a cruelty in her features and her yellow-flickering eyes stare balefully into him. Her lips curl into a sneer. He realizes she is alive. The young woman bends toward him, hungrily. Her lips part to expose sinister white teeth.

"Franklin . . ." she purrs, touching his forehead with her slender fingers. "Take me, Franklin. I'm yours. . . . "

He flees along the long corridor and bangs frantically against the door. It will not open, so he sits down and begins to cry. The woman from the painting sits beside him, puts her arms around his shoulders. He shrinks away, but she follows.

"Isn't it wonderful, Franklin? Just the two of us — forever."

He pulls away as her flesh begins to sag, her face aging. His mother clutches at him with knobby hands.

He feels warm pavement beneath his feet and smells automobile exhaust. The dark city streets around him are comforting in their normality.

He rushes toward the sounds of crowds and sirens in the distance, shouting happily, "I'm awake!" At last he has escaped the nightmarish world of sleep. He skids around a corner and sees the outline of a hospital, a few blocks ahead. There he will be able to find someone who can help him understand and overcome his troublesome dreams.

A giant sun — several giant suns — explode, and the city churns and rolls/boils about him. The buildings topple inward, toward him. He tries to run back toward safety, but the leaning buildings are everywhere. They crumble, silently showering him with a deadly torrent of metal, stone, glass.

"I'm going to die!" he thinks, and it is almost a pleasant, a welcoming thought. . . .

The dust of chaotic devastation becomes a smoke-filled moviehouse. An old Charlie Chaplin film is playing. The moustached comedian capers across the screen, mugging at his unseen audience.

A sharp elbow pokes him in the ribs and he gets up to leave, but a heavy hand slams him back into the hard seat. "No one leaves before the end of the picture." He huddles down in the seat, and someone shoves a bag of rancid-smelling buttered popcorn into his hands. "Eat, Franklin!" His mother leans over his shoulder. She forces a handful of the greasy-cold stuff into his mouth.

Wavering phantoms zig-zag across the screen. Although he hasn't seen the end of the first picture. A different movie is playing. Garish cartoon monsters zoom out over the stage, pointing accusing fingers at him. He covers his ears as their voices screech maniacally around him. "He doesn't appreciate us anymore. After all we do for him!"

Angry hands tear at him as the shadowy mob presses in upon him, grumbling angrily. His mother chuckles in the gathering darkness. . . .

At last he awakes sitting straight up in bed, breathing heavily. From outside comes the sound of crickets. A full moon slants its shimmering light through the curtainless window.

He gets out of bed, goes to the window and rests his palms on the sill as he leans forward to inhale the warm night air of summer.

Gazing out at the familiar neighborhood, he sees cars parked along the street but the houses are all silent, their windows unlit.

A strange, morbid feeling falls upon him. He blinks his eyes, straining to see the dark houses better. They stand out starkly, like stubs of rotten teeth, in the moonlight.

Then he remembers. The houses are empty. The neighbors have been gone a long time. The cars are old and crumbling into rust, and only he has been left behind.

Sobbing, he turns from the window and falls back into bed. He settles in, oblivious to the remains of the rotting room which surrounds him. He pulls at the ancient sheets, and they fall apart in his hands. No matter. There are other places — where man and man-made things have not crumbled away. Places where he has a mother with a knobby mahogany cane, beautiful paintings, and moviehouses with Charlie Chaplin films. There is also the deep well with the slime-covered bottom. But that does not matter. At least someone — or something — alive is up there pushing the cover over the well.

He closes his eyes and lets the silent darkness enfold him. He waits patiently for the dream to continue, so he will not be so damnably alone. ❧

Drifting Atoms

MARY ELIZABETH COUNSELMAN

illustration by

CHARLES SCOGINS

originally presented in WEIRD TALES, 1941

The whole business began at Ray Chetham's, the night of July 2nd. Just shows you how close we are to the weird and unbelievable even in the most ordinary of settings. But whenever men get together and start thinking, really *thinking* — well, anything can happen. Anything.

We had met, as usual, for our weekly poker session. Just the five of us, pals since high school days. Chet, Perry Lester, Tom Scofield, and Boyton Greer. And me, Joe Littleton.

There we were, five ordinary American businessmen. Lounging around the table in Chet's apartment, sleepeyed, in shirt sleeves, drinking and smoking companionably and arguing about things in general.

Perry was popping off about the next election, Boy griping about the hand Tom had dealt him, when Chet suddenly remarked out of a clear blue sky:

"Joe — suppose someone could change the spots on a card merely by willing them to change. See what I mean? Simply by *thinking* about it. And why not? Look here. Everything we see in this room is nothing but a collection of atoms, held together by — what? Some kind of centrifugal force. If that force were all at once destroyed, everything in the universe would fly into particles of matter and go spinning off into space."

Perry grinned at him, reaching for a glass. "Here, pal," he drawled. "You need a drink. Put this under your belt, and you'll feel a lot better." He winked at me, describing a rotary gesture at his temple. "Nutty as a fruitcake! Poor old Chet!"

Chetham ignored him. He took the glass of whiskey, held it to the light, regarding it lazily. "Atoms," he murmured. "Nice little glassful of atoms. Pretty soon they'll be a part of me. It takes iron, leafy vegetables, fat, and what-not to make a man's hand . . . you morons know what I think? I think all atoms are exactly alike — and it's only the way they're put together that determines whether they'll be wood or flesh or metal or what-have-you. All matter is composed of the same basic material." He grinned and struck an attitude.

"Screwball!" Lester snorted pleasantly, fishing for cigarettes in Greer's coat pocket. He lit one, blew smoke rings into the air. "Look at that," he jerked his thumb at one gray spiral. "You mean to say that I and that smoke are composed of the same stuff?"

Absolutely, Chetham nodded, jabbing a forefinger through one of the rings. "More atoms went into you Perry, and they're stuck together in a special way — that's the only difference. If I could get that smoke to stay put in the shape of a red-headed, pug-nosed reporter, your own fiancée couldn't tell it from you except for the density of atoms. And if I could get enough smoke together to supply the same amount of atoms as you have in your homely carcass — why, presto! You'd have a twin! It wouldn't be alive, of course; couldn't move or speak. Just a big blob of matter that looks like you. See?"

"Two Perry Lesters for the price of one!" Greer piped up, laughing. "I've been swindled!"

We all chuckled drowsily — none of us very much concerned or interested except Chet, a science professor, and me, a fiction writer, who enjoyed crazy flights of imagination. Tom Scofield, moody and quiet since his hardware business had failed, looked on with a forced smile. Boyton Greer, a nervous young bank clerk with a hobby of indoor photography, shuffled the cards impatiently. Perry Lester, who covered the courthouse beat for the *Globe*, openly yawned.

We might have gone on from there with never a thought beyond our own humdrum lives, had not Chet leaned back in his chair, sipping his highball, and voiced the crazy idea that was to launch us all on this incredible journey into the unknown.

"You know something else I think?" he drawled. "I think that, before Creation, some *Force* — call it by any religious name you like — collected a lot of atoms out of space, threw them together, and called them planets or stars or what-have-you. And when men were created, they were given a small portion of that Force, or Power. Call it Will, or Intelligence; call it Soul; call it anything you like. But I believe there is enough electrical power in the human mind to draw and hold atoms together, in any form we choose!"

Scofield laughed uneasily. Greer snorted. Perry Lester and I said nothing, but I leaned forward with greater interest.

"Ghosts, now," Chetham expanded. "Materializations of any kind at a séance. They're simply a collection of atoms gathered together by the sheer mind-power of a group of people concentrating on one thing."

Lester's cigarette burnt him; he dropped it with a curse, still blinking at Chet. "I never heard anything so completely screwy!" he exploded. "You mean a group of people, ordinary people, can create something out of thin air, just by thinking it? Why, you're —"

Chetham waved him to silence. "Now, now, keep your

shirt on, Perry. I didn't say exactly that. I said the atoms already exist. The very air around us is full of them — microscopic particles flying around until the gravity pull of some larger solid draws them to it and they become part of that solid. But . . . you've seen a magnet pull a heavy piece of metal to it? If our mind power was developed enough, we could draw atoms *away* from solids. I could take you apart and reassemble you on my body, except that your mind-power would be pulling against mine. Or we could both concentrate on dissolving that chair, atom by atom, and sticking it onto this chair over here. . . ."

Perry winked at me. "See?" he whispered. "I told you he was nuts! Of all the crazy — "

"But that degree of mind-power," Chet went on, ignoring him, eyes narrowed dreamily, "could probably never be attained by the human brain in its present state. If it could — think of the chaos! Right now, though, I'm convinced we could materialize any familiar object out of detached atoms that are not yet caught by any centrifugal force. Your watch, Perry, for example, could be duplicated. . . ."

Our reporter snorted. With a flourish, he took out his new watch his aunt had given him last Christmas and laid it down on the table, clearing a place among the cards and chips.

"All right!" he waved at it. "That turnip cost Aunt Mag a hundred and ten bucks. I know — I've hocked it. Make me one like it, Chet my friend, and I'll give you this one!"

Scofield, Greer and I were leaning forward now, interested and amused in spite of ourselves. But we laughed openly at Chet, who stared dreamily at the watch, running a hand through his shaggy black mop of hair.

"You think it's so funny?" he said quietly. Those black

eyes, sliding over our faces, were serious and unsmiling. "Listen, you knot-heads!" Chet snapped. "Ancient necromancers — the Medes and the Persians, the old Magi — could create anything you'd like to name, simply by the power of thought. They were able to change the atom formations at will: Water into wine, wood into stone, inanimate objects into animate ones — the way Moses turned his rod into a snake — they way Lot's wife, by her own mental turmoil, turned her own flesh into salt. They could *do* it, I tell you! And their minds were no better developed — in fact, I'd say they were much less developed — than yours or mine. We have a knowledge of electrical force, chemistry, physics that those old ducks never had. . . ."

We four were not laughing now. Chet's mood of gravity and growing excitement was contagious. Lester peered at him, one eyebrow cocked at a quizzical angle. Boyton Greer gaped at him, unwinking. Scofield, however, seemed the most affected. He was staring at Chet strangely, wringing his hands in that nervous way of his until his knuckles cracked. A little muscle in his mouth twitched. Tom was always high-strung.

Unexpectedly he blurted: "Chet, I — I've got a book at home —"

All eyes shifted to him, and he reddened like a small boy caught showing off.

"That is," he stammered, "I just thought it might amuse you fellows. Just for a laugh, of course. I mean, what you were saying, Chet; this book tells how —"

Chetham sat up with a jerk, his eyes bright with interest.

"Huh? What kind of book, Tom? You mean, this crackpot theory of mine has been thought of before? Not seriously?"

Scofield nodded shyly. "Y-yeah," he stuttered. "It's all in this book. Uncle of mine willed it to me with the estate. . . ."

We fidgeted uncomfortably. Each of us knew about his uncle — he had died in an insane asylum last year, and any mention of him brought a flare of panic to Tom's eyes. Hereditary insanity is not a pleasant thought for a jittery chap like him. But, with a moribund eagerness:

"Uncle had a lot of crazy books," he was saying now. "Used to collect them. Banned stuff, dealing with witchcraft and so on. This one I mentioned is a compilation of rituals stolen from a Parsi temple. Persian fire-worshippers, you know. Chet, your saying that about the Medes and Persians awhile ago made me remember it. Those Parsi *mobeds* — priests — really had thought-control down to a fine art, even better than the Yogis of India. In this book are all sorts of formulae for impossible tricks, like setting a bush afire with a glance, or making water spurt out of a dry rock. They could do it, too, in those days. Nothing supernatural about it; just sheer science."

He stopped for a breath, glancing from one face to another, then back to Chet for approbation that was certainly forthcoming. The four of us blinked at him, intent and fascinated by such a weird conversation coming out of shy, moody Tom Scofield. As for Chet, he was grinning like a kid with a new toy.

"Say!" he burst out. "I'd like to see that book! Can I borrow it tomorrow?"

"And me next?" Perry Lester chimed in, and mugged at us. "Gentlemen, won't you join us in a padded cell?"

I remember that was the very crack he made. Perhaps if we had realized how prophetic it was, we would have dropped the whole thing like a hot brick. But we didn't realize, of course. Chet was full of fantastic theories which he and Perry were always squabbling about, for nothing more than the sheer pleasure of popping off. Boyton, Tom and I had always trailed along, putting in our two-cents-worth, until the "debate" ended in a big laugh. Life on Mars, the construction of a stratosphere plane, the physical changes of a psychopathic "werewolf" — these were some of the crackpot matters we had taken apart, for the fun of it. Naturally, then, our fancy was caught by this new idea of Chet's while, as naturally, none of us took it seriously.

We had not forgotten it by the next time we met, this time at Boyton Greer's because his wife was out of town. Perry mentioned it almost at once. And Tom, shy but eager for attention, brought out the promised book. There was a clause in his uncle's will, he said, preventing his ever letting it out of his possession; but we could see it, anyhow, in his presence.

It was an ancient-looking volume, inscribed on vellum and sloppily bound. Pages were missing, and the whole thing was in Sanskrit. But Tom's uncle had translated the passages here and there. In fact he must have been working on this very translation when he lost his mind — from overwork and too intensive study, the doctors said. I doubt that diagnosis, in view of what was in the translations — and what happened later.

We didn't play any poker that night. After Chet had read aloud a few pages of that book, we were too interested for ordinary thoughts.

The wording was obscure. There was a lot of stuff mixed in about *Ahura Mazda*, the Parsi deity of light and *Narasamsa Agni* — fire — in his various forms.

But between the lines there was a curious sort of scientific theory, hinted at now and then — something about the non-existence of matter except as held together by "the Law of Eternal Mind." It was very vague. There was still more about all phases of earthly matter being akin, and that caught Chet's attention at once.

"There!" he pointed out eagerly. "That agrees with my theory! Look how many plants seem to be almost animal, and how many insects are nothing but animated twigs and leaves. And don't plants eventually turn into mineral form? Petrified trees — that's one marked instance. Then, there's that disease science has no cure for, when flesh hardens slowly into stone and can be chipped off. . . . Yes, there's a link somewhere, and I believe it's in the atom. Hmm! . . . You know, I think we've stumbled on something revolutionary!"

Lester, Greer, Scofield and I were reading over his shoulder, scanning the neat translations appended to each vellum leaf. Suddenly Lester indicated one paragraph, and murmured the words aloud:

"*. . . And he shall make, with his own mind and the Power thereof, a likeness unto that which is. And the likeness shall be, it shall exist, until the Power is withdrawn. Yea, what though Life is not given and Growth forbidden, it shall be seen, and touched, it shall have weight and color and substance, according to the Will of him who thinks. For so it was in the Beginning. . . .*"

"What do you get out of that, Chet?" Lester muttered. "And look; further down, it tells how to — "

We all read those next few paragraphs, forming the words silently. Simple words — but with a meaning that struck one like a blow between the eyes.

"Why, there's nothing to it!" Greer murmured, frowning. "All you do, according to this, is sit and put everything else from your mind, and concentrate on something."

Chet smiled. "Yes, sure. But that's not so easy as you might think. In fact, it's damned hard to concentrate on any one thing for much longer than ten to twenty minutes. Almost impossible for the average person."

Perry nodded. "Yeah. Little sounds distract you. Other thoughts creep in. But you can train yourself to do it. It was devilish hard for me to turn out copy in the news room, with everybody yelling and the teletype going. But it can be done — and so could this."

I grinned at them, nodding at the card table Greer had previously set up for poker. "Let's have a séance," I chuckled. "Perry, does that offer about your watch still hold good?"

A murmur of laughter greeted this, but it was uncertain laughter. The phrases of that Sanskrit translation were thrumming in all our heads. Could it be? *Could it be?*

Still laughing, Boyton Greer swept cards and chips from the table and gestured solemnly to the chairs drawn up to it. I sat down. Perry snorted. Tom Scofield ran a nervous glance over our faces, smiling shakily. Then, as Chet sat down opposite me with a clowning gesture of pressing forefinger to forehead, eyes closed as in a trance, the others sat also. With a flourish Perry Lester took out his watch and plunked it down in the center of the table.

"There!" Chet laughed. "That's our pattern, gentlemen. Take a good look at it, get the picture of it firmly fixed in your mind. Because — we're going to materialize one exactly like it!"

After a moment we controlled our levity and got fairly serious about the thing; though, of course, each of us thought the idea was absurd. We were merely amusing ourselves, as people do with an Ouija board, not laughing only because that was part of the game.

We took a good look at the watch, shiny white and gold-rimmed against the black table top. Then, with a swift gesture, Chet removed it. For a few moments we could still see the "light image" of it against the dark surface; then even that faded. But, by agreement, we still sat motionless, concentrating every thought on the spot where the watch had lain.

No one moved. No one spoke. Five men, from varied walks of life, no different from any five you might see on the street every day. But we sat there around a card table that night, tampering with physical laws as a child might toy with a sleeping cobra. . . .

We sat. We stared. We concentrated.

Five minutes. Ten. Twenty. . . .

Perry was the first to break. With a snort of laughter, he suddenly sat back in his chair, fishing for cigarettes.

"This is silly as hell," he burst out. "Goes against every known law of science. . . . Aw, come on. Let's play some poker! . . . Smoke, Chet?"

The rest of us, at his words, had relaxed, laughing. Chet, blinking eyes that watered after our concentrated vigil, shrugged and leaned across the table, bracing himself on a bare elbow for support.

Instantly he jerked back his arm, rubbing it and cursing. All the laughter had vanished from his eyes as he put out a hand gingerly and touched the table top where his arm had rested.

"Huh!" Chet exploded. "Feel that — the place where we've all been staring! It's — it's *hot!*"

Wide-eyed, we felt the spot. And there was no mistake — it was warm, that one round spot in the center of the table top; warm, but cooling rapidly. We gaped at each other blankly. Greer shivered. Scofield swallowed noisily. Perry tried to grin, and shook his head like a punch-drunk fighter.

"Say!" he breathed. "Do you suppose — ?"

Chet's narrowed eyes stared at the spot, bright with elation. "Do I suppose? Hell yes! Do you know what happened? Our combined mental attraction was collecting atoms at that point of focus — and welding them together! . . . Perry, put out that cigarette," he snapped. "Tom, sit back down — we've got to try this thing again!"

We glanced at Scofield, who had half risen from his chair. Sweat dewed his high forehead, and his pale eyes were frightened.

"Chet, I — I don't like this," he blurted. "They — they say my — uncle was babbling about something like this when — when he — do you suppose he was really mad?" His voice rose pathetically. "I mean — could such a thing — ?"

We were all looking at him, which made him flush and stammer as usual. But Chet spoke calmly, very scientific and detached again.

"Yes," he answered quietly. "It could be and is, Tom. Sit down. We're going to prove it."

But Tom Scofield was pushing his chair back, shaking his head. That little muscle in his cheek was twitching more violently than ever, and his face was ashen. His eyes were wide and glassy.

"No!" he jerked out harshly, groping for his hat. "No, no, I won't try it any more! I — don't like to *think* so hard about things, Chet. When I do, I — I feel dizzy. My head aches. . . . Please! I want to go home. I — get the jitters like this sometimes." He broke off so pitifully that Chet frowned at us and slapped him on the back.

"Okay, sure," he laughed. "Don't take this thing so seriously, old son — ye gods! After all, it's just a screwy experiment. Why should it frighten you?"

I'll never forget Scofield's eyes as he stopped at the door and turned back to us. Those pale eyes stared at the table top for a moment, then veered away like a scared bird.

"Why?" he whispered. "It's the — the uncertainty,

Chet, don't you see? That's what got my uncle — the doctor told me, and I — I visited him once at the asylum before he died. You see, he — got to worrying about — what we are and why we're here. Are we really here, after all? Where, exactly, is the thin line between imagination and reality? The human mind — it's so tricky, so easily fooled. . . ."

Chet scoffed at him reassuringly. Perry gave another of his down-to-earth snorts, though I saw Boyton Greer staring oddly at Tom as he opened the door.

"Nuts!" said Perry. "Don't try to tell me I spend forty bucks a week trying to clothe and feed a body that doesn't exist! I don't know *why* I'm here, but I know damn well I *am!* I'll slug the guy that says I'm — "

But Tom Scofield had gone.

We looked at each other for a moment before speaking.

"I didn't like the look in his eyes," Chet murmured. "Tom's such a queer duck. Goes off half-cocked over the slightest thing. Guess we shouldn't have stirred him up with a screwball theory like this."

"Rot!" Perry exploded. "Nothing wrong with Tom; he just took one too many, that's all. And as for your fine theory, Mr. Chetham, I can explain that 'hot spot' on the table. It wasn't there. But you put on such a good act that we others believed it was, after you said so! Pure suggestion, that's the answer. 'Materializing a watch'!"

Chet grinned at him, eyes narrowing in that stubborn way of his when someone — usually Perry — betters him in an argument.

"Think so?" he snapped. "Well, it so happens, my idiot friend, that I *did* feel heat at that point. Listen; let's meet at my apartment next week sometime, and we'll try this little experiment again. I think I've got a way to disprove this 'suggestion' theory of yours, Perry."

We grinned at his vehemence and agreed to come, debating whether or not to ask Tom, since he had appeared so easily upset by the thing. . . .

But the question was settled for us next morning. Poor old Tom — wandering about the streets all night until the police took him in! They thought he was drunk at first, but later he was transferred to the psychopathic ward. We heard the details via Perry: how he had kept beating his fists against his head, and mumbling about a watch that kept ticking in his brain. Only we four made any sense out of that, and we kept our mouths shut after a short discussion.

For, as Chet pointed out, everyone knew there was insanity in Tom's family. Anything was likely to set him off, and it had just happened to be our crazy discussion the evening before. Explaining Tom's aberration would not help him and would only bring a lot of unpleasant publicity.

We had our meeting at Chet's the very next night, full of talk about Tom's commitment to the state mental hospital. Perhaps, had it not been for that, we might have lost interest in our fantastic "experiment with mind-power," as Chet called it. But anything capable of driving a man mad holds a sort of morbid curiosity for the normal man. Like a magnet, the subject drew us once more as we lounged around the apartment, drinking up Chet's company-Scotch and fogging the air with cigarette smoke.

"Of course," Perry drawled, "you've been clowning about the whole thing, Chet. Take off your beard; we know you!" He chuckled. "Come on now — 'fess up! You didn't really feel that hot spot, did you?"

Chet, leaning back in a deep leather chair, squinted at him thoughtfully. Then, with a crooked grin, he solemnly raised his right hand as we used to in our kid days.

"Honor bright, I felt it," he said flatly. "But the more I

think about it, the more I — I wonder if I didn't hypnotize myself into believing I felt it. Try pressing your fingertips together hard, with your eyes closed, and tell yourself there's a pane of glass between them. You know damn well it's not there — but you can feel it! I'm wondering if my 'hot spot' wasn't something of the kind."

I glanced at Boyton, about to make some jeering comment. But his serious, almost frightened eyes stopped me. He leaned forward, eyeing Chet. Suddenly he blurted:

"I've got to know. This thing — it gets under your skin, doesn't it? Worries you. . . . Listen, you three. There's a way we can find out for sure. Have someone else, someone who doesn't know a thing about our — our watch idea, feel the spot after we've concentrated on it."

Chet grinned, and reached for the phone. "I thought of that too," he nodded approval. "I'll phone the drug store and get them to send some ginger ale. When the delivery boy comes — well, he's our guinea-pig. Okay?"

He phoned the order, then beckoned us to sit in a circle around the table as on that night when Tom showed us that weird book.

Seated in comfortable chairs a moment later, we prepared to repeat our crazy "séance." Conditions this time were more favorable. A lamp threw our faces in shadow. It did not hurt our eyes so much, illuming only the dark table top. And Chet stuffed our ears with cotton to shut out any noise.

We sat. We stared. We concentrated, as before on that night Scofield had been with us, mentally forming the shape of Perry's watch.

Ten minutes. Fifteen. A half-hour. . . .

If you have tried it, you'll know the strain of concentrating every faculty on one spot for any length of time. It's nerve racking. After a very short time, my head began to ache. My eyes burned unbearably from the fixed staring. My muscles, tensed to the nth degree, began to stiffen painfully, and I am sure the other three felt as I did.

But we did not move, nor did we speak. With every fiber of our beings, we concentrated on the formation of a flat gold watch at the same point on that dark table.

And suddenly. . . .

Boyton Greer drew a sharp breath, visible but not audible to our cotton-stuffed ears. All of us tensed. We leaned forward, gaping at the table's center, concertedly tearing the cotton out for audible speech.

"Do you see what I see?" Perry whispered sharply. "Good Lord! I'm losing my mind! Or else —"

"You're not," Chet rapped out. "I see it too! Boyton? Joe?"

We nodded, dazedly, and continued to gape at it.

It was fading slowly now — a round shiny-looking blob, the size of Perry's watch, white with a yellowish rim. The numerals were blurred, however, and there was no stem.

"Say!" Chet whispered, pointing out this last oddity. "I wasn't thinking about a *stem* for the darned thing! Were you?"

Perry, Greer and I shook our heads, stunned. That was why the part had not materialized! We had all been concentrating on the *face only*.

Blinking at the shadowy thing, we saw it flatten out, become ovoid, then slowly begin to dissolve. Gingerly Chet poked it with a pencil, and the dent left in the thing's surface was like that one might make by poking a pat of wet sand. Fine sand, almost powdery — that is what the blob appeared to be made of. As we looked, it seemed to melt into the table top. . . .

And once more we all touched the spot where it had been. It was *hot*, as hot as the hearth in front of a blazing fire!

"Well I'll be a — " Perry sat back, mopping sweat from his forehead.

Boyton Greer huddled in his chair, shivering, shaking his head dazedly.

Chet grinned broadly, spread his hands. The light of scientific triumph glowed in his thoughtful eyes — though there was bewilderment in them, too, and not a little healthy fright.

"It's true!" he breathed. "It works! In a minute, I'll realize it, but right now I — I just feel slap-happy! It *was* there, wasn't it, Perry? We *did* see it?"

Perry Lester nodded vaguely, slumped back in his chair. He ran a tongue over dry lips; then he scowled.

"Hypnotism!" he exploded. "You know what we've been doing? Sitting up here like a bunch of dopes, hypnotizing ourselves into seeing a watch! We haven't proved a thing . . . and personally, my head aches! I feel like the devil. Nuts to the whole thing! I'm going home to bed!"

"No, wait!" Chet seized his arm, forcing him back into his chair excitedly. "We've got to bring it back, Perry — and find out whether the delivery boy can see it or not! Then we'll know."

Perry sat down again slowly, running a finger around under his collar. "Well — okay," he growled. "But much of this concentrating business is going to make us all sick. The strain is too great."

"Quiet!" Chet snapped. "Concentrate! The boy will be here in a few minutes. Now, get this. When I get up to let him in, keep concentrating. Replace your ear cotton, and bring it back!" he whispered. "With the hands pointing to — a quarter to ten. Everybody must agree on that hour."

Fifteen minutes later — minutes that made my head ache sickeningly and my eyes burn with staring — there was that watch-like blob at the table's center again, as solid as before. It shimmered slightly, like an object seen under water. But the numerals were clearer — and this time, it had a stem and slender black hands pointing the hour Chet had planted in our minds before the thing materialized.

There was a knock at the door, and Chet rose quietly to open it.

With tremendous effort of will, Perry, Boy and I kept our eyes glued to the table as the black delivery boy shambled in. The watch quivered as Chet maneuvered him into the dusky room. Cautiously I removed my ear-stops to hear as his light voice murmured:

"That was quick service, boy. So, for a tip, you can have anything you see on that table! Fair enough?"

The boy grinned at him, then shuffled over to the table, eyeing us curiously because we sat so still and did not glance up at his approach. Sniggering, he peered at the table, then turned to Chet.

"Aw," he grinned. "You's jest funnin' me, ain't you Cap'n?" I heard, and relaxed — but stiffened again as he added, "You-all wouldn't gimme no gold watch for a tip, now, would you?"

A moment later, when he had slipped the beaming kid a dollar and hustled him out, Chet whirled on us again. We were all leaning back in our chairs, exhausted and stunned . . . all but Perry.

With savage energy he stood up and reached for his hat, scowling. "I've had enough of this," he snapped. "I'm leaving —"

He stopped short, however, blinking quizzically as Boyton rose, eyes wide with a child-like terror of the dark.

"Chet," he whispered. "He *did* see it! It's — true! Then,

you and I — all of us — are nothing but a bunch of tiny particles, held together by — what? And we could dissolve, like that watch! Fly into atoms and go drifting off into space! I wonder," he muttered. "Is that what death is? When our bodies disintegrate into dust —"

Perry stared at him, then flashed a warning look at Chet and me. He laughed lightly, reassuringly.

"Oh, come on, Chet — this has gone far enough. Boy, don't take him seriously. Why, that delivery boy seeing it doesn't prove a thing! It's nothing in the world but thought-transmission, coupled with mass hypnotism.

"We were thinking that watch so hard, we made the kid see it. Some kids are very sensitive, like dogs. That's the answer: telepathy and hypnosis. Eh, Chet?"

Chet glanced at Boyton's white face, and shrugged. "Sure," he drawled. "That's all there is to it. The watch didn't really exist at all."

Greer stared at him fixedly, then forced a grin. "You're — quite sure? Wow!" he laughed shakily. "This thing — had me going for a minute! The idea of —" He shook himself like a terrier, and faced us, more like the old Boyton. "Well, good night, atoms!" he drawled. "I'm going home and get some shut-eye. If I disappear in the night — *pouf!* like that — you'll know what happened to me! See you tomorrow."

But we didn't see Boyton, not ever again, alive.

I was sitting in the office the next morning, nursing a blind headache caused by our mental strain the night before, when Chet phoned. Perry had just called him with the news via the city room, about a clerk, one Boyton C. Greer, who had been walking along the street on his way to lunch. Suddenly, without a word, he had leaped in front of an oncoming truck, to be killed instantly. Greer's wife was prostrated with grief, at a loss to explain the suicide except that Boyton had seemed very nervous and depressed the night before.

That afternoon we met — only Perry, Chet and I now — in a downtown restaurant. A deep gravity hung over us like a cloud as we sat discussing Boy's suicide, following so closely upon Tom's mental collapse.

"Chet," Perry blurted, "it was this watch-thing that got them both. Boy was such an impressionable kid, and poor old Tom was a psychopathic case. We should never have stirred them up with a crazy idea like this, and left them to worry over it."

Chetham met his eye queerly. Sweat beaded on his high forehead, and his hand shook nervously, holding his coffee cup.

"No?" he drawled. "Perry — Joe, I've been thinking about this damn business all night . . . and I'm not so sure! We started this as a gag, yes. Half the time I was pretending, of course — like the time we found the formula for witch-ointment, and rubbed the stuff into cuts on our arms. The aconite and belladonna in it did give a sensation of flying and high excitement, and we did have hallucinations; so I pretended we had really flown through the night to a witch's Sabbat. I actually had the rest of you believing it for a while, but of course there was nothing to it. . . ."

Perry nodded, grinning faintly at the memory of five small boys camping out together under the stars.

His grin faded as Chet's quiet voice went on:

"But this thing — I'm not so sure. Franklin was playing a game with a kite and a key, when he stumbled on the truth about electricity. And we five nitwits, clowning around, may have actually been performing a valuable scientific experiment — with mental electricity. It scares me, the way it scared Tom and Boyton. But — I decided last night that we must go on with it. We owe it to those two to find out if there's anything to it besides telepathy and hypnotism. Don't you see? If they've given their lives for something of real value to science, Boy's and Tom's names will go down in history. And so will ours — if we can prove that watch was real!"

Perry and I stared at him. The noise and clatter of the small café faded into nonexistence at his words.

"It can't be," Perry blurted out, almost desperately. "Chet — it's a scientific impossibility. Besides, there's no way to prove it. Why, good Lord, if a man can't believe his own senses, what can he believe?"

Ray Chetham pushed back his chair, and rose from the table, his dessert untouched.

"A camera," he replied flatly. "I'm going to Boy's now, to try to cheer up his wife — and borrow that pet camera of his and some stuff for developing. You know that old vacant house of my uncle's on Beecher Street? There's an old table and some chairs in the attic. I'll meet you there in an hour, and we'll test this crazy thing once and for all!"

He strode out of the restaurant. Perry and I sat for a minute, staring at each other. He grinned at me shakily, and ran a finger around under his collar.

"I have a feeling," he said, "that we've gone quite far enough with this screwy business, Joe. Tampering with the Law of Creation, that's what we're doing — in case there's anything to it, which I doubt. But — suppose there is? What effect will such knowledge have on the world of tomorrow? Cripes!"

He jerked to his feet, glancing at his pocket watch, and I saw him wince slightly as he did so.

"Be seeing you in an hour," he muttered. "I've got to hock this thing to pay my rent."

He laughed oddly. "Sordid down-to-earth thought

isn't it? Maybe if I waited, I could hock — *the other one.* And tomorrow, the pawn shop owner would look for it, and —" He strode out, laughing queerly.

I sat for a long time, almost the whole hour, thinking about what he had said. Thinking and thinking about it, imagining the possibilities. . . .

I felt funny and light-headed, and a little sick at the stomach, when I got up finally and headed for that old house on Beecher, to join Chet and Perry — and a camera.

They were already there when I arrived. Sunlight streamed through a curtainless window, full on the table around which Chet had placed two rickety chairs and a packing box. On another chair he had rigged up Boy's camera for a time-exposure.

The half-open door of a spacious closet across the room revealed a second smaller table, with pans of acid ready for developing the picture of — whatever was to be on that table.

My head was spinning now. My heart pounded, and I felt a crazy excitement, similar to the effect of a marihuana cigarette I once sampled. The room appeared all out of focus, and Chet's and Perry's faces looked distorted and unfamiliar. If they had looked at me, perhaps they would have noticed something in my expression. But they were intent on the experiment; merely waved me to my chair, and sat down at the table.

It took a long time, this meeting, to make the blob of matter appear on the table top — evidence of my mental state, and perhaps theirs, too.

We sat, stared, concentrating for almost a full hour. And then —

There it was, quivering as from an electrical current but clear in every detail. I wondered if the thing was solid, a hollow shell, or whether the vague rudiments of a mechanism were hidden there inside — distorted, perhaps, by minds unfamiliar with watch-works. I wondered. . . .

Then — click! Chet had pressed the camera release, and registered on the sensitive film whatever really lay on that bare table top.

The sound was loud in the silent room, so loud that it startled me, and made the watch-image quiver and lose its shape. Slowly it dissolved as Perry leaned back, rubbing his smarting eyes and stretching tense muscles.

Chet stood up dizzily, taking the camera with great care. I felt rather than saw him make a bee-line for the closet; heard the door shut behind him. . . .

It was then that the roaring began in my head, deafening me, blinding me. I could see that door across the room, looming large and forbidding as the door to a death-chamber of a prison. Behind it a man was moving swiftly, dipping a section of film into a pan of acid — and thereby, perhaps, solving the eternal mystery of Creation.

And men would be gods, pitting their brain-power one against another — creating images that did not exist in the normal scheme of things, creating even women that did not exist — until no one could tell the true from the false, and madness would sweep the world. . . .

Terror shook me like an ague — a blind sick terror of space and mystery and things beyond our ken. In that moment it seemed that Boyton and Tom stood beside me. I thought I could see them, waving frantic arms and screaming something at me, shoving me toward that monstrous door. . . .

I heard someone — Perry — cry out:

"Joe — what's the matter, Joe? You look so — wait, Joe! Take it easy, old boy; you're — *Chet! Chet! He's gone mad! Look out!*"

Vaguely I remembered picking up a chair, feather-light, and raising it above my head, and smashing with it — smashing at a monster wearing a white mask made to resemble Perry Lester's face.

Then the huge door burst open, and I was smashing again, wielding the chair with no effort, until a second fiend, masquerading as my old friend, Ray Chetham, went down like a felled ox.

Something in his hand — a piece of film, ready for developing, but ruined now by exposure to light. . . .

That's about all, Sergeant. You'll find the bodies in that second-floor room, in the old vacant house on Beecher. I came straight here, the minute I realized there was nothing I could do for poor old Perry and Chet — after I came to myself, you understand, I saw what I had done.

I thought of suicide at first, longed for it, bending over them and crying like a baby. Old Chet and Perry were more like brothers than friends. . . . I couldn't stand the thought of what I'd done. . . .

Then I knew that suicide was the easy way. What I had to do was give myself up, so that I could tell someone about our experiments before they do — whatever the state is going to do to me.

Someone else may want to try what we tried — a scientific mind — not a bunch of untrained helpless laymen like the five of us. Someone not afraid to find out what was on that undeveloped film.

I don't want to know, myself. I hope to God nobody ever finds out! 🙠

Dream People

JOHN GREY

dream people
are very tiny
live under fronds
carry certain diseases
which they pass on
to children who
play in thick forest

children grow
into odd young men
who confuse reality
with the tugging of
the dream people's seed

I lie in bed
playing with your shadow
as you sleep
and I feel like a
silent speck of horror
a finger-nail that
scratches a thousand times
its size

you bleed on white linen
slowly slowly
not sensing me drag
you through the forest
as you push into the pillow
without light
I tuck you under a leaf
the dream people make love
to you with the harsh
burn of runaway stars

Late Bloomer

JANET FOX
illustration by
ELIZABETH A. SAUNDERS

Kirsten's hand on the smooth wood of the bannister led her step by step down the staircase. Sunlight against her right side told her when she passed the narrow window. Her feet, accustomed to the stairs' dimensions, carried her, without a misstep to the bottom where the sound of her footsteps was muffled on the Persian carpet. She could almost remember the design on it, but when she concentrated, the patterns and colors always blurred.

The clink of dishes and utensils told her that she was late for breakfast, but Aunt Francine said nothing. She sat down, and using the familiar pattern of silver and dishes, began to eat.

Francine cleared her throat, as if to make her presence known. "I hope you won't mind, dear, but I have a club meeting this afternoon. I'd appreciate it if you'd turn on the spray in the greenhouse."

"Sure."

There was an uncomfortable silence. "And I'm sorry about our argument yesterday," Francine went on. "I suppose you know best, but —"

"I know you think I should stay here in this house where everything is safe and familiar, but that's the point. I can't spend the rest of my life here. There are things I can learn at the school. And if I were in a larger city, maybe I could even see a — a psychiatrist."

Aunt Francine said nothing, but Kirsten could sense

that the old woman's thin form was ramrod straight, the patrician features disapproving.

"If someone could only help me remember what it was that made me lose my sight. Sometimes in dreams I can almost remember, but then it slips away, and when I wake up I'm always . . . afraid."

"Losing both your parents in that plane crash would be bad enough, I'd think, without imagining something mysterious."

"That might explain it on a temporary basis, but it's been three years."

"It's never easy. I know how I felt when your uncle died."

"Uncle Charles," she said, almost in a tone of surprise, and then was embarrassed at not having any better memory of him than she did.

"He died only the week before you came to live with us. He'd been ill so long. So much death."

"Then why don't I remember that?" Kirsten asked herself, but only silently. It was possible she'd been so grief-stricken she'd forgotten the events of her first few weeks here. Losing her parents had been hard, she knew, but she'd not become blind until several weeks after their deaths.

"Well, I must go. Don't forget about the spray. You'll be sure and lock the door behind you? Those blooms are priceless. I don't want even the servants to see them."

Francine's voice grew strained and fanatical whenever she talked about her orchids. Kirsten was always partly amused by it, yet it was pathetic in a way. Francine had more passion for her rare flowers than for most people. "I'll tend to them. Don't worry."

A narrow walkway led to the greenhouse's heavy

wooden door. The padlock was a cold weight against her palm as she searched her pocket for the key. This was only another of Francine's odd preoccupations with her plants. Even if the orchids were rare, she couldn't imagine any burglar passing up the antique silver or other costly artifacts in the house in favor of bark-encrusted bulbs or parasitic blossoms.

As the door swung back she was almost overcome by a fetid, organic smell. Though Francine could spend hours here it made Kirsten uneasy, though she could not have said why. She reached out and gently touched the surface of one of the leaves, rough-textured, slightly adhesive to her fingertips. Of course there was no wind in here, but sometimes, in the silence, the leaves rustled as if something small and furtive moved among them. She almost felt watched by unseen eyes.

She found the controls of the sprays and water hissed, a damp mist rising to bathe her face. Water droplets fell among the leaves with a sound like a faint sigh.

After a few moments she turned off the spray and listened to the water dripping off engorged blossoms and leaves. The thick scent of growth and decay was almost palpable and she wished futilely that she could only look around. That would dispel whatever lurked there in her own personal darkness.

The lock spoke an implacable click and she felt glad to put the place behind her. She stepped out onto the front porch, the sun hot and clean on her face and arms, the grit-laden wind washing away the closed-in smell and the sense of anxiety she always felt in the greenhouse. She felt for the padded porch-swing and began to swing back and forth, into the bright hot sunlight, back into shadows cast by vines growing on a lattice at one end of the porch.

She heard the angry voices at a distance, growing

more distinct as whoever was arguing crossed the lawn. One voice was the guttural growl of the gardener, a man of one syllable or less. She didn't recognize the other voice until she heard the footsteps on the wooden steps of the porch. It was a local character BEM Haskins, who'd earned his nickname by indulging in his hobby of investigating flying saucers. BEM, of course, being short for Bug Eyed Monster.

It was his weight, creaking the boards of the stairs, that had identified him for Kirsten, and now he confirmed it, his deep, slurred voice and the constant faint smell of alcohol about him. She remembered Francine and her friends laughing about the way he roamed the area in his van, tracking down saucer sightings and trying to prove his weird theories.

"But look, I found it. Look at it, I —" BEM's voice trailed off as he realized she couldn't see what he was probably holding out toward her. "Oh God, sorry, I didn't mean —"

"That's all right; I'm used to it. What's that you've found?"

"Just a piece of junk," said the gardener in disgusted tones. "BEM, you got no call to be bothering Miss Hastings."

"I found it with my metal detector, a broken piece of something bigger, something made outta metal, black and twisted like it might have come down through the atmosphere."

Kirsten put her hands out and touched the thing. It was as he'd described it, crusted with dry earth, irregular and pitted as if it'd gone through some burning. She tried to feel the strangeness BEM seemed to find in the object, but it seemed like an ordinary piece of metal.

"A few years back there were all kinds of sightings

around here, a regular flap."

"He's a looney," said the gardener. "I'll throw him off the place."

"No, let him look around if he likes. He won't hurt anything."

With an obscenity blurred by growling tones, the gardener departed.

"Thanks," said BEM. The porch railing groaned as he settled his weight on it. "People don't always take me serious, I know, but one of these days —. They kid me. 'Little green men from Mars,' they say. Hell, I know there's no life on Mars, and why do people always say little green men?"

BEM went on in this manner for awhile and then decided to take another sweep around the grounds with his metal detector. Sunlight against her arms and face had grown weaker and the wind was beginning to grow cold, so she went back inside. Listening to BEM's wild theories had given her a headache; she could feel tension building at the back of her neck, behind her eyes. And that night she dreamed.

There was the tree-of-life design on the carpet in rich purples and blood red. Oddly, she could see again in dreams, but sometimes she couldn't recall upon awakening what it was she'd seen. Now she saw her own reflection in the tall mirror. A tall woman, slender in a leaf-green dress, a tense grace, as of something startled, ready for flight, eyes large and almost haunted in a pale face, tendrils of light brown hair straying around her cheeks, her white throat. Like seeing a stranger.

In her dreams the stairs were beneath her feet and she could see the dark polished walnut of the bannister. At the top of the stairs was a door of darkly varnished wood. Confusedly, she recognized the door to the greenhouse, its large padlock.

Despite the lock, when she pushed on the door it swung inward, giving a view of a spacious bedroom decorated in antique furniture. The room was dim and shafts of light slanted downward, dancing with golden dustmotes. It took her several moments to realize a body lay upon the bed — nude, emaciated, bones delineated by dry and fragile skin. She also began to notice the cloying greenhouse smell about the place. One might almost have said that it was a corpse which lay on the bed, except that it writhed and shuddered continually as if in pain, though there was no outcry and the papery eyelids stayed closed. There was a slithering noise behind her, and as she whirled to look, she woke up.

It was almost a full minute before she realized she could not see. Fragments of dream with their confused imagery clung to her mind, but the more she reached after them, the harder her heart beat and the more frightened she became until fright had driven all memory of it away. All she could be certain of was that she had had this dream before.

Francine snapped shut the catches on Kirsten's suitcase. "That should do it."

"You're still not angry, are you, now that we've made all the arrangements?"

"I suppose not," said Francine, her voice betraying a nervousness that had been increasing over the last few days. "Before you leave, I wish you'd visit the greenhouse with me. There's really been such a blossoming. I'm so proud of my little ones; not for three years have I seen such gorgeous blossoms."

"I, uh —" began Kirsten, reluctant to spend her last evening at home in that fetid, decay-laden atmosphere.

"I can describe them to you, dear, the colors, and you could touch —"

"All right," said Kirsten, relenting, thinking, *Maybe she'll be lonely here when I go, just her all alone with her plants.*

There seemed more noises than usual in the greenhouse, rustlings of leaves, water drops condensing and falling; there was somehow a restlessness. Kirsten rubbed her arms, against the clamminess of the atmosphere. Francine was talking in a vaguely hysterical undertone, "Don't I givems just what precious needs? There's a pretty. There's a love." It was ludicrous, but somehow didn't seem that funny.

"Tell me what the blossoms are like," said Kirsten quickly. "You said you'd describe the colors. I can smell them." She didn't add that it was an overpowering stench, the sickly scent of too many bouquets at a funeral. "Aunt Francine?" she asked, as she heard the receding tap of high heels across concrete. She turned to follow the sound, but the slam of the door, the click of the padlock stopped her.

"How . . . stupid," she said aloud, but she was beginning to catch the undercurrent of fear the place always held for her. The rustling of foliage was like sinister whispering, and then she heard a slithering sound behind her. The same sound she'd heard in dreams. She bolted but hit one of the tables, numbing hip and thigh, and fell onto the damp, grainy concrete of the floor.

"Who is it?" she shouted. "Who are you?" Something round and cool slid across her wrist. As she jerked away something like thorns caught in her flesh. She screamed and tore herself free, but already she could feel a heaviness as if the thorns had been tipped with a poison or a drug. Another damp tendril slid about her throat with a caressing motion. Leaves, fresh and delicate fluttered against her cheek. The smell of blossoms was suddenly all around her as if she were being smothered in them.

A questing vine slid across her knee, pushed past the hem of her skirt. Despite the feeling of heaviness spreading through her body, she began to struggle. The tendril about her throat tightened perceptibly as something feathery and cool moved with the persistence of growth along the inside of her thigh. And then it was pushing past the flimsy material of her panties and a moment later she was penetrated by something that felt like a small closed fist, something that began slowly to uncurl — to open.

Whatever the thorns had injected into her caused her to lose consciousness and she was immediately back into her recurring nightmare, climbing the long staircase, approaching the door with its heavy padlock. This time as the door swung back, exposing the emaciated body on the bed, she realized the face was barely recognizable as that of her Uncle Charles, though the sunken cheeks with their translucent stubble, jutting beak of nose made it seem a caricature of the man she'd known. The skeletal body writhed monotonously, and she rushed to his side to see if she could comfort him. His mouth was working, as if it took some immense effort of will just to open the dry lips. She leaned closer as if to hear his last words. . . .

Only to awaken on the hard floor of the greenhouse. A cold numbness was in all her limbs, and she stirred, disturbed by what she'd seen in the dream. Patches of color danced before her eyes, amber to gold to flame to silver-pink as if the hues lay just a bit beyond the visible spectrum. She closed her eyes tightly, opened them again. "I can see!" she shouted, her words answered only by a faint sigh as of wind through foliage. "I can see," more quietly, her hands going to her abdomen as she saw the flowers standing erect on their cobra-like vines. It had been a shock that had taken away her sight, and now another had brought it back.

The dream was still with her. All she had to do was close her eyes to picture the atrophied figure on the bed, moving slowly, monotonously as if something within it surged with life. Her uncle's lips opened as she waited for his message. Something poked out like a blackened tongue, a line splitting across it from which light leaked — amber to gold to flame until it had outrun the spectrum.

Out of a new feeling of calm that had taken possession of her, she considered it a beautiful sight. ❧

A Trick of the Night

S. K. EPPERSON

A sleepless urge waits alone in the dark,
To live a piece of a dream.
And on your screen he's bigger than life,
Not living at all, but breathing;
Like a body in a casket will sometimes,
It is merely a trick of the light.

The fantasy slips between the sheets,
Crying shamefully aloud to be fed.
Begging fulfillment it chafes and whines;
My God how you wish this man dead!
Guided by yearnings that reek of revenge,
You take up the knife and plunge it in. . . .

He breathes yet beside you, but simply
Amazing is how much better you feel.
Dead on the screen of your innermost dreams
Is this faithless, adulterous heel.
Preparations are swift, the funeral hurried,
One minute more and the bastard is buried.

The burn that made this murder due
Has dissolved with an echoing sigh.
The fantasy has passed for true
On the blade of this vengeful wife.
Like death in dreams can be sometimes,
It was merely a trick of the night. . . .

ঽ

On the Blue Guillotine

GREGORY NICOLL

illustration by
TODD RILEY

He had no idea how he got there, or how long it had been. He knew only that he was tied securely — hands and feet — to the upright frame of the blue guillotine.

And he was in pain. Fierce, searing, undreamable pain.

The thick hemp ropes which bound him to the device were old and worn, and the thousands of stiff black threads woven into their fabric picked and tore at the flesh of his wrists and ankles like clusters of rusty needles. The slightest movement brought a thousandfold increase to his suffering.

His muscles burned. His arms, tied to the framework above his head, and his legs, spreadeagled out below, ached with the unmercifully *deep* agony of musculature forced to remain in one position for hour after grueling hour.

Hunger burned a hole in his stomach, and thirst tore at his throat.

Above him hung the guillotine blade, a gleaming Sword of Damocles poised to strike the deathblow which with each passing hour he desired more emphatically. Death, he reasoned, would bring an end to the torture.

Yet it seemed that each successive time his eyes fluttered weakly open and his gaze turned skyward, the great blade and the crossbeam from which it was suspended were somehow *higher* than before, as though the sides of

151

the guillotine were growing upward toward the sun like the stalks of some gigantic poisonous plant, hoisting its beautiful but deadly flower up farther from the earth with each new dawn.

After what might have been days of this, the lethal blade was no longer visible — lost somewhere in the unreachable heights of the blue sky, having long since passed its vanishing point.

On that day, *they* came.

The two doctors looked down at the patient thrashing futilely against the restraining straps.

"It's such a tremendous waste of a good mind," said one of them. "He was quite a scholar."

"Oh?" said the other. "I wasn't aware of that."

"Yes, it's true. He was nearing the end of a major translation project when the symptoms struck."

"What was he translating?"

"It was an obscure French text. I'd never heard of it before this case came to my attention. The title of the book was *Cultes des Goules*."

He did not know what to call the creatures he saw through the burning haze of his dry, stinging eyeballs. He decided to call them demons, for that is what they seemed to be. They cackled hideously at one another as they formed a circle and danced in grotesque motions around the base of the blue guillotine, pointing from time to time at him with their web-fingered hands.

And as they frolicked, they sang.

Guillotine, guillotine, guillotine blue
Flesh for me, flesh for you!

Their voices were high, like the squealing of animals, yet evocative of reptilian hissing.

"Is he ever cogent?"

"No, not since he's been with us."

"Well, does he respond to questions or to direct stimuli — to touch?"

The doctor shook his head sadly. "No," he answered. "Only to pain."

The demons daubed him with a sickly-smelling blue paint, which they smeared across his body and rubbed firmly into his skin with their coarse, knobby hands, tearing away what was left of his clothing in order to cover *all* of his body with the pigment. He screamed hoarsely when one of them dragged its claws across his genitals, and the scream caused the creature to pause for a moment. It then resumed its painting with renewed interest.

When the demons finished, they danced again. This time their cries sounded even more inhuman.

Guillotine, guillotine, guillotine blue
Flesh for me, flesh for you.

There was a disturbance in the surface of the blue sea.

The orderly stood meekly before the doctor. "I swear to you, sir, I don't know *anything* about those marks on him. It *might* be rats, but I've never seen any rats in that ward."

The doctor regarded the young man carefully. "From now on," he said, "I want you to look in on him *every* time you walk past his cell. No matter what you're over there for or how big a hurry you're in. If there are rats — or *any-thing* — in that man's room, I want to know about it. Do you understand?"

The orderly nodded. From the gravity of his supervisor's tone, he understood all too well.

The gargantuan thing from the sea breathed its putrid seawater breath on him as it tore the ropes loose. Lifting him from the blue frame in one gigantic web-fingered hand, it forced his neck down onto the lower half of the block. Several of the little demons slipped the wooden companion piece in place, trapping his head in the path of the guillotine blade.

Amidst an ear-piercing cacophony of demonic laughter and chanting, the great blade descended from the sky. It whistled downward with the velocity of a cannonball, ever increasing its fearsome speed as it lashed toward its inert blue target.

The guillotine was blue. The sky was blue. The ground was blue. The sea was blue. The victim was blue. Even the blade was blue, for its polished mirror-like steel surface reflected all the blue around it.

With a hideous THOK! of steel embedding itself in wood, the blade ended its fall.

There was a splash of crimson.

The orderly's scream echoed through the entire building.

They found him amidst the chaos of broken serving-ware and splattered food from the tray he had dropped outside the door. He was shuddering and jabbering incoherently, his eyes wide with a peculiar blend of terror and amazement.

"It *talked*," he gurgled. "It talked. I heard it."

Inside the cell, where the lifeless body still lay secured by the straps, they found the patient's severed head face up in a puddle of blood beneath the bed. The lips appeared to twitch for several moments after its discovery, as though the patient was attempting to speak.

"I heard it!" shrieked the orderly as they led him away. He cackled dementedly and, as he reached the elevator door, a tiny fragment of what seemed to be a half-remembered song escaped his lips.

Guillotine, guillotine, guillotine blue . . . 🙠

Red Rover

GLEN R. EGBERT

illustration by
P. J. MEACHAM

"**G**et your mangy ass outta my chair!" Jeb swung a meaty fist, missed the dog's head and collided with the lamp instead. It smashed into the wall. "Now ya done it."

Red Rover jumped down and scurried under the sofa. Jeb got down on his hands and knees and reached in to grab it. The dog growled and snapped at him.

"Why you . . ."

"Jeb? What's goin' on in there?"

Jeb jumped up. "Nothin' Ma."

His mother stood in the doorway. "Somethin' break in here?"

"Stuart's dog knocked over the lamp!"

Mamie Ashe stood under five feet in heels, had hair like iron filings and a glance as sharp as a boning knife. A year before she'd had steel pins put in her hip in three places where she broke it. Jeb was convinced the doctors replaced her insides with metal.

"I don't care if he is Stuart's dog. I'm tired of cleaning up his messes."

"Don't even know if it is Stuart's dog," Jeb remarked, not really paying attention to Mamie.

"Shits everywhere. Not shit either. Smells sick or somethin'."

"Just shows up on the stoop one day. Big old crate with our address. Could be from anybody."

"Just the other day," Mamie continued, "I stepped in a

157

big pile out by the back door. Tracked it all over the rug. Almost made me puke."

"Stuart's all the time gettin' into trouble. I mean, Ma, a crate from Columbia! Could be anybody sent it, not just Stuart."

"Did you here me, Jeb? Tracked all that shit from here to Sunday."

"Huh? Oh, yeah, I remember." He chuckled, then stopped when he saw his mother's face.

"Stuart's not gonna be back for another month, damn fool, traipsin' all over South America lookin' for potions and magic spells. I got a magic potion for that dog of his."

Jeb grew pensive. "Last time he's here, seemed scared or somethin'. Kept talkin' 'bout trouble with witch doctors, curses and such. Silly shit, huh?"

Mamie glared at him. "You listen up, Jeb, or you're gonna feel a curse crost your cheek."

"Yes'm. What do ya want I should do to the dog?"

"Get rid of it, Jeb. Drown it, strangle it, or somethin', but don't let me find it here tomorrow."

"Stuart's gonna be awful mad."

Mamie, all ninety pounds of her, swept into the room on steel ball bearings and struck her son across the face. Tears sprang into his eyes.

"Gee, Ma, whyja hit me?"

She glared at him. "My son don't talk back to his Ma, that's why! I know what I'm doin'."

He took a deep breath to keep his angry words from finding voice.

"Lose the mutt, Jeb. I don't want anymore dog shit in this house."

"Okay, Ma, whatever you say." He waited until she was out of the room before he crouched in front of the sofa. "Come on, Rover. That's a boy." He reached in and grabbed the dog's collar. The dog hunched his back and dug in his claws. When he had the dog out, he stood up and cradled it in his arms. "Red Rover. Don't see why Ma called you that. Stupid name. Stupid dog." The dog growled. It didn't look like any dog Jeb had ever seen. Squinty little eyes, no ears to speak of, and fur the color of red clay. Jeb had told his Ma it reminded him of Stuart which earned him a split lip. "Does so resemble Stuart, the sonovabitch."

The dog's ears perked up.

Jeb carried Rover through the kitchen to the back door where its leash hung on a nail. He clipped the leash to the collar. Now that was a pisser, that collar. Jeb wasn't sure what it was made of, but it was all sorts of colors, browns, blacks, even some yellows, and it seemed to be braided. Sure felt like hair, Jeb had decided right off.

He dragged the struggling dog on the end of the leash to his Chevy half-ton, got in and pulled the dog up into the cab. For just a moment, Jeb thought the collar was going to break; there was a dry snapping sound. But it held. The dog twisted at the leash once, then was inside panting, glaring at Jeb with murder in his eyes. But no dog scared Jeb the way his Ma did. He started the pickup, backed out of the drive with a splatter of gravel, and roared off down the road. The dog whimpered next to him.

"You know what's goin' down, don't ya boy?"

The dog growled. Jeb hit him on the side of the head, sending Red into the far door with a thumping sound. The dog lay still.

Jeb knew just the way to get rid of a dog. Kinda fun, too. He'd done it once or twice to cats when his Ma had gotten tired of changing litter trays and vacuuming up cat hair. Course, he hadn't told her what he did to the animals. She probably thought he just choked them or drowned them. Something unimaginative like that. But Jeb had brains, you bet, and when it came to getting rid of pets, he was hard to beat for inspiration.

He rolled down the window and sucked in cool air. L.A. had been one bitch of a place, but a cold front had bloomed off the coast, lowering the temperature several degrees. The moon shone near the horizon, a bloated yellow clown face. He glanced at the dog once or twice, but it was like Red Rover had given up. Jeb wondered whether the dog suspected this was its last night on earth. He shrugged. Dogs weren't that smart. Jeb decided he didn't care whether his Ma's brother found out about Rover or not. Maybe he'd tell him himself. That'd frost his ass! Yeah! His Ma would be proud of him then; maybe she'd treat him better.

The freeway sign pointed left, and Jeb spun the wheel, using the illegal steering wheel knob he'd put on himself.

The truck bounced once as he entered the onramp and Rover moaned. At least it sounded like a moan. Jeb brushed his hand over the dog's back and jerked his hand away. He didn't like that a bit; felt like the dog was already dead.

"Few more minutes, boy," he said, cursing himself for the quiver in his voice. He tried to convince himself it was plain excitement, but something about the feel of the dog had disturbed him. He glanced over quickly when the truck passed beneath a freeway light, and noticed that part of the collar had been torn away. The dog looked bad. Its color had changed some, its original bright red coat more magenta than red. And the dog's head looked swollen. Maybe I hurt its neck some, Jeb thought. Tissue got all swollen up from a bruised neck. That made sense.

Light traffic hustled by. The few cars in Jeb's way scurried aside as he sped across several lanes to the fast lane.

He liked it best right there, hurtling along at seventy. "Come here, boy," he said, trying to keep the excitement out of his voice. He reached over and pulled on the dog's leash. Red Rover growled. "Easy boy, easy, I'm not going to hurt you."

A brand new Vette pulled up behind Jeb's Chevy and flashed its high beams. Jeb gunned his truck up to eighty. The Vette dropped back.

"See, Rover, that guy thinks he's hot shit. We'll give him a little surprise, huh? Just you and me." He considered that and chuckled. "More you than me, I bet." He pulled the leash some more. The dog strained against the leash, making it difficult for Jeb to keep his eyes on the road. The Vette pulled up within a foot of his rear bumper and blinked its brights again.

"Sonovabitch!" Jeb braked enough to scare the pee out of the Vette's driver. Sure enough, the car dropped back again. "Fucker could go 'round." Red Rover lurched to the far side of the cab. Jeb wrapped the leash around his hand several times and gave it a yank. He heard snapping fibers and guessed the dog collar had broken more strands. "I don't give a shit 'bout your collar. You ain't gonna need it where you're goin'." He gave it another tug and the dog ended up in his lap. Jeb had a brief impression of glaring eyes, flaring nostrils, and teeth that seemed too long.

"Jesus Christ! Get offa me!" With a mighty heave that almost made him lose control of the truck, he pushed the dog out the window. Jeb wasn't sure what happened next, things unfolded so quickly.

He still had hold of the leash, wrapped around his right hand. The dog's weight almost pulled him out the window. He could hear Red Rover flopping against the truck's side, each impact sounding like somebody was hitting a fifty-gallon drum with a four-by-four. He shook his hand and the leash came loose, but it got caught on the steering knob.

The dog smashed into the truck again, then the leash pulled the steering wheel over to the left. Jeb fought for control, but ended up racing at eighty miles an hour right up against the center divider, sending up a shower of sparks and a squealing sound so loud it made his head ache. Was that the dog making that sound or the truck? For what seemed hours he wrestled with the wheel, gritting his teeth against the sound of tortured metal, cursing steadily. Then there was a sudden absence of pressure on the steering wheel that sent the truck into the next lane. A VW bug angled away, blaring its horn. Jeb looked in his rearview and saw a curious thing. For just a moment, before the Vette went out of control and smashed into the center divider, Jeb was sure that Red Rover was standing on the Vette's hood.

"That's fuckin' crazy!" He swerved across three lanes just in time to catch the next offramp, bounced like a maniac off the freeway and down a dark neighborhood street. He'd barely missed hitting several cars, but he was certain no one would have been able to describe him or get his license. As he drove home, he decided he'd find some other way of getting rid of animals. At least the big ones. The image of Rover standing on the hood of the new Vette came back. He shook his head. Even if the dog had landed there, no way would it have been able to stand up. The impact alone would have killed it. Still . . .

He shook steadily as he drove home. Hell, the damn dog had almost got him killed. He decided he'd tell Stuart the truth and to hell with the consequences. Besides, it was Ma's idea to waste Rover. Stupid name for a stupid dog. He pulled into their driveway, parking with a squeal of brakes that reminded him of the sound on the freeway. He pulled the leash off the steering wheel knob and found what was left of the dog collar at the end. The remaining strands had snapped from the dog's weight. Jeb shook his head. If that wasn't human hair, then his hemorrhoids didn't hurt.

He dropped the collar and leash beside the porch. His Ma was sitting at the kitchen table, drinking herb tea that smelled like swamp water.

"Get rid of that damn dog?" she asked, looking up at him with her fierce stare. Once more he felt four years old gettin' set for a lickin'.

"Course I did, Ma." He started to tell her how strange everything had been, then decided against it. No telling how she was going to react even when he did what he was told. He walked past her into the living room, turned on the television and flopped down on the sofa. The images on the television calmed him. Then they seemed to blur and run and before he knew it, he had dozed off. Sometime during the night, he was vaguely aware of something standing over him. He groaned. Red Rover had come back for him, he was sure of it. But then the figure moved closer and he saw his Ma. Before he could say anything, she was gone. He rolled over on the sofa, trying to gain some comfort on its bumpy cushions, too much asleep to get up and go to bed, too much awake to be comfortable. It must have been about two or three in the morning when he heard the first sounds. Still, he was so out of it, he couldn't be sure that what he heard was really happening.

There was the sound of breaking glass near the back of the house, near Ma's bedroom.

"Jeb?" Ma sounded strange. He could tell just from the way she said his name, she was scared! He'd never known her to be scared before.

A low growling sound made Jeb sit up and stare into

the darkness.

"Oh, my God!" Ma shouted. "Get away from me!"

Jeb tried to speak, but couldn't. He heard scuffling and grunting coming from his Ma's bedroom, like a big boar hog rooting in the ground, then the sound of something thumping against the wall. Then silence.

Jeb swallowed. He strained to see in the darkness. Was the doorknob turning? Had the door opened a crack? He spoke in a whisper. "Ma, you okay?" He didn't expect an answer. A heavy sound came from her bedroom as though the bureau had been pushed aside. Then a crash reverberated throughout the house. Whatever was moving around in there had pushed the door off its hinges. As he sat frozen on the sofa, something came down the hallway toward the living room. He could tell it was big by the sound of its footsteps. They set up vibrations in the floor that sent chills up through his spine. No man carried that much weight.

He stood up feeling as though his joints were frozen and went to the door to the hallway. Something was on the other side, he was sure of it, some presence, some thing that pressed against the door. He put his hand on the door. It seemed warm! But maybe that was just his imagination.

"Uh, who's th . . . th . . . there?" he said, his voice so tiny he could barely hear it himself.

The pressure on the other side of the door seemed to increase. He heard a whimper.

"Rover? That you boy?"

There was a low growl.

Jeb knew it was Rover. And that it wasn't. The contradiction didn't bother him one bit. The hallway door seemed to press inward, but of course that was impossible. He bolted for the kitchen an instant before the hallway door splintered into a billion slivers. He made it to the back door as something hit the kitchen door so hard it rocked the whole house. He wasn't about to turn and look at whatever was behind him. No way. He leaped the porch steps, hit the gravel drive running and was into the cab of his truck before he knew what he was doing. Some deep dark portion of his mind had taken over, taking him back to an ancient time when reflex controlled a man's behavior. The key was in the ignition. The truck stuttered, then caught. Jeb slapped it into gear, spun the wheel hard over, and backed up straight into the porch. He heard the crumpling of masonry, the splintering of wood. He sent the truck peeling out of the driveway, risked a glance in his rearview just in time to see the porch roof collapse onto the ground. Then something pushed the roof aside as though it were a pile of rags. Something big. Two red shiny points of light glared into Jeb's eyes in the rearview, then were gone as he spun the wheel, the truck slipping and sliding into the street. He accelerated, a bubbling sound of apology and regret coming out of his mouth.

"Oh, Lord, I'm sorry, sorry, most humbly sorry." Then he was mouthing gibberish as he streaked down the street.

He looked in his sideview mirror and began to relax. Then he jerked forward, staring in shock. Something was coming up on the left side of his truck, thirty yards back, coming fast, something with red points of light for eyes.

He pushed on the gas and the truck leaped ahead. But like the Vette, the thing following increased its pace, edging up nearer.

Now he could hear the thud and scrape of its clawed feet on the road. He looked once again, and caught a glimpse, just a moment's brightness in a passing streetlight, of a thing out of a psychotic's nightmare. He could almost make out its contours, could almost see Red Rover's original outline in the monstrosity keeping pace with his truck, could almost imagine it was just some dumb dog protecting its territory against his pickup.

The freeway onramp loomed ahead like some fabled entry to paradise. Jeb chuckled. He was going to make it. Once on the freeway, he could lose this thing. Maybe even turn it on someone else. He sped up to sixty and sailed onto the ramp. For just a moment, he nearly panicked. His tires slipped and squealed on the pavement as they fought to hold the road; he almost crashed into the guard rail. Then his radials caught and he was home free.

Without looking, he sent the pickup racing across to the fast lane, the sounds of crashing metal and horns fading as he reached eighty, then ninety.

"Sonovabitch!" he yelled. "Whoeee!" Nothing on earth could stop him now.

A hundred.

He'd make Dago by first light, then stop for a bite to eat, and race for the border. Nothing could catch him there. He laughed, an hysterical sound, womanish and shakey.

"Wish I had a beer," he said. But damned if he was going to stop until he put a hundred miles between himself and that thing.

He jerked the steering wheel just a bit, sailed into the next lane to pass a Porsche doing ninety, then pulled back into the fast lane. He glanced in the rearview to catch sight of the driver's face. Burned his ass good, he thought gleefully. Everything made him feel bigger, like he'd won some ultimate contest.

Except . . .

A shadow of massive proportions edged past the Porsche, ignoring it. The driver must have seen it though, for suddenly it dropped back a hundred yards. Jeb thought he saw it rear-ended back there, its headlights veering crazily sideways then into the sky. But he had no time to wonder about that. The shadow dropped behind. Gonna make it, Jeb thought to himself. No beast could keep up with him now. He was home free.

Almost.

Something grabbed the truck's rear wheel. A tire blew and the nose of the pickup twisted into the center divider, sending a shower of sparks back of him like a comet's tail. Impossibly, the truck slowed, then stopped. Cars whipped by, their screaming horns dopplered into mournful sighs.

Jeb kept his eyes closed, thinking maybe Red Rover would leave him alone if he played dead.

Something the size of a bull reared up next to Jeb's door, stared at him with eyes of brilliant coral light, then pulled the door off its hinges with its teeth.

For just a moment before the thing bit through Jeb's neck, he had the impression he was looking at Stuart.

"Stu?" There was no answer except an awful grunting.

Finished, the thing looked briefly around the cab, then spun daintily and tottered across the freeway, ignoring the cars that swerved to miss it. A brief flurry of bushes at the freeway's edge announced its passage, then it was gone. ❧

The Wind Has Teeth

G. WARLOCK VANCE AND SCOTT H. URBAN

illustration by
DARRYL ELLIOTT

I.

Autumn is an insidious season.

Unlike winter, which pounces paws-down like a white-pelted jungle cat, or spring, which drives off the rear-guard of snow like a victorious general, autumn creeps up on summer slowly, treacherously. A subtle, sinister season, it enacts the same back-stabbing assassination every year and leaves no witnesses. Autumn spreads its infiltrating tendrils through an unremittingly naïve summer like a nacreous cancer, and by late September, it has all but usurped the year.

At no other time of the year is death so colorful. Chilled breezes plummet through a purple sky, lined with orange and crimson along its western edge. They carry with them the cinnamon smell of decayed and burning leaves. The leaves themselves are tinged with rich brown, pumpkin orange, lemon yellow and sunset red. They achieve the pinnacle of their beauty only in death.

Like the kaleidoscopic leaves and the hastily-covered flower beds, the day is dying too. A punctured sun, leaking crimson on the horizon, drowned in its own ruddy magnificence. Coolness wrapped its north-wind fingers around outdoor thermometers — not with the mind-numbing cold of winter, but with a soft, vague hinting of the nip of the grave.

169

The leaves, the flowers, the day — all these were dying.

People were dying as well.

II. 9/21/8-. 11:15pm.

"Here Philip. I thought you might be able to use this."

Startled, Philip Howard jerked back from the window. For a moment, he stared incomprehensibly at the brandy snifter in his best friend's outstretched hand. It seemed like something that had no part in a world where you could say 'good-bye' to a companion — and find him dead a half- hour later. Philip forced a small laugh to show that he was all right and accepted the snifter.

"Thanks Craig. I could use it at that." Philip was content for the moment to sip the liqueur and study his companion's features, wondering how two such disparate individuals could form an insoluble bond. Philip considered himself fair and lanky, nonchalant in manner and emotionally distant. Craig Quiller, on the other hand, possessed dark features and a dark shock of hair. He was quick to rise in passion, but could fall easily into numbing depressions. Linked by their mutual penchant for collecting and creating stories of the macabre and supernatural, they had eventually formed an organization comprised of individuals with similar tastes.

"Don't much feel like joining the party, I guess, right?" asked Craig sympathetically.

From the distant corner where they stood, they turned and looked back into the broad lounge. When Craig had initially formed The October Society, he had the good fortune to meet Benjamin Casprak. Casprak, a retired widower, owned the meat-packing firm just outside of Durham, Ohio. Although he had removed himself from active management of the company, leaving such details to his oldest son, now president of the firm, Casprak had made his money and then some. A mutual acquaintance had introduced Casprak and Craig, and they discovered a shared affection for pre-code EC horror comics. When Craig had informed Casprak of his intention of starting an organization devoted to literature of the weird and grotesque, Casprak had been willing to donate the use of one of his mansion's rooms one night a week. Casprak's mansion lay outside the Durham city limits on its own acreage a good twenty miles away. Casprak maintained there were certain peculiarities about Durham residents he did not care for.

At the moment, the chairs and couches of Casprak's lounge were occupied by October Society members. Unlike most meetings, when Craig, as secretary and only existing Society official, had to threaten to fire a gun to bring them to order, tonight's gathering had a muted, somber atmosphere. It was not a regularly scheduled meeting; it was, in fact, a wake.

Philip nervously swallowed some brandy, relishing the liquid warmth.

"I know," Craig said dejectedly, "I wish they weren't all so downcast. Believe me, I'm shaken by Paul's death more than I can express. Still, I'd like to start a meeting, tell some stories, just to get our minds off it. I'm afraid they'll take it the wrong way, though."

Philip had turned back to the window and was trying to look past the glare into the tangled woods beyond the lawn. "No, don't force it. If the guys want to talk, we'll get around to talking . . . eventually."

Craig scrutinized Philip for a while, concerned. A small ridge where Philip's jaw met his skull was dancing in and out. Philip was clenching and unclenching his teeth. Craig put it down as normal. After all, it had been Philip who had discovered Paul Ansare's mangled corpse last night.

Craig then noted Philip's pupils growing wide, his lips paling, and his fingers turning white against the stem of the snifter. "What is it, Phil?" Craig asked anxiously. Philip didn't answer and Craig gripped his shoulder. Leaning over and squinting out the window, Craig tried to see what had jolted his friend.

Through his fingers, Craig felt Philip's muscles relax. "It's all right, Craig. It wasn't what I thought it was." He paused, drained his brandy. "At least, I don't think it could possibly have been what I thought it was."

Craig nodded, trying to understand and empathize. "Get you a refill?" he asked, pointing to the empty glass. Philip rather absently handed it to him. Craig began walking towards the open bar which Benjamin Casprak provided to the Society for a token monthly fee. Pulling himself up short, he swiveled back towards Philip and affected a cheery tone. "By the way, Phil, wanted to tell you . . . it's Monday. September 21st. It's the solstice. Welcome to the first day of fall."

III. 9/20/8-. 9:45pm.

Smirking, Leonard Talbot was circling the room, showing all who would spare a glance his newly-acquired signed copy of Stephen King's 'Salem's Lot. As Philip Howard entered the room, G. Gordon Gregor, Durham's resident novelist, was describing a proposed film adaptation of one of his novelettes. Benjamin Casprak was making the rounds, checking to see that everyone's glass was full and that they all knew where the hors d'oeuvres were located.

The twenty-two assembled revelers forgot the chill

September night, only a wall away. Wine, brandy and rum tumbled freely, a liquor-waterfall, augmenting the joyous mood and making everyone's voice just a little louder than normal. A five-log blaze crackled in the fireplace, more to spread brightness than warmth.

Philip headed across the room to confer with Craig, passing a small group centered around Paul Ansere. Paul was just coming to the punch-line of another insufferably ribald joke. His listeners chuckled appreciatively: Paul's jokes weren't always the most inventive, but he had an inexhaustible supply of them.

Paul's low voice, which carried all too well in the paneled lounge, brought Philip up short. "Phil! Hold on there a second! I wanna talk to you!" Philip turned to wait. Although not his favorite Society member, Philip didn't have anything against Paul personally. Paul probably needed to cultivate a dominant personality and slightly overbearing manner in his real estate developing firm.

Listeners drifted away from Paul, who moved to Philip's side and clapped a heavy palm on his shoulder. Philip felt as if his left side had lost half an inch. Maybe just a little too much brandy, Philip thought wryly.

"Hey, how ya doin', Phil?" asked Paul, baring a toothy smile. "We gonna watch *Nightmare on Elm Street* tonight?"

"I'm fine, Paul," Philip replied. "No, I think Craig is going to give a short talk on the image of death in M. R. James's work." Philip wasn't surprised to see Paul's face fall momentarily in disappointment; reading wasn't high on Paul's list of hobbies.

"Wonderful," slurred Paul, unobtrusively guiding Philip into an unoccupied corner beside some bookcases. "Look, I got something I want to talk to you about."

Philip had no idea what he and the developer had in common besides the Society, but he was willing to give

Paul a couple of minutes. "Okay. Shoot."

"Well, Phil, you know, this Society is a fun deal and everything, you know, but not everyone here is a mental giant, if you catch my drift."

Philip couldn't help but chuckle at Paul's wharf-rat stare. "If that's a back-handed compliment, thanks; but we really shouldn't put down anyone in the October Society. I mean, everyone who's a member is an expert or respected member of his or her chosen field."

"Yeah, well, what I meant was, you got a lot more horse sense than a lot of the rest of them. And I think that these meetings can be an excellent way to drum up some business — trade ideas — further our own careers. This ghost business is a lot of fun, but it can only go so far."

Philip was beginning to get a little bit irritated. "Look, if you're getting bored with the meetings, then for God's sake, don't come anymore. Now look, I've got to see Craig. . . . "

Paul's rather stout forearm shot past Philip's chest, barricading his way. "Hold on, I'm ramblin' a bit, but I've got a very concrete proposal to make to you. Something that could help make both of us a lot of money."

Philip drew in a deep breath and stared down his nose at the developer. He didn't encourage the man to go on, but Paul did anyway.

"It has come to my attention that a vast amount of land may shortly be up for sale. With my knowledge of the market and my real estate connections, I stand in an advantageous position to acquire this land." Philip noted how Paul's words underwent a startling transformation as he made a pitch. He could see how Paul had become so successful even with such a gruff exterior. "I don't own this land yet, but I am already lining up potential investors to join me in a fortune-making opportunity."

Philip fended off his words with a waving hand. "Hold on, hold on. First of all, where is this land?"

"Most of it falls in the territory of Durham Woods. You know, the forest that most everybody in town calls St. Elmo's Wood? It is *prime* real estate, let me tell you, *prime* real estate."

"And what are you planning on doing with it?"

"Well, knowing the area as I do, I would have to say Durham — and our neighbor city Outerville, too — are only going to grow and prosper in the future. I believe we're looking at a major population influx shortly. Casprak's meat packaging plant is small potatoes to some of the industries I've heard are considering the Durham-Outerville area. There's even talk of a computer programming place coming in. Now, the way I look at it, any influx of business is going to mean more people. And people need a place to stay, a place to live, right? So I am considering the installation of condominiums on that land. I'm not kidding when I say I believe we could all become very rich off this."

Philip's brow was wrinkled with unanswered questions. "Wait a minute. St. Elmo's Wood? Isn't that . . . isn't that the ancient site of those old Ohioan Indians? What were they called — the Itiqua? Yes, I believe they were the Itiqua."

Paul looked puzzled for a moment, as if he couldn't see what Philip was getting at. "Yeah, I guess I've heard of the Itiqua. I don't know if that's where they lived or not. What difference does it make anyway? I mean, last I heard, they were extinct, wiped out. That was centuries ago. I'm talkin' about the here-and-now, about something that could make us a ton of dough."

Philip was shaking his head, a rueful grin on his face. "Paul, look, I really appreciate your offer, but quite frankly,

I think you're appealing to the wrong man. I'm certain I don't have the kind of money you need to invest in your project. You're probably asking me because I have my own advertising firm in town. But believe me, when the bills are paid off at the end of the month, I barely have enough left over for Kraft macaroni-and-cheese."

"Won't take much to get you in on the deal, Phil. Yeah, I probably wish you had more, but only a ten-thousand dollar investment will buy you into the group. *You* just keep your mind on the profits."

By now, Philip was laughing outright. "Ten thousand dollars?" His head went back and his voice got louder. *"Ten thousand* dollars?" A hand on his arm and a sharp look from Paul made him remember where he was. He quieted down again. "Look, Paul, if I had ten thousand dollars to simply invest wherever I wanted, I don't think I'd be sitting in this pit of a town."

A sour look grew on Paul's face. "Okay, Phil, but I think you got more capital than you really let on. I'll tell you what. I may talk to some other people here tonight about this deal. But I'm still willing to consider you if you want to come in. So you think about it, all right? You could be missing out on the chance of a lifetime."

Philip shook his head. "How many times have I heard that line? It's usually printed on an envelope with Ed McMahon's face."

Paul pretended to be abashed. "No, I mean it. You think about it. Look, I gotta go talk to some other folks."

Paul started to turn away, but a nagging thought caught on the back of Philip's mind. To get rid of it, he called out to Paul, stopping him. "Paul, in that part of St. Elmo's Wood you're talking about . . . isn't that also where the Old Stones stand?"

Paul mused for a second, trying to recall the layout of

the land. The Old Stones were perhaps the only things Durham offered that could be called a tourist attraction, though very few outsiders knew of their existence. A ring of erect stones perhaps thirty feet in diameter, they stood in the untrammeled silence of St. Elmo's Wood, rather far from town. An unusually deep shade of black, no geologist had yet determined the exact nature of the Old Stones. In addition, no one knew whether they were a natural formation — or whether the Itiqua, a peculiar native American tribe spoken of primarily in mad Joseph Durham's *The Black Sermons*, had wrestled them into place.

"I ain't exactly sure," Paul replied slowly, "but I think that's where they are." He shrugged, as if to show how inconsequential the matter was. "Of course, they're going to have to come down. That's right where I want to put my condos."

IV. 09/21/8-. 11:49pm.

By the time Craig was through refilling Philip's glass, Philip had moved away from the window. Concerned for a moment, Craig at last sighted him standing in front of one of the many bookcases in the lounge. Philip's head was cocked at an odd angle, like a puzzled animal, as he scanned the spines for a particular title.

"What are you looking for?" Craig inquired, holding the snifter out for Philip to take.

Philip waved away the proffered drink, too intent on his search. His eyes passed over novels, anthologies, magazines and Penny Dreadfuls while his lips silently mouthed their titles. He paused to shove his glasses back to the bridge of his nose and said to Craig, "You know, sometimes I think our little crew has amassed *too much* material on the supernatural. Trying to find the title you want is nothing short of maddening —" He bent back to his search while Craig started to say something about a new filing system. Before Craig could finish, however, Philip muttered, "Ah, here it is; I found it." He pulled out a thick, heavy tome with a dark, rich moss-green binding.

Craig recognized the book; it was from his own personal collection, on loan to the Society's library for the members' benefit. *"The Collected Short Stories of Algernon Blackwood,"* he recalled aloud. Philip didn't reply, merely nodded his head in assent. He was thumbing through the introductory pages, at last lighting upon the table of contents.

"Blackwood had an extraordinary vision," Craig said, trying to elicit comment from his distracted friend. "He imbued Nature with a fascinating, and at times terrifying, immaterial Force. As in 'The Willows.' . . . "

"Yes," Philip agreed in an off-hand way, without raising his head. "I'm trying to recall the details of another of his stories, one almost as famous as 'The Willows'. Coincidentally enough, I believe it also starts with a 'W.' . . . "

Knowing Philip's moods better than Philip himself did, Craig unobtrusively backed away from his friend. It was not that the two never had squabbles — they did, and many times over the most inconsequential of matters — but Craig had learned when Philip wanted to be left alone. This was one of those times.

His index finger trailing down the page, Philip didn't even notice Craig's exit.

V. 9/21/8-. 7:55am.

Luke Matthews stepped through his front door, coffee cup in one hand, unlit pipe in the other. The morning's chill helped clear his head, for which Luke was grateful —

he'd had maybe a *little* too much to drink at the October Society meeting last night. He was glad he had some time before he had to get ready for work, time wherein he could make his peace with the always-troublesome Monday.

Luke took a deep, to-the-bottom-of-the-lungs breath and began to make a mental list of all the things that had to get done that day. At the same time, an excited, shrill voice cut through his thoughts.

"Mr. Matthews! Mr. Matthews!" The voice was young-boy high and slightly out of breath.

Luke turned and saw his next-door-neighbor's son running up to him. Roland "Rollie" de Witt, clad in scuffed Levi's and a Chicago Bears sweatshirt, skidded to a halt in front of the puzzled adult. "I gotta ask ya som'thin'," Rollie blurted out. Rollie had just turned five. Luke wished he could greet Monday morning with such enthusiasm.

"What's that?" Luke asked, noting that Rollie's fingers were red with chill. His clothes were damp too. His mother must not have warned him to not roll in the dew-wet grass.

"My Dad doesn't smoke a pipe," Rollie explained. "I was wonderin' if I could borrow yours."

Luke smiled a patronizing smile, fingering the briar pipe in his hand. "Little young to start smoking yet, aren't you, Rollie?"

Rollie screwed his face up into an expression that said 'grown-ups never understand'. "I don't want to smoke it," he cried, "I need it to go with my snowman!"

It took several seconds for Rollie's words to penetrate Luke's still-stirring consciousness. Then he leaned back, as if Rollie might be carrying something contagious. "A snowman? In September?" Even though Luke liked Rollie, he couldn't help but snort. "Rollie, there's no snow now, won't be until November at the earliest."

"Is *too* snow in September!" was Rollie's indignant rejoinder. "You come see!"

The day no longer seemed clear and sharp to Luke. He followed Rollie around the side of his house to the rear, feeling as if he were moving from sunlight into a shadowed dream-realm. The house's shadow enveloped both of them, intensifying the illusion. Luke had a strong notion to jog back inside and start the day all over again.

At last they quit the shadow and emerged in the wide backyard. There was no fence separating Luke's yard from his neighbor's; Rollie often played in each as if he owned both. Not watching where he was going, Luke almost stumbled over a partially uncoiled watering hose. His eyes were transfixed by the unnatural scene before him. Coffee slopped unheeded over his cup's rim; his expensive briar pipe slipped between his fingers unnoticed.

To the left and right, cutting across his and the de Witts' backyard, as well as the yards of all the adjoining neighbors, ran an uninterrupted swath of shimmering, glittering snow. The pure white trail *had* been mussed-up: a tri-sectioned snowman, obviously Rollie's handiwork, stood in the middle of the slowly melting path. Rollie's feet had left prints; there were even the remains of a 'snow angel', explaining Rollie's wet clothing.

As Rollie stooped scavenger-like and snatched Luke's pipe, interpreting its fall to mean he could use it, Luke realized the snow path was consistently fifteen feet wide with a sharp boundary. No cloud could have left a trail so precise, so exact. *A snow-making machine?* he thought. No, he would have heard any loud mechanical racket in the night. Not only was the swath consistently wide, it was uniformly deep — about three feet, Luke estimated. It couldn't exist; like the spoor of an angel, it couldn't exist — and yet it did. Luke could feel the freezing cold radiating from the running mound even where he stood some six feet away.

As Rollie speared the pipe's stem into the snowman's mouth, right below the two Quik-Lite charcoal briquette eyes, Luke came to the awareness that somehow, some-way, this was connected with the October Society . . . and that he hadn't seen or heard the last of the business yet.

VI. 9/21/8- 4:06am.

"Craig?"

"Wha .. What? Who is it?"

"Craig, it's me, Philip. God, I'm sorry, I know what time it is . . . "

"You're doing better than I am; I don't know what time it is. Umm, what time is it?"

"Hell, uh somewhere 'round four I think. . . . "

"God, Phil, what's going on? What're you calling me at four a.m. for? And what's all that noise in the back-ground?"

"Well, I'm down at the police station — "

"*What the fuck!?*"

"Hold on, hold on, I'm . . . I'm all right, I just thought I should be the one to call you and let you know. . . . "

"To let me *know*; let me know *what*?

"Just, just calm down. Uh, on the way back home, I came across Paul Ansare's car. . . . There'd been a wreck. . . . "

"So what you're telling me is. . . . "

"He's dead, Craig. Paul Ansare's dead. There's more to it, but I can't go into it over the phone. I'm sorry to wake you up; I thought you'd want to know. I'll talk to you later today, okay?"

"Sure, sure, fine; my God, Paul's dead; I don't believe it. Hell, are you all right? Do you want me to come get you?"

"No, I'm fine, the police are going to drive me home as soon as I finish my report. I know you've got to teach this morning, so I'll let you sleep. I'll talk to you later, Craig."

"Okay, Phil, give me a call if you need anything."

"I will. 'Bye."

"'Bye. . . . "

VII. 9/22/8- 12:11am.

Either Philip had immediately found the information he needed or he had given up the search, because he replaced the Blackwood volume with an agitated gesture minutes after Craig had slipped away. Philip caught up with Craig halfway across the spacious lounge.

"I took a trip in my mind for a bit," Philip said. "I'm back now." He gave Craig an apologetic look. "Sorry I snubbed you."

"N.A.N. No apologies necessary. But take this god-damn second drink I've been carrying around for you before it becomes a permanent fixture in my hand."

Philip took the snifter and knocked back better than three-quarters of it. "I imagine someone's spoken with Paul's wife today," he said as they continued walking between soft-spoken groups of people.

Craig nodded. "Oh, yes. As you know, the police broke it to her; you were there. But I had Martin Danforth get on the phone with her immediately afterward and offer to handle all the necessary arrangements. She was very grateful. You know, I didn't get any sleep at all this morning after you called. I was on the phone a better part of the day, calling our members, pulling in favors, trying to make things as humanly comforting for her as possible."

"Good. Glad to hear that."

The two had come to the head of the group's table. Near them in the wall was the crackling fireplace. Pleasant tendrils of warmth laved the pair, belying the early autumn morning. The glowing embers threw an orangish cast over them as Craig turned to Philip with a somber countenance.

"When you called last night to tell me about the accident, I remember you saying there was 'more to it'. We haven't really discussed what happened last night — do you feel you can talk about it?"

Philip faced the leaping flames. With a start, Craig noticed the reflective glints at the corners of Philip's eyes. "I'm not quite sure I . . . " Philip began.

A voice interrupted Philip's feeble protest. "Phil, please, tell us what happened." Without even attempting to, Arianne Sprecher, a journalist and four-year Society member, had overheard the men's last few comments. "Really, Philip. Look at all of us, moping in this oversized room, claiming we're honoring Paul's memory, and all of us too scared to even say his name. You were the one who found him last night; you're the only one who can tell us about it. Why not get it out in the open?"

Other members had by now overheard Arianne's impassioned words, and they made sounds of agreement. The clamor was not loud, but it was persuasive. Without spoken directions, the October Society members began to gravitate to the long oaken table around which they customarily sat. Tonight, Philip found himself at the table's head, the seat usually reserved for Craig as recording secretary.

Philip made a deprecating gesture. "I confess, I've known all of you on the order of years now. Yet I'm not sure I can tell you what happened yesterday without everyone laughing at me, claiming I'm pulling your legs.

You'll think I'm making up a story and smearing Paul's name. I don't want that to happen to me or to the group."

Voices were immediately raised in protest, but Arianne's cut through most clearly and convincingly. "Listen, Phil. The motivating factor for this group is our appreciation for what most others scoff at. We all love the strange and the supernatural, even though most of us consider it a purely intellectual pursuit. If something out of the ordinary occurred last night, I don't think you could find a more accepting and open group than the one gathered here tonight." Cries of 'hear, hear!' accompanied the short speech.

"All right." Philip spoke with obvious reluctance. "I'll tell you what happened as I perceived the course of events. I've said you won't believe me and I still think that's true, so I won't argue with you afterwards or defend myself."

Philip turned away from the group momentarily and stared into the fire. He seemed to wear a hellish halo with red and gold rays. Losing himself in the flickering fire, Philip's mind slipped the grasp of time and returned to the previous morning. Then he shook himself, as if to lose the mantle of madness, and looked back to the table.

"As you all know, we've lost Paul Ansare. I found him last night, dead by the side of the road." Philip contemplated the fireplace for a moment: how the fire inside seemed to writhe with a curious intelligence, as if it were aware of its own purpose, and its purpose was to dance. He wondered what other seemingly unthinking forces were possessed of emotions, desires. "Our regular Sunday night meeting broke up somewhere around 12:30 in the morning. We had all said farewell to Benjamin. Paul was one of the first to leave. He lives . . . sorry, *lived* . . . in Outerville, as I do, and so was traveling down '36' on his way to the junction that would take him to Route 224 and on into town."

Philip's eyes became glazed, as if not focused on any one thing in the room. "I was doing a little better than the speed limit to get home as quickly as possible. My wife doesn't like me to be out too late and I don't like to make her worry. Since I was traveling fast and was already tired to begin with, I almost didn't see the accident. I would have missed it entirely, were it not for the fact that my car . . . fishtailed at that moment. I'll come back to why I fishtailed in a second. As the car swerved, I recognized in my headlights' beams Paul's Celica off the side of the road. It had slid into a culvert, hit a brace of trees, crumpled the front end and turned on its side.

"I regained control of my own car, although it took me almost a mile to come to a complete stop. Praying there would be no traffic that early on a Monday morning, I made a U-turn and slowly cruised back to the accident site. My own lights blinded me, reflecting off the Celica's mirrors and chrome.

"In the weak light, I could see the beginning of the Celica's skid. The wide, greasy marks stood out sharply on the pavement. Then I saw what had caused him to lose control of his vehicle. *And* what had made my car fishtail. Don't ask me to explain yet. But believe me when I say that it was a road-wide patch of solid ice."

Open mouths and arched eyebrows met Philip's statement, but if he expected anyone to challenge him, he was disappointed.

"Now, I had made it across the ice patch, so I know Paul could have made it as well. There was something that had made him slam on his brakes just before the ice. Could it have been the sight of the ice itself? I don't think so. It was perfectly clear, like a layer of glass surfacing the road. No, something else had made him veer."

Tiny beads of sweat stood out on Philip's forehead, either due to his proximity to the fire or the intensity of his recollection. He wiped them off; somebody coughed, then he continued.

"The ice on the road was enough to tell me something out of the ordinary had happened. The morning was cold, but not cold enough to freeze standing water. Of course, all of these thoughts flashed through my mind in a matter of moments; my primary concern was Paul's condition. Within seconds, I had switched off my motor, clicked on the emergency flashers, and stumbled out of my car door. . . ."

VIII. 9/21/8- 1:07am.

The eye-aching glare of headlights reflecting off the Celica brought a throbbing migraine to Philip's head and neck. His dress shoes, worn for the meeting, didn't give him much traction on the road's slippery surface. Nearly falling more than once, he inched to the berm and slid down the short, slick embankment.

Paul's Celica had crossed both lanes and now lay on the driver's side. Philip dropped to all fours in the rime-coated grass, soaking his pants. Muttering prayers, he peered through the windshield to determine Paul's condition. For a moment, a scream welled up in the back of his throat. *Paul's body had no head!* Then an errant breeze blew some cloud-cover away and a moonbeam lit the ravine. Paul's head was still attached to his neck. Philip felt no relief: from the body's condition, it was obvious no life remained.

Philip refused to accept this fact at first. Ignoring the cold, the discomfort and the horror of the scene, he scurried rodent-like to the exposed underside of the car. Using the drive-shaft and muffler exhaust as ladder rungs, he clambered up to the Celica's passenger side, now a plateau. The automobile shifted a fraction of an inch, then moved no more. Philip felt it wouldn't overturn — and felt that saying a few prayers to that effect couldn't hurt either. The car's surface, smooth and glossy to begin with, was now covered with a frosty sheen. Philip knew he was more in danger of slipping off the top than of having the car tilt.

As Philip secured a position on the elevated side and began tugging at the door handle, something tiny but insistent broke through his concentration. He was not alone at the accident scene — and whatever else was there with him, it did not feel as if it were of human origin. Philip didn't pause in his exertions to investigate the uncanny feeling; he worked harder at the door handle. The passenger side door had buckled when the front end collided with a tree trunk. Philip feared it wasn't going to surrender to his efforts.

The deep night's wind was picking up with each passing minute, whistling fiercely through the swaying, rickety branches. If wind could be said to have a destination, Philip thought, it seemed to be headed his way. The whistling increased in volume, becoming a howl. The wind possessed a rhythmic quality, as if it were pulsing in and out stentoriously. Like a mystic conveyor, it brought other sounds to Philip's ears; echoes of footsteps, huge and resounding, more heavy than a man's could ever be.

The lights of Philip's car seemed to dim and fade out, leaving him bereft of illumination in the middle of the night. Kneeling on the car's treacherous surface, Philip felt as if the ground around the Celica had slipped away, leaving him adrift in a shadowy void. His lower lip trembling, his throat pulsing with sobs that would soon break free, Philip threw his head back. There was some small comfort to be found in the jagged silhouette of the pine tops against the clouds. But even that ease became a curse when the clouds parted once more, allowing the bone-white moon to shine through.

Philip *saw* at that moment, and in the very act of seeing, he made himself forget. Although somewhere, in a spider-webbed corner of his subconscious, the image would remain forever, Philip could never again call that sight to the surface. To do so would have been to invite madness. Because just then, Philip realized he was being *watched*, observed by something that had no part of the ordinary, common world. Instead of even acknowledging the fact the something *else* was out there, he bent back more furiously to the task at hand. As he did, the clouds slid into position once more, eliminating the moon's glow.

His brush with the unexplainable lent Philip the strength of dread. With an upward tug that almost dislodged both of his shoulders, as well as his precarious perch, he opened the passenger door. The crushed metal screeched raucously, a sound totally at odds with the forest surroundings. It seemed few things of Man had penetrated this far — and those things that had did not last long.

The door swayed into an upright position and held itself there like a sail set to catch a propelling wind. Philip lowered himself into the awkward opening, taking care to place his feet just so. It was an effort not to trample Paul's body in the narrow, cramped space. Philip knelt over Paul's form, still frantically seeking some sign of life. He moaned Paul's name over and over, knowing there would be no response. The gear shift stabbed his ribs. The dashboard pressed against his back. And the steering wheel was just damn in the way. Paul's body was still held in position by the shoulder harness, which it took Philip several minutes to release. Philip held his fingers to Paul's neck and wrist, seeking a pulse that would indicate there was some hope. Nothing happened.

Afterward, Philip would never remember just how he got Paul's body up and out of the crazily-canted Celica. Somehow he did, although it took the remainder of his waning strength. Philip carefully stretched Paul's corpse on the torn, muddy turf, amid newly fallen leaves. Philip's car's headlights were visible once more, and Philip inspected Paul's body. There was an open gash on his forehead, several ribs were obviously crushed, and a leg was broken. But from Paul's pale, bluish pallor, Philip tentatively guessed that Paul had suffered a heart attack just prior to the accident.

Not a single car had passed since Philip had found the accident. He felt as if he had left the rational, work-a-day world and crossed into a primeval countryside inhabited by dryads and satyrs. His isolation was intensified — when he realized, again, he was not alone.

Hair prickled at the back of his neck and his thoughts ran so quickly they tripped over each other. "Jesus, it's the Watcher, the Watcher returned, he's come for me, not just Paul, and it was the Watcher that Paul saw, the thing that caused him to have a heart attack, just before his car veered across the patch of ice into a tree. . . . "

Philip whirled around, wishing he had some weapon in his hands and knowing the most modern automatic rifle would have no effect on whatever he encountered.

It wasn't the Watcher. In a way, it was almost worse.

Paul Ansare stood beside the pummeled automobile, an indecipherable expression on his faintly luminescent features.

"Good Christ," Philip said. He could barely breathe. He checked at his feet to make sure Paul's corpse was where he had placed it. It was. "My God, what are you?

What *are* you?" Crashing waves of faintness washed over Philip's mind, threatening to pull him into blackness. He resisted, but couldn't help staggering backwards erratically.

A voice that spoke without words buzzed in his ears like a staticky radio receiver. Paul was speaking, but his mouth did not move. It remained frozen in an enigmatic line.

"Philip. I'm glad it was you."

"Paul? What — how can you — "

"If it were going to be one of the club members who found me, I'm glad it was you. I think you will best understand what has happened to me. You see, I've now been doubly freed." Paul sounded meditative, as if now he finally had a chance to think about things he had no time for before. "The accident freed me from life, and you freed me from imprisonment."

Philip suddenly realized he was looking *up* at Paul's lambent visage. He'd somehow stumbled and fallen backward on his rear.

"I've learned that mankind was not meant for what he calls 'civilization'. The life and the flesh are out there, in the woods, in the wild places. The Master taught me this by deliberately causing my death while I was still in the car. I discovered I was released from my mortal body — but that which survives death was trapped in a cage of steel. I came to understand much more while I screamed without a voice, hammered away without hands. And then you freed me."

Philip wanted to ask Paul questions: How could the dead man communicate with him? How could he see the Celica through Paul's otherwise substantial form? But he literally could not form the words.

"Now I wish I'd listened to you earlier this evening. I wish you'd been a bit more forceful in your objections. But the past is as lingering as the autumn wind. And I must go join the Master as the newest hunter in his pack." Paul's head turned away momentarily, as if he were in silent communion with a distant someone in the unlit woodlands. He then continued, "By the way, Philip, you would do well to stay away from this stretch of the woods in the future. Warn the others away, too. The woods, and this road, have been claimed by another."

"Paul — " Philip finally managed to stutter, his hands making vague halting motions.

"I have to leave: the Windwalker calls and his patience is short. Dispose of the flesh as you will. My new companions inform me it makes good eating." A disquieting pause. "Farewell, Philip. Know that we wait for you to join us too."

A choppy gust burst through the twigs, pushing Philip's hair down across his forehead. It licked around the edges of the spectral image and seemed to tear at Paul as if he were a papier-mâché dummy. As the rushing air whittled at him, Paul did not move, his expression did not change.

Philip, too, was mute and immobile. He sat in the roadside slush, watching his former friend disintegrate wisp by wisp, and when nothing was left of Paul, he sat there still, wondering who and what rode on the breezes around him.

IX. 9/22/8- 1:36am.

"Finally," Philip concluded, "I recovered enough presence of mind to get Paul's body into my car and drive it to the police station. I think you all know the rest." He folded his hands: a punctuating gesture.

Any other group, at the end of a narrative so bizarre,

would have broken into a heated babbel of exclamatory voices. The October Society members, however, remained still, calm, as if consciously mulling over some new discovery of science. A log popped in the hearth, a solitary intruder on the silence.

"Windwalker," murmured a pensive voice.

Craig's head darted up. "What was that, Rachel?"

Rachel Carson, farther down the table, shook her head. "I'm not sure. It's something Philip said about Paul's new 'Master'. Paul also referred to the Master as 'Windwalker'. That reminds me . . . reminds me of the stories my great-grandmother used to tell me. She was a full-blooded Iroquois. On cold autumn nights — nights such as this — she used to speak of the Wendigo, the Windwalker . . . The Bringer of Snow."

"'The Wendigo'!" Craig interrupted excitedly. "That's what you were looking up in the Blackwood book, Phil!"

Philip merely nodded in agreement, his eyes focused on Rachel. He knew Rachel was a professional secretary, and he could see the concentration as she searched through her mental files, looking for stories and legends that had been whispered to her in toddlerhood. "The Wendigo is a great native Indian deity," she continued. "He — or It — apparently has a great deal to do with the natural elements and the guardianship of the forest. His tales are primarily told in Eastern Canada, New England and the Mid-West."

"Itiqua . . ." spoke up another member, Lionel Granger. "Itiqua and . . . Ithiqua! My God, I wonder if it could be possible!"

"What, Lionel?" asked Philip. "What are you saying?"

Granger, overweight and retiring, found himself the center of attention. But he seemed not to notice; his voice was quivering with barely pent-up emotion. "As you know, I'm a collector of Lovecraft stories and Lovecraftian material. In the body of writing known as the 'Cthulhu Mythos', there are references to a 'Windwalker'. But his name is more ancient than that of 'Wendigo'; he is called Ithiqua. He controls the storms, the clouds, the realm of the air. And don't you see . . . "

"Of course," cut in Philip, realizing where Granger's line of reasoning was taking him. "That's so close to the name of the Indians who lived on the site of Durham! The Itiqua!"

"Right!" agreed Granger. "The similarity is too close to be coincidence. It might only have been the crazed Joseph Durham's feverish mind that transcribed the name of the tribe from 'Ithiqua' to 'Itiqua'. We might even conjecture that the tribe took on that name to appease their god. They were the followers, or the Children, of Ithiqua, the Windwalker."

As if the heat were leeching the very blood from his form, Philip's face suddenly became albino pale. "Jesus, and the Itiqua . . . the Itiqua worshipped at . . . " He ran a savagely palsied hand through his damp hair. Craig's hand shot out and grasped Philip's shoulder to steady him.

"Philip, what is it? Damn it, what is it?" Craig tried to convey both reassurance and urgency; the combination was unnerving.

Philip was hurriedly casting his gaze around the assembly, nodding at each member in turn and counting as he did so. His voice, cracking under his breath, was enough to chill Craig. "Nineteen, *twenty*!" Philip finished counting with a cry. "Twenty! With Paul in the Society, we had twenty-two members! We should have twenty-one here tonight!" And again, he began his inexplicable attendance count.

"Phil, what are you getting at?" Arianne asked. "Calm down and tell us what's wrong!"

Philip didn't seem to hear Arianne's anxious words. He leaned over and frantically clutched the lapels of Craig's suit-coat. "Who couldn't make it tonight, Craig?" he demanded. "Who begged off from this meeting!"

Craig shook his head in confusion. "It, um, it was . . . Rick, Rick Wrightson. He said he couldn't make it tonight. Said he had something else to do. Something about a prior engagement."

"We've got to get a hold of him." The intensity of Philip's voice, the fixedness of his gaze, paralyzed Craig; he'd never seen his friend in such a state. "We've got to call his house and make sure he's all right."

The other members were watching the scene with a mixture of revulsion and unquenched curiosity. They alternately moved in more closely and scooted their chairs back away from the table.

"Why call him now, Phil?" Craig asked, puzzled. "Christ, it's the middle of the night; I'm sure he and his wife are long asleep by now. I don't want to wake them up —"

A jagged-edged moan broke from Philip's bloodless lips. "Just do it, Craig," he pleaded. "Damn it, call him! Call Rick — now!"

Benjamin Casprak wasn't caught up in Philip's hysterical outburst. Acknowledging Philip's serious tone, Casprak retrieved a cellular telephone from a nearby desk and handed it to Craig. "Go ahead," Casprak assured him. "It's all right."

Craig brought out his Society notebook and riffled through to the directory; his less-than-steady finger began to punch out the Wrightson phone number. As Craig finished dialing and put the phone to his ear, Philip faced the Society members. With breathless, barely intelligible phrases, he began to describe to them what he had omitted from his earlier narrative: his talk with Paul Ansare that Sunday past and Ansare's unorthodox business proposal to him.

Craig was meanwhile engaged in a more-or-less one-sided conversation. On his part, there was a lot of 'uh-huh'-ing and head nodding. Finally Craig concluded the conversation by saying, "Very well, Mrs. Wrightson, I can assure you that if any of us hear anything, we'll let you know immediately." Craig pressed the button that severed the connection.

"Please," said Philip, in a voice that almost became a sob, "don't let it be . . . "

Craig locked Philip with a leveling stare. There was compassion in his eyes as well. "You know what's happened, don't you?"

Tears began to well up in Philip's eyes. "I didn't know then! I had no way of telling! All I remember is that before the end of our meeting Sunday night, Paul cornered Rick Wrightson and began talking to him. I guess they were talking about the real estate deal; but Christ, for all I knew, they were talking about the latest ball scores! Paul was doing a lot of fast talking and Rick was doing a lot of head nodding, as if in agreement. . . ." Philip shrank in his chair, his features falling in on themselves even as his friends watched.

"Mrs. Wrightson," Craig addressed the remainder of the group, "was not in bed — she was still awake, and is very nervous. She said her husband went out this evening to check out some land, some property he was considering buying. Rick told her that, with Paul's unfortunate but timely death, he, Rick, now stood a very good chance of . . . making a killing in real estate. He was going to drive out to St. Elmo's Wood . . . where Paul had told him the land would be coming available — "

"Right near the Old Stones," Philip finished for Craig in a now-toneless voice. ". . . near the Old Stones, where Paul, and then Rick, were going to set up condominiums . . . the Old Stones, where the Itiqua tribesmen spilled the blood of their enemies to worship the Windwalker. . . ."

X. From *The Outerville Observer:* 9/23/8-

Following a four-hour manhunt early yesterday morning, Outerville police and searchers have recovered the body of Outerville resident Richard M. Wrightson. Wrightson had been missing since Monday night. His body was found by the stone Indian monuments in the Outerville-Durham forest, popularly known as St. Elmo's Wood.

The cause of death has yet to be officially announced. Sources close the Police Department have informed the *Observer* that Wrightson died from exposure and shock due to extreme cold. Monday night's low did reach the lower 40's, but there is still some question as to how Wrightson could have met his death from this temperature.

Additional reports from witnesses at the scene reveal further unexplained details. "Sure, it had been real cloudy that night," said Horace Yardley, owner of several tracking dogs the police make use of. "But I know there hadn't been any rain or sleet or such. And yet, there was new-fallen September snow melting all around Mr. Wrightson's body." ❧

Graveyards In The Dark

S.K. EPPERSON

She danced with insanity
The night of the funeral.
She was swept up in its arms
With the aid of bourbon,
And borne into the darkness,
Away to the graveyard.

On a bitter cold terrace
Her fingers clawed the earth.
She kissed him in the moonlight;
Her lips tasted dirt.
Every promise broken,
She shrieked out his name.

Dancing through the night,
Always the same refrain,
Her feet sliced the air,
Knees dug deep in grime,
Until insanity left her.
There was never a reply.

❧

For Ray

MICHAEL N. LANGFORD

For one whose bright and dark eyes have
Seen so much summer,
Breathed so much autumn,
Drunk so much fine dandelion wine:

Will I ever be half
The Martian you are?
Could I ever create a carnival with even a quarter
The pandemonium of your porch?

And if I awakened in Waukegan
And waited one hundred boyhoods in
The magic stillness of a summer's first dawn,
Would grandparents wake and cook my hotcakes?
Or should I rise and cook them for myself?
Clearly?

And if pedestrians viewed only screens at night,
Would something wicked their way come?
Impossible!

Every boy has his own Whale to wrestle
Into sub-submission.
Such is our mission.

So now before the ferris turns again,
I must run to board the Rocket.
The firemen follow close behind.
Ray knows his book.
I must learn mine.

ಜಿ

The Old Marsh Road

JAME A. RILEY
photo by
ERIC TURNMIRE

$\mathbf{J}$t happened quite a few years ago, but it still scares the hell outta me like it was yesterday when I think about it. I don't remember though when it all began. It was that way as long as I can remember. Nearest I can recall though, it was Smitty's brother, Jay, that really started making a big thing about it when we were real young. 'Course Smitty probably knows different now. Been strange not havin' him around these last few years since he and I were practically inseparable when we were kids.

Smitty's older brother, Jay, used t' let us ride in the back of his old pick-up truck. Sometimes it would get dark when we were heading back home and he'd take a detour through the marshes for the fun of it. 'Course he'd do it just to scare us.

He'd say, "Man, there's a thing out there in them marshes that is mean and scary as hell and one of these days, he's gonna fly up and snag you guys right out of the back of my truck. So when we go through there ya better hold on tight."

Then he'd detour through there and be speedin' down that dark and misty old marsh road until we'd get about to the middle of it and then he would slow down. Then me and Smitty would start bangin' on the truck cab and yelling, "Come on Jay, let's go!" and he'd start laughing and all and slow down even more. Well then Smitty and I would duck down in that truck bed and stare at the sky.

It was real bad when the moon was out and the shadows would move around in the overhanging trees.

Smitty would say, "Aw there ain't nothin' out there but frogs and birds and stuff. Jay's just full of it. There ain't nothin' else." So we'd get brave again and start bangin' on the truck cab and finally Jay would take off outta that marsh and head for home.

I'd say, "See I bet he even scared himself."

So when we'd get back home we'd tease him about being scared and he would tease us and say, "You guys were the ones bangin' and hollerin' back there and saying, 'Let's go, Jay!'" Then we'd finally get him to admit that there wasn't any horrible monster thing in the marshes and we'd forget about it for a few days.

Well, I bet ya think, if we were scared of it then why did we keep riding in the back of Jay's truck? He didn't always do that, and so most of the time it was just a lot of fun. We'd be cruising down those country roads and feeling the wind and the warm summer evenings, occasionally dropping pebbles out and watching them hit the road at 60 miles an hour and having a good time. But then we would be heading back home from the next town over where Jay had to pick up something for his dad and it would be getting dark. We made Jay promise not to go into the marshes and then most of the time he wouldn't. But sometimes we'd forget to make him promise and so if he felt particularly mean or something, he'd just suddenly take the detour and we'd find ourselves on the old marsh road so we'd start banging on the cab and yelling at him.

Once he'd started, though, he never would turn back. He'd be up there laughing and looking back at us and so Smitty and I would grab the old tarp he kept in the back and get it ready to pull over our heads just in case some horrible dark taloned beast would suddenly loom over our heads on huge leathery wings. Those were some other stories that Jay and his friends would tell us about them ol' swampy marshes.

"Big huge nasty winged beast. He has a face that is so hideous, that it would stop a man's heart right dead to ever see it." Then they'd start to laugh after they had really gotten us going. After that we'd realize it was all just a big joke.

On those rare occasions, though, when Jay was feeling rather nasty and would take off into the marshes, we'd try and prepare ourselves even if it was all a joke. It couldn't hurt to be a bit cautious . . . just in case. But we never did see or hear anything except the croaking of those fat old frogs and stuff, and Jay would have a good laugh.

When we got older we thought less and less about that old nasty winged thing in the marshes. After Jay went off to college we never rode through that part again until I got a car of my own. My dad bought me an old junker to run around in so that I wouldn't be using his the way my sister did when she was that age. Smitty and I were still best friends so we'd drive around together.

Every once in a while we'd have to drive through the old marshes. Smitty'd look over at me and say, "Do you think there ever was anything to those stories that Jay used to tell us? Do you think that there might really be something out here?"

"Naw," I'd say, "I think it was all just a bunch of bunk. They were just stories that ya tell to little kids to get 'em scared."

We'd sorta laugh a bit halfheartedly and Smitty would say, "Yeah, a bunch a bunk. Jay was really full of it." But I would push on the gas a little harder and check my mirrors more often. Smitty never said anything about this. I think if he'd been driving, he would have done the same thing.

When we were eighteen, (our birthdays were only two and a half months apart) Smitty got his own car. He only had it about two months before he got killed. It seems that he had to drive to the next town south of us to pick up some stuff for his grandfather, who was sick, and couldn't go himself. Well, you may have guessed already that he had to drive back through the marshes.

It was about 10:30 when he was coming through there and ran right off the road and into a ditch, finally hitting a tree. From the skid marks on the road, the police estimated that he'd been doing at least 95 miles an hour when he hit. Nobody ever could figure out why he crashed. I was there right after it happened 'cause I heard it on my dad's police radio. I helped identify the body. It was a mess. The man that drove by it and first reported the accident and helped pull Smitty from the wreck said he'd never seen anything like it. His hands were locked tight on the steering wheel and there was an absolute look of terror on his bloodless face with his eyes still open and staring.

I'm glad I didn't see that part. The thing was, later on when they did the autopsy, they said he'd had a cardiac arrest and he'd been dead when he hit. Must've died of fright but they said it was really odd that someone that young would have a heart attack from running off the road. But of course I don't believe that was what scared Smitty to death. There were marks on the car roof and around the front windshield that looked like they were made by huge, powerful talons ripping at the car. Even yet to this day I know something else scared the hell outta Smitty. And I will not drive on that road at night no matter what. Because it might still be out there. 🙢

Trip

MICHAEL N. LANGFORD

Childhood, Death
    Dreams, Drugs, and
        Madness
All ride together in the same Car.

Childhood bounces
Up and down on the back seat.
Madness tries to tell
Death how to drive,
And the other two play
Out-of-state license plate games.

Pinto Rider

CHARLES L. GRANT
illustration by
RON AND VAL LINDAHN

It was warm that day, warmer than late October had a right to be. The Sandia Mountains were already touched with snow at the heights, the aspen had already gone to gold and beyond, but there was nothing on the near slopes but brown from straggling brush to blowing sand to hard piles of thrown dirt that once had been mud. The air, if it had been right, should have told of a cooling, the sky should have been more fragile a blue, and there should have been at least a taste of something more on the wind than the ash of dry dust.

But it was warm.

And in the air, a waiting.

Ray Maxton shifted uneasily on his chair, sniffed, scratched his chest without feeling it, and hooked his tired boots on the porch's sagging rail. A sheen of sweat on his brow; he wiped it off with a thumb. He shifted again and leaned forward a bit to stare at the sky. Nothing. Not even a cloud. But he still didn't like the feeling he'd had since waking that morning. It excited him, and it frightened him, without him knowing why. It made him snap his fingers in impatience every few minutes; it made his throat constantly dry.

At first, after breakfast and cleaning the cracked dishes under the pump in back, he blamed it on his imagination. Dreaming, he told himself, will do that to a man — it'll fire the mind until the mind finally provides what really isn't there. It'll make ghosts from the fog and demons from the clouds. Dreaming has a place; too much of it is a curse.

Then the day warmed up, became downright hot, and the road through town shimmered with specters no one saw but him.

Getting old will do it too, he thought wryly as he rubbed his face with a callused, bony hand; only, when you get old, they call it getting crazy.

Beside him, on the floor, was a dark-stained stone jug half-filled with water, and the fingers of his right hand trailed absently over the cracked mouth as if he couldn't make up his mind whether to take another drink. Across the road, in a low building not much more of a stone shack than his own, except that it had a crooked sign over the door that said Tavern, he could hear two men laughing over the hesitant sound of an ill-tuned guitar. Down the street a pair of bearded miners crouched in the dirt beside a mule, arguing about something that had one of them pointing angrily at the sky.

The creak of a door on poorly fastened hinges that had gone to rust last winter, and he looked over his shoulder. He didn't have to. It could only be Jon.

"What do you see?" the younger man asked, sitting on the top step and hooking his knees with his hands.

"Not much," he answered. It was the best answer he could give. He'd been sitting here since sunup, and not a soul had come through. Not a wagon, not a rider, from either down country toward Albuquerque, or up and around the hill at the placer mine in Dolores.

Not a hawk in the sky.

Dust devils only, and a blue-tail lizard that skittered across the road just past noon.

Jon, wider at the shoulders and a head taller than his

father, scratched his light hair mightily, scratched under his arms, across his stomach. Then he sighed loudly and picked up a stray blade of grass. Brown. And dusty.

"You're gonna grow to that chair," he said, forcing a laugh, not looking around. "You keep waiting like that, they're gonna think you're part of it."

"Have to admit, sometimes I feel like it."

The young man said nothing. He no longer asked why because the answer was always the same.

"I was thinking," he said a few minutes later.

Ray nodded without moving his head. Thinking was about all anyone could do these days, what with the gold in Dolores and San Pedro coming and going like summer rainstorms, without nearly half the pleasure. It made everyone uneasy. No one could predict if any more would be found.

"I was thinking maybe I could take Raro down to Albuquerque. It would give the poor critter some exercise, you know? And I was thinking . . . might be work."

Ray stared at his left leg, board-still and supporting the right. Whenever he stood, it was an effort; whenever he walked, he felt like he was hopping. Not much for a man like that to do. A hell of a way to bring up a son.

"Dammit," Jon said, twisting around, his face beginning to flush. "Dammit, everybody around here knows there ain't enough water for those stupid mines. The place is practically deserted, for god's sake. Why the hell . . . oh hell." He spat into the road. "I'm going, that's all." He spat again. "I want you to come with me."

Ray smiled. "You think I can ride all the way down there? You crazy, boy?"

"Dad, it's not —"

"Besides, here I got a place. There, I got nothing. It'd be easier for one man to find what he needs than one man and a cripple."

Jon's face darkened in disgust. "You're not."

Ray slapped his wooden leg. Hard. Ignoring the pained expression on his son's sun-dark face. "I'm dreaming that?"

There was no self-pity in his voice; acceptance had come a long time ago. "I'll stay."

"And do what?" Jon demanded.

"Wait."

"You're —"

He grinned. "Maybe."

Angrily the young man flung himself to his feet and stomped across the road, raising dust that covered his ankles and clung to his hips in a poor reflection of a cloud. He reached down once and picked up a stone, whirled and threw it as hard as he could into the arroyo behind the house.

He almost lost his balance, threw up his hands and stalked away.

Ray didn't smile.

The wind blew and he turned his head, covering the jug with his hand until the dust passed and the air settled. Then he shifted his buttocks again, shifted his heels, and folded his hands across his stomach.

Two men laughed. The guitar snapped a sour chord.

Jon started for the tavern, changed his mind, and kicked his way around the side of the house.

With a groan loud enough to be heard in Sante Fe, one of the miners got to his feet and grabbed the mule's reins, trying to tug it into going with him. The mule didn't move, and the man still on the ground rocked with silent laughter.

Ray watched them for several minutes, enjoying the mime show, until he saw the shadows crossing the road, felt the sun setting, and braced himself for the cold air that would cover the town in place of the snow.

It didn't come.

A lantern in the tavern window, wavering behind muslin. The miners hobbled off to the boarding house, the mule straggling behind. The guitar in new hands, this time birthing music. The creak of Ray's chair.

But the cold didn't come.

Not like it had on the night he'd lost the leg. A bitter, wind-driven cold slashed through with snow that made his eyes water and froze his breath on his mustache. Made his gloved hands too clumsy to bring the gun out when the faceless man on the steam-snorting pinto brought out his rifle. It was over in less time than it took for the thought *god I'm dead* to cross his mind; a single shot (he was told), a lucky hit (they all said), and by dawn he was unconscious in the doctor's office, minus the leg from just above his knee.

Jon had been nine.

Ray had been a decade younger, and the beard that he had then had gone gray a year later. It was all gone now, and the mustache, and now Jon was leaving too. He supposed it was only right and natural. But that didn't make it any easier.

When the boy left, there'd be nothing left but the waiting.

"You are a jackass, Maxton," he told himself then. And he agreed. He had spent ten years each October waiting for that pinto to return, working the placer mines as best he could, working a tiny farm that barely grew weeds, selling bits and pieces of whatever he owned to be sure the boy didn't starve.

"A jackass, pure and simple."

Dreaming.

Getting old.

"You want to know something, Raymond?" Lilly had said wearily as she'd thrown all her things into the battered steamer trunk a year after the shooting. "You want to know what I think?"

He hadn't said a word. All their arguments had been long done with, all their nights long since buried.

"I think you're too damned scared to admit that you did a lousy job, that's what I think. I think you're using that damned leg as an excuse not to get up off your butt and find yourself decent work."

Lilly, in all the years he had known her, had never bitten back a single word.

"I think," she'd gone on, "that you are too goddamned proud to admit you made a pisspoor sheriff. Strutting and loud talking, polishing that stupid badge ten times a day, and the first time you get a chance to prove the walk and the talk, you knew you couldn't do it."

"I didn't get shot on purpose, Lil," he'd said.

She nodded as she dragged the trunk to the door. "I know that, Ray." Her smile was sad, was final. "But Lord, in the middle of a snowstorm? What were you hoping for, a miracle?"

A lucky shot, he'd thought then.

Stupid, he thought now.

But Lilly had left him, and hadn't written him a word since, and he and Jon behaved as if she'd never existed.

Darker then, and warmer.

Two men barged out of the tavern, arms around each other's shoulders, and careened off walls and hitching posts all the way down the road until they vanished into an alley between a pair of adobe buildings that used to house a bar and a store. Like the men, they could barely stand now, and Ray was sure that the first good winter storm would blow them down. Like all the others.

He yawned.

A light danced from the doorway as Jon set up the lanterns inside, a rusty creaking as the pot was set on its hook over the fire.

Maybe, he thought —

And the snow began falling.

At first he thought it was insects drawn out of the hills to the flames; then he thought it was his eyes, from staring too long and wishing too hard. Then he heard someone curse, heard someone else shout and whoop a laugh, and he saw snowflakes settle on his boot, melt to a lingering dark stain, and vanish a moment later.

"Jon," he said without raising his voice.

Big, fat, wet flakes pushed by a light wind.

"Son, come out here."

The light on the porch floor was split by the boy's shadow.

"Holy . . . good god!" Jon said, and stepped to the railing. He held out a hand, pulled it back and stared at his palm. "How can it? It's . . . how can it?"

"It's October," Ray said.

He could feel the young man staring, not believing, as he slowly lowered his feet from the railing, reached to his left and picked up a gunbelt. Jon saw and shook his head. Ray smiled at him, pushed himself out of the chair and winced at the stiffness in his good leg. He strapped the belt on, fingers deft, leather oiled and supple.

"Dad, don't be stupid. It's only —"

Ray eased the gun from its holster, double-checked the ammunition, and nodded to himself. He cocked the hammer, eased it back, closed his eyes for a moment.

Dreaming.

The guitar still playing while the miners raced up and

down the street, shouting, laughing.

Jon shook his head slowly. "Dad."

Ray looked at him and shrugged. "You never know," he said.

And Jon grinned at him. "You're crazy, you know that?"

He smiled back, and cocked his head when he heard the hoofbeats on the road. Slow. Walking. Out there in the dark; out there in the white.

The guitar played.

The wind strengthened.

Ray eased his son to one side and stepped off the porch.

"Dad?"

The snow was sharp against his cheeks, made him squint when he looked north, and he wondered why the pinto rider had taken all this time to come back. He'd never known the man's name, had once in a long drunk convinced himself he had been the Angel of Death; but angel or demon, it didn't matter anymore because there he was again — patiently waiting in the middle of the road just the other side of the tavern. A shadow on a horse, framed in dashing white, the pinto snorting, pawing the ground, its mane blown and its tail lashing.

"Dad!"

If I miss, he thought suddenly . . . and drew and fired.

And felt himself struck by a brand that made him scream, lifted him and threw him and pounded him to the ground. The gun was gone from his hand. The snow was in his face, slapping him while he heard Jon shouting his name.

And the burning, no longer dreaming, and the pinto rider walking past him, hooves sharp as the cold, a shadow still until it was gone.

And darkness.

"Dad?"

And light.

"Dad?"

And he opened his eyes and immediately looked down, wanted to scream and didn't, wanted to laugh and couldn't, took his son's hand and squeezed it until the young man grimaced and tried to pull away.

"He's good," Ray said, though feeling packed with grit. "But at least now they match." Then he pulled Jon lower, closer, to see his eyes. "You saw him," he said, not asking, demanding.

Reluctantly Jon nodded. "I think so."

"You saw his face?"

"No. It was too dark. And the snow . . . I just saw the horse."

Ray sighed, and coughed, felt the pain and felt nothing.

"Who else?"

"No one," his son answered. "Just you and me, that's all. The rest were in the tavern."

Damn, he thought.

Sleep came and went between tides of pain.

No dreaming.

Just the dark.

"Dad, who is he?"

Ray didn't answer. It didn't matter. Lilly was gone, Jon would be gone, and it didn't matter a damn because the pinto rider was all he had left in the world.

Jesus, he thought; and listened as his boy left to find him a new leg. 🙿

Snow Dove

BRAD STRICKLAND
illustration by
DARRYL ELLIOTT

Miss Agatha Adel rose in the crisp dark that cold Wednesday morning, looked out the window at Green Street, and felt fifty years slide off her back. The neighborhood was again the way it used to be all that time ago, neat houses with homogenous families living in them, yards not cluttered with discarded tires and trash but as level as careful tending could make them.

Gone were the angular, rusted cars of doubtful utility; in their places stood the graceful humped domes of the cars she had known as a girl. The paint-starved house at the end of the street, the one that now belonged to sour old Mr. Hirschel, had been restored to its youth again, to the happy days when the twin Gerard girls lived there. And Miss Aggie's heart beat with the freedom of a girl's heart, too, and was glad: no school for Aggie today.

For in the night snow had fallen.

Miss Aggie raised the sash and bathed in the glorious cold air, feeling it tingle her nose and redden her cheeks to perky winter apples. She tipped her face up to the gray heavens and saw the flakes still spinning down. First they were dark against the flat gray clouds and then they disappeared against the snow-covered roofs, and finally they were in sight again against the dark walls of the run-down houses, snowflakes marvelous and outrageous in their whiteness. Pirouetting and swirling, whirling and tumbling, they hurried past like children sledding on Vickers

Hill (but the Hill of her youth, not the site of the Wal-Mart and Revco and Bi-Lo, not the graded and asphalted mesa that existed today). Miss Aggie remembered, oh, she remembered.

No school today. It was rare enough to see snow on any January day this far south, and the snows she recalled from the last ten years had been paltry, stingy snows, half an inch or an inch, adding to the creeping ugliness of the neighborhood instead of transfiguring it. Shallow snow was only a grotesque icing on rusting junk discarded in front yards. That kind lay a dingy white, spiked with the unmowed grass in the neighbor's yards, to be slushed by noon, melted by evening. And there had never been enough snow on the ground to cancel school, at least not in the last decade.

But this — this was a real old-time snow, easily nine inches deep. No, deeper, deep enough to keep her and all of her charges out of the classroom for one, two, maybe three whole days, and then the weekend.

Aggie laughed aloud, and the chuckle did not sound as if it could possibly have come from the throat of a sixty-four-year-old second-grade teacher serving her last term before retirement. She leaned from the window to glory in the thick white coats adorning the firs, in the jagged range of miniature white Himalayas running the length of each leafless branch of the oak tree in the Clements' yard across the way. The Clements, with Miss Aggie the last remnants of the old neighborhood, were both in their eighties and would not stir from their snug home on such a cold day. They were old. Aggie laughed once more, and again the laugh said the calendar was a liar. It was easily the laugh of a mischievous fourteen-year-old. The telephone rang and for a giddy moment Miss Aggie almost thought it was laughing with her.

But the second ring pulled her away from the window and back to the bedside table. "Hello?" she said into the receiver, her voice bright.

The caller went "Harrumph." That was enough; she knew him immediately — Mr. Wilkinson, the principal. "Ah, glad I caught you at home, Miss Adel. No school today, I'm afraid."

"None tomorrow or Friday either at this rate," she said with high good cheer.

She heard him sigh. "It's just a terrible mess. Well, I have to call the others. We'll discuss ways to remedy this situation at Monday's faculty meeting."

She hung up and stuck her tongue out at the phone. A terrible mess, indeed. Imagine! Looking for ways to remedy a wonderful snow, just as if a snowfall were a stomachache and not a gift from heaven! Mr. Wilkinson wasn't more than thirty-five, but he was older than Miss Aggie Adel, ages older.

The bedroom door creaked open and both cats, Augustus and Gustava, came padding in, meowing their readiness for breakfast. "Look at this," Miss Aggie said, holding Gussie up and touching her paws to the mound of snow on the window sill. Gussie reacted with outraged dignity, squirming down, stalking across the rug, shaking each forepaw with every other step. Miss Aggie laughed at her, but at the same time she found herself wishing that the other two cats, Dinah and Clara, had survived the summer to see the snow. They had been the adventurous ones, and they would surely have loved the transformed world.

Aggie heard voices from below and again leaned out the window, with Gus writhing and purring as he wound himself against her ankles. The neighborhood children, the three that the old street could boast now, had spilled out, freed from the tyranny of the school bell. Aggie cupped her hand beside her mouth and called down, "How is it?"

Little Brazil, his face a Caribbean brown, laughed his sunny laugh. "Oh, mon, Miss Aggie, it great!" His voice rolled and rose with the musical accent of the island where he had been born. "Look what I can do!"

He stooped — no easy task for one so bundled as he — and crunched a double handful of snow into a mass, then rounded it until he had a beautiful smooth ball. He held it up for her to admire.

"Well," Miss Aggie said, "don't just hold it. Throw it!"

Gomez, at nine, a year older than Little Brazil, urged, "Yeah, man, throw it!" Little Brazil was persuaded, cocked his arm, brought it down hard —

Smack! the snowball struck the wall above Miss Aggie's window, and showering fragments of it found their icy way onto her bare neck and down the front of her nightgown. "Ooh!" she squealed, squirming and giggling at the same time.

"You tried to hit Miss Aggie!" doe-eyed Paloma shrilled out at her brother, her chocolate-brown eyes wide with indignation.

Aggie laughed until the cold tears ran down her cheeks. "You silly girl. Boys don't throw snowballs at you unless they really, truly, deep down inside like you — haven't you learned that yet?"

"C'mon out, Miss Aggie," Gomez said, grinning up at her. "It's great snow."

She let delicious temptation curve her lips into a smile. "Well —"

"Please," Paloma said. She was too young for her voice to have kept the island lilt; she sounded like any ordinary six-year-old from a poor neighborhood. At times, though, Miss Aggie had noticed that Paloma sounded — different. Her voice could seem disconcertingly old at times. Now, though, it was just young, excited, and happy: "Please come play."

"Maybe just for a minute." Miss Aggie closed the window and at the same time caught sight of Mr. Hirschel staring out his bedroom window down at the corner. A sour old face he had, beak-nosed, beetle-browed, jowled. He was dressed as he always was, winter or summer: a greasy dark vest over a dirty T-shirt. Miss Aggie had suspected once that he owned only the one vest, but on the unpleasant occasions when she had been close to him, like last summer, when she was trying to find her missing cats, she had discovered that he had an assortment of vests, dark blue, maroon, or brown, but all of them so nasty that they looked nearly black from a distance.

Miss Aggie, seeing him at his window, paused. Mr. Hirschel's glare of disapproval at — what? The children? The snow? Miss Aggie herself? The world in general? — almost ruined the morning, almost made her stay inside.

But no light-hearted fourteen-year-old lass can stay in when snow lies thick and heavy, ready to frost braids and dust fur collars with a million prisms of diamond-shimmer ice. In a few minutes Miss Aggie had dressed herself and had fed Gus and Gussie, who showed no inclination to explore the white world outside. In a few minutes more she had a steaming cup of cocoa inside her and her galoshes and heavy quilted jacket on the outside of her, and then she went out among them, the three children who waited for her.

She showed them how to make snow angels, and together they turned her front yard into a Christmas card, with a big Miss Aggie angel in the middle and three small Paloma and Gomez and Little Brazil angels spreading their wings above and on either side of her own. As they stood admiring their work, Miss Aggie said, "Paloma. Your name means 'dove.' Your angel looks just like a pretty white dove."

Little Brazil laughed. "Oh, mon! My gran'mere is a dove!"

"Is Paloma your grandmother's name too?" Miss Aggie asked.

Paloma nodded shyly, smiling as if pleased to share such a pretty name. And still the snow sifted gloriously down, so Miss Aggie knew that before long the deep angels would be filled with the new fall, almost as if by the grace of God Himself.

She showed them how to make really good snowballs, and they threw at the telephone pole on the corner of Rampart and Green Streets until they pelted it at every toss, even from ten yards away. And oh, how they took to every frigid game she could summon from memory: all of them, even Paloma, whose island days were remote but who could remember no significant snow at all.

Little Brazil (how did he get that nickname?) separated himself from the others and began to amass a small mountain of snow just across the street from Miss Aggie's house, in front of the Clements'. After awhile Paloma wandered over to him, leaving deep blue tracks like lopsided figure eights behind her. "Whatcha doin'?"

"Snowman," he grunted, his nose glowing even through his dark complexion.

"No," said Aggie, laughing. "Oh, dear, no, no, no. Haven't you ever made a snowman before?"

Little Brazil wiped his nose with the back of one purple mitten and shook his head. "Seen 'em on TV is all."

"Well, you don't heap up a snowman. You roll it. Watch."

Gomez, who had one last snowball ready, donated it. Miss Aggie dropped it into the snow — it sank more than its own depth — and she began to roll it. Wonder of wonders, it grew, fattening as it went, until it was as big as a head, then as big as the large globe in the school library. It made a crunching sound as it rolled down the sidewalk, and when it got too big for her, then Gomez, Little Brazil, and Paloma took it over and rolled it a few steps more. Finally it was too big for all of them together to move, a wonderful irregular white clump of snow half the size of a compact car. "Now smooth it!" Miss Aggie shouted, clapping her mittened hands with midnight silence.

They smoothed and shaped it until it was a perfect sphere, whiter than any white they could name. Then Gomez was off to roll a torso, which was ready in half a minute. They boosted it up into place, and Paloma laughed to see that the snowman's shoulder was as high as Miss Aggie's chin. And then Little Brazil stooped, his grin steaming, to roll the head —

But Mr. Hirschel came out onto his snow-covered front porch. He came with his bald forehead wrinkled forward into a scowl, his beaked nose jutting over a cigar clenched between stained teeth, his bare arms swinging, his black vest flapping in the breeze. "Get the hell out of my yard," he said.

Paloma, who had been sketching buttons on the snowman's chest with her finger, barely glanced around. "Ain't in your yard. We on the sidewalk."

Mr. Hirschel's face went the color of eggplant. He stormed down the steps, his slippered feet kicking lilliputian blizzards, and he waded through the snow on his walk, his expression looking more and more dangerous. Paloma backed away, coming toward Aggie, and Aggie put her arm around the girl's shoulder. Gomez and Little Brazil had been bringing the head to the body. They stopped twenty feet away, the uncapitated snowman's cranium cradled between them on their linked hands.

Mr. Hirschel put one foot on the snowman's spine and pushed. The body toppled over, the torso splitting and spilling. Another kick gutted the abdomen. The boys dropped the ball of snow and fled up the street, and Paloma tore after them. "Goddamn niggers!" Mr. Hirschel yelled. "Niggers and spicks. And you, you damn fool old maid. Get into the house with your stinkin' cats, you damned old bitch."

Aggie ran away from him, ran with her mittened hands pressed against her burning ears. She slipped, skidded, and came down with a jolt that sent fire through her left hip. She got up somehow and stumbled on, up her own front steps, into her hallway. The door slammed behind her. Gus and Gussie raised their backs at the noise and ran up the stair, leaving her alone. Trembling, Miss Aggie had to sit for a long time on the bottom step. Then she rose and with a stitch of pain in every step she dragged her way up the stair and to her bedroom.

She let the sodden coat lie where it fell. She peeled herself out of sweater and baggy jeans, out of the wet green argyle socks. She put on her fuzzy pink robe and huddled deep inside it, crying.

After a long time she crept to the window. The angels on her lawn had vanished, obliterated by another three or four inches of snow. Even the ruins of the snowman in front of Mr. Hirschel's house had been blanketed, had become merely another undulation. The children were nowhere to be seen. Aggie leaned her forehead against the freezing glass and let her breath condense, hiding the white world outside. Gus came and she scratched his ears, but he seemed to sense her mood and wanted no part of it. He stalked out again.

Old, Miss Aggie thought. He had called her old.

She didn't mind the other. Not fool. Not old maid. Not even bitch. Those things she could bear, for she never believed other people's lies. But old was heavy with the truth.

The phone rang, making her start. She groaned her way up, pain twisting like a thin blade in her injured hip. She all but collapsed on the bed as she lifted the receiver. "Hello?"

Someone breathed at her, a heavy snuffling sound. She felt colder than she had in the snow. "I'm warning you," the voice growled, and it was his sure enough, was Hirschel's furious grating voice. "If I catch them in my house I'm gonna kill them. I got a right. I'm sitting here with a loaded shotgun on my lap and I got a right to protect my property."

She heard the tremor in her voice: "I don't know what you mean."

"Them goddamn black pickaninnies!" he bellowed. "Thieving little bastards come in through my kitchen window. Slipped it open slick as shit. I nearly caught them — heard them slam it to when they went out again. You keep them brats away from my house, you crazy old bat, or I'll shoot them just like I shot your damn —"

Her hand tightened on the receiver, but Hirschel banged his phone down on the hook. She hung up, too, and after a moment took the phone off the hook and left it there so he could not call her again.

She remembered how Hirschel had denied ever seeing the cats last summer. Clara and Dinah had disappeared within a week of each other back in July. Adventurous kittens they had been, eager to explore the neighborhood. Miss Aggie wept some more.

She went downstairs a step at a time, catching her breath at each new stab of pain. She shook as she opened a can of vegetable soup, as she stood heavy on her good right leg and stirred the simmering pot on the stove. She could not stop crying.

The rising steam bathed her face. Potatoes and peas and carrots floated and sank; the brown soup bubbled and blurped. Blending with that sound, so soft that she thought she might have been hearing it for a minute or more without really noticing it, came the sound of a child's hesitant knock at the kitchen door.

Aggie tore a paper towel off the roll and wiped her eyes and blew her nose. She opened the back door. Paloma stood there. "Hi," she said gently.

Aggie's smile felt wrong on her face. "Hello."

"It's not snowin' as hard now."

"No." Miss Aggie sighed. "Everything ends."

Paloma tilted her face up, her chocolate-brown eyes big and solemn. "Not everything. Some people can be young and then old and then young again."

The voice was so different, so aged and wise, that Miss Aggie shivered. "What?" she asked in confusion.

"I said we built us another snowman," Paloma said.

Aggie clutched her robe tight at her throat. "I misunderstood you. I thought — what? Another snowman? Oh, no. You'd better not. Mr. Hirschel —"

"Not in front of his old house." Paloma wrinkled her nose. "Beside yours. Look."

In her fluffy slippers Aggie took a tentative step out onto the little back porch. The new snowman stood next to the house, sheltered from view. He stood in an angry pose with his back to the house, sculpted arms akimbo, bald head tilted forward. Aggie could see the white left ear and part of the cheek. But that was enough. She pressed her fingers against her lips to hold a giggle in. Gomez waved from the other side of the snowman; Little Brazil stepped back from the flapping vest. "Oh, dear," Aggie said with a titter. "It's — it's quite a likeness." Then the cold breeze hit her again. "Where did you get the vest?"

Paloma rubbed her nose. "We just . . . found it." That tone again, that voice that was too old. *Don't ask me where*, it seemed to add silently.

"Well, I — I suppose — oh, he'll never see it there, will he?" To the boys she called, "Come in! Soup's on. We'll have some hot cocoa."

She dumped a second can of soup into the pot, and they made a little luncheon party at the table. The boys grinned and snuffled and petted the cats. Paloma was curiously dainty as she set the table. She paused once, her wide brown eyes on Miss Aggie. "He hurt you," she said.

"I fell and hurt myself," Aggie replied, feeling as if she were a little girl guilty of some mischief and reporting it to her grandmother. They ate, and when they had finished Paloma wouldn't allow Aggie to stump about on her injured leg. Instead the little girl cleared the table, rinsed the cups, washed the dishes.

"Oh, dear, look at the time. It's past noon. Your parents will be worried about you," Miss Aggie said, luxuriating in not having to rise and walk on her red pain. "You'd better go home."

"Can't," said Little Brazil. "Mama and Papa both workin."

"On a day like this?"

Little Brazil shrugged. "Papa drive an ambulance. Mama, she's a maid at the motel. Gotta work."

"My papa," Gomez said with a grin, "he's drunk."

"Miss Aggie," Paloma said suddenly, "would you give me a carrot?"

"A carrot, dear?"

"Not to eat." Paloma's eyes were all Aggie could see,

deep and brown and old. "For the snowman."

Of course. The final touch, the orange nose. Every snowman deserved one, and this snowman deserved a bigger nose than most. "Look in the refrigerator, dear. The drawer on the left, I think."

Yes, there were the carrots; and one of them was grand indeed, a foot long easily, a lovely tapering vegetable spike that would be just right for the purpose. "Take it," Aggie said, unable to contain her laughter. "Please take it."

The three children went outside. Aggie sat for a moment. It's wicked, she told herself. God forgive me, it's wicked. But he called me old. And he did something to Clara and Dinah, I know he did.

The groan and slipping whine of a passing car brought her out of her reverie. She stood carefully, took hitching steps through the house to the front door, and looked out through the glass. A car with chains thumped its laborious way up the street, leaving nasty gray ruts behind, spoiling the snow in a way that the wheeling tracks of the children did not. And now the snowfall was spotty and faltering, too light to repair the damage. Aggie sighed, and her breath steamed the cold window. Everything ends.

She went upstairs, her hip hurting terribly. She had prescription tablets in her medicine chest, left over from a painful tooth extraction a year earlier: she had taken only one, because it gave her an unpleasant woozy feeling. But now she swallowed two. She lay on her bed beneath a thick down comforter and dozed.

She dreamed of her mother, as she had been in the last year of her life: an old white-haired woman, spare and straight of spine. "This will help," she said, and her soft hands stroked the painful hip.

"Your eyes weren't brown before," Aggie said.

The woman smiled. "Change is woman's nature. I will show you secrets: you have grown old, but accept me and you will grow young."

Miss Aggie came suddenly awake, but she was alone in the bedroom. She slept again, this time without dreams. When she woke for good, it was because a screaming noise had broken her sleep. The wail faded: it had been a siren, coming from not far away. Aggie looked at her watch. It was nearly five. Twilight had fallen outside; the early night of deep winter was almost on Green Street.

She rose and dressed in the jogging suit she wore for warmth instead of exercise. She put on a pair of sneakers and noticed only when she was halfway downstairs that her hip was much better. The kitchen was frigid. She had not shut the back door properly, and the wind had blown it open, had fanned a thin white drift across the linoleum. A child's footprints showed there, little lopsided figure eights. Gussie came in, went to the open door, and stared outside, her tail twitching her disapproval of snow. Miss Aggie went to close the door, reflected that she ought after all to have one good look at the snowman, and she edged out onto the narrow back porch, shivering from the cold.

The snow had ceased to fall. The dusky sky was a flat gray slate overhead. She crunched down the steps, holding the rail with both hands, and then out into the yard, her feet sinking into more than a foot of snow. She had to take short steps to keep the small lingering pain at bay, and she began to pant in the bitter air.

Little by little the snowman's face revealed itself as she circled him. Bald high forehead. Beetle brows, deep-set eyes. A beaky nose sculpted from snow. A real spit-black-ened cigar butt protruding from an angry mouth. Jowls.

"Perfect," she breathed. "Oh, he's perfect."

A nose sculpted from snow.

Her heart fluttered. Aggie heard another siren sound, just a single whoop! from down toward the corner. Breathing even harder, she limped to the front of her house and looked down the street. A small crowd stood in front of Mr. Hirschel's house. She saw the Clements, an almost identical couple, both small, bent, and birdlike, standing a little apart from the darker neighbors.

The red and white ambulance must have come south on Rampart. It was up on the sidewalk now in front of Mr. Hirschel's house; it had rolled right onto the mound of snow marking the first snowman's resting place.

The front door opened and a swarthy man and a black man came carefully down the snowy steps of the Hirschel house, carrying a stretcher between them. The sheeted body must have been heavy, for the black man who brought up the rear had to hunch down to make the burden more nearly level as they came down the steps. He said something to Mrs. Clement, and Mrs. Clement shouted to her half-deaf husband: "Real quick, he said. Must have been a heart attack."

The two men came slowly down the walk, slid the body slowly into the ambulance. Mr. Hirschel needed no haste, not now.

Aggie's head was whirling. No one down the street had noticed her spying; the dead man occupied their eyes and thoughts. Looking behind her, Aggie carefully stepped backward, putting her feet just exactly in the tracks she had made. She teetered on a high wire of her own imagining, and the whiteness was a thousand-foot drop without a net. She did not fall.

She left only one track that seemed to end nowhere, as if the girl who had made it had been snatched from earth by a soaring angel. It was an old joke of hers, a trick she had often played in the snows of her girlhood, making a mystery of passage to baffle the prosy grown-ups. When Aggie had backed all the way to the snowman, she changed direction and went around it to look at it again from the front.

The carrot had not been meant for a nose.

The blunt round stump of it jutted from where the breastbone would be. The deep-thrust tip must have pierced the snowman's heart.

The snowman was so white that, staring at it, Miss Aggie had an illusion of color. To her it seemed, just for a moment, that a red stain flowed downward from the carrot, a translucent icy scarlet that reminded her of a cherry snow cone.

But the flavor would be bitter. Miss Aggie did not care to sample it. She blinked, and the snowman was white again. For a short time she stood in the freezing cold, thinking of Paloma, of young-old eyes, of hands that must have practiced making images, perhaps in wax, decades ago on some sunny island where snow never fell. And she felt herself beginning to — accept. The young could do that, could accept as true all the things old folks would call impossible.

But now she was shivering in the deepening twilight. She had had enough of the snow and the cold. She stuck her tongue out at the snowman's angry glower, went behind him, and pushed him to ruin. She tugged the vest free, wadded it into a ball in her right hand. Flannel would burn to ash in her fireplace. The snow would melt with warmer weather. The sodden cigar butt would disintegrate in time. The carrot would remain, perhaps food for a hungry squirrel when spring came.

Gussie and Gus stood in the open doorway watching her. Aggie took the back steps two at a time, laughing. The cats gave her an incredulous look and scampered inside ahead of her. Her hip hitched once, just as she stepped over the threshold. The twinge passed immediately. Miss Aggie pressed the palm of her free hand over the joint. "Just a growing pain," she decided, and then she went inside and closed her door against the cold and the rising dark. 🕭

Carousel

S. K. EPPERSON

He loved carousels in the moonlight.
The pale glow of a dozen frozen steeds'
thrashing legs, bulging necks, bared teeth
and silvery manes, whipped by a wooden wind
that went nowhere.

He loved to ride the carousel at midnight.
The visceral thrill of clamped knees,
clinging hands, open mouth, and sweaty hair
teased wild by a wind that went nowhere
and took him along.

❧

The Window

ELIZABETH CONKLIN

illustration by

P.J. MEACHAM

"Irene won't approve, of course," Momma was saying on the phone to Aunt Remy in the kitchen, "but we should hold a séance. They say it's a half-breed Indian girl who was jilted by a white man. People been hearing her ghost cry on that mountain for thirty years. And still some don't believe. You know what Irene said to me? She said people go to heaven or hell when they die. Ain't no in between. Have you *ever*?"

I rolled my eyes at Grandpa, who chuckled softly. He don't believe in nothing, which is why he's not afraid of ghosts. To make him laugh out loud I whispered, "I hope it don't scare off the fish!"

When we finished winding the line on the reel we stowed the gear in the back of the pick-up. Grandpa hid a couple of packs of cigarettes in his tackle box while I stuck my toy bazooka behind some suitcases.

"Get off that phone, Eva Fay, and pack up the food," Grandpa ordered as we came back in. Momma obeyed, though she'd been flipping fried chicken out of the pan with a pair of tongs as she talked and had a pan of tea brewing on the stove. She swung her long hair back and forth like a curtain.

Ross was slicing boiled eggs into the potato salad, wearing only his glasses and a pair of paisley bell-bottoms. Grandpa'd been giving him a hard time ever since he burned his draft card and I hoped the old man wouldn't start anything but sure enough he suggested Ross put an apron over his pretty trousers. Just like himself, Ross didn't blink but tied a blue apron with a duck on it around his waist. I stuck my head in the refrigerator quick but Momma laughed right out loud.

That's how we began our trip up to Lake Conasauga with Grandpa in a rotten mood. I should have known right then that something was bad wrong about the whole thing.

Momma paused as she was getting into the cab of the truck and looked at Grandpa, who had insisted on riding in the back with me. "You feelin' okay, Daddy?"

"I'm perfectly fine," he said shortly.

"I put your medicine in your shaving kit."

He nodded without looking at her.

Holding Grandpa's bird dog Slick by the collar in one hand and eating fried chicken with the other I watched Atlanta disappear like time going backward.

The mountain road wound forever upward in a cloud of red dirt. I closed my eyes and tried to imagine how a lake could sit on top of a mountain without running off. I thought about a lot of things because the whole time in the back of my mind I was trying not to think about the ghost. Grandpa said hogwash, but Momma said no one really knew whether there was such a thing or not until they experienced it for themselves and she for one intended to keep an open mind because you just never knew. I tended to side with Grandpa until I woke up in the middle of the night scared silly and wondering if the old man might be wrong for a change. Then we got to the lake and suddenly Momma was screaming and throwing her arms around her sisters. I let both my aunts kiss me, shook hands with my uncle and hid from my giggling girl cousins.

Grandpa rescued me. "Guy, let's git this truck

unloaded," he said. "The sooner Momma can cook dinner the sooner we can eat. Slick! Get down from there. The sooner we eat the sooner we can go to bed," he continued, handing me down a suitcase as the dog scampered off. Then we hollered together, "The sooner we go to bed, the sooner we can get up and go fishing!" Momma just rolled her eyes.

Aunt Irene sounded like she was pleading with God when she said grace before dinner. We were in the cabin her family was sharing with Aunt Remy. I looked up at Aunt Irene without lifting my head—Grandpa never sounded like that when he prayed. She looked like she'd been tired for a long time, as though she'd waited all her life for something that never happened. Her husband, Uncle Willis, was the opposite. He laughed loudly and immediately whenever someone made a joke and didn't stop until Aunt Irene tugged on his madras sports coat. The little girls, Jill and Abby, were their daughters.

"The old man who sold us these says he heard the ghost wailing last night clear down to Ellijay," said Aunt Remy at one point, passing a dish of apple rings she'd taken off the pork ribs. What I could see of her eyes under her wedge of orange curls were bright like stars.

But Irene spoke again. "Most likely the wind. Have some more butterbeans, Aaron."

Momma gave her younger sister a look that said they'd talk about it later and changed the subject. Uncle Aaron pushed his peroxided bangs off his forehead and obediently helped himself to more butterbeans but he didn't look too happy about it. I pitied him, since I'd managed to scrape most of my vegetables onto Grandpa's plate while no one was looking. But I grinned at Aunt Remy when Grandpa wasn't looking. Grandpa's never smiled at a woman.

After dinner, Grandpa showed me how to use his camera and I took several group photos, feeling important.

I got tired early and wandered back to our cabin as soon as Jill and Abby were put to bed. Grandpa was already there, standing in front of the picture window in the main room smoking a cigarette and watching the sun go down. He didn't seem to notice me. His eyes looked sad and far away but the sunset was pretty, sparkling on the water between the straight pines, so I stood beside him and watched too. The lake was very still, except for a sort of shadow on it near the bottom of the window that climbed to a crest in the middle and then disappeared.

Grandpa shook himself and turned to walk off. "Hey, Guy!" he said, starting at the sight of me. "We got our own room. Right through here."

The sound of a guitar from the cabin down the road came to us for a long time after we went to bed. Momma was laughing when she came in late with Ross and smelled like wine when she kissed me goodnight. I listened to Grandpa's wheezing and Slick's long snores until I wondered if I had any breath of my own; then I felt sleep coming at me like a freight train.

It seemed like a few minutes later that Grandpa's clock went off. After nudging each other for awhile we quit dozing off and got out of bed. Outside, the brisk night air woke us all the way up. I shone the flashlight through the trees and Slick danced ahead as we made our way down to the lake.

White mist was rising from the water. The only sounds were the creaking of oars, the scuffing of Slick's paws as he made himself comfortable and the plip of fish jumping near the boat. "Just smell those fish," I whispered, breathing deep. My only problem was solved when Grandpa stood up in the boat. Gratefully, I followed his example and peed beside him into the dark water.

I don't know when I first became aware of the sound but it seemed like it had been going on for a long time, only so far away that I didn't recognize it at first. It was a woman crying. "Grandpa," I said. "Do you hear that?"

He did, then, just as I said it and looked back toward the cabins. A square of light glowed in Aunt Irene and Uncle Willis's cabin. "Women," said Grandpa, lighting a cigarette. "Don't ever try to understand 'em, Guy. Young men today don't know how to treat women."

"It didn't sound like Aunt Irene," I said. The sobs, which had been pitiful like a child's, grew louder as though the crier was getting angry. Soon they sounded loud enough to shake the roots of the trees.

Grandpa continued what he was saying as though he didn't hear either me or the crying. "Women don't know what they want. They need to be told what to do," he said. As he spoke, the sobs reached their highest peak, so loud that they sounded right next to the boat, and stopped.

I wanted so bad to get out of there that I almost grabbed the oars. "Grandpa!" I shouted, then bit my tongue. If I told him I thought it was the ghost he would think I was a fool. I sat there shaking in the silence for a long time, and looking at Grandpa's still back.

Since I had forgotten to watch my float, Grandpa caught the first fish as the sky began to lighten and the birds started singing. After that I paid attention to what I was doing. My first nibble got me so excited that I forgot about everything else.

In the end, Grandpa caught more than me but I caught the biggest. When we finally headed back for the dock, the sun was flashing white on the big front window of our cabin and it hurt my eyes. I turned back around to face Grandpa and we both grinned. Sharp across the water came the smell of bacon frying.

Aunt Remy was in a tizzy at breakfast. She'd heard the crying this morning and was sure it was the ghost. Momma was sad that she'd slept through it but Aunt Irene said she heard it and it wasn't nothing but a cat in heat. Before I could disagree Grandpa broke in. "Irene, honey, have you put up your pickles yet?" he said just like no one was talking.

Aunt Irene took the girls back to their cabin for a nap after breakfast. I scraped plates in the kitchen while Momma washed and Aunt Remy dried. When I heard the men settle themselves on the porch, I pulled Momma's arm like a little boy. "Grandpa and me heard the crying too, Momma. It wasn't no cat."

Momma looked at Aunt Remy hard and pursed her lips. "I brought some candles," she said.

I looked quickly between their faces. "You're going to have a séance, aren't you?" I said. "Momma, I don't think you should. I think we ought to go home."

Momma looked at me in surprise. "Oh don't worry, Guy," she said like she was talking to a baby. "It's just a game, like the Ouija board. Anyway, if there are such things as ghosts I'm sure they can't hurt you."

"How do you know?" An enormous yawn ended my sentence. Without waiting for a response I went back into the main room and flung myself down on the sofa. I was a little relieved for once that Momma didn't take me seriously. I didn't really want to go home yet. Still.

Before I knew it my body felt as though it were rising and drifting away but I could hear Momma finishing up in the kitchen and, later, Jill and Abby giggling outdoors. I heard Uncle Willis's deep voice asking them if they wanted to go for a boat ride and their shrieks all the way down to the lake, all mixed in with my dreams. Then the rest of the grownups went for a hike and it finally got quiet, except for Slick's snores.

Either my eyes were partway open or I was dreaming because I kept seeing the window across the room, with broad daylight streaming in. That's when I saw the shadow for the second time. It was completely black. It always started at the bottom of the window and bulged higher in the middle. Sometimes it was just a line at the bottom and sometimes it wasn't there at all. But it kept coming back, slowly so that I only noticed it gradually swelling, covering the light. There were little black specks at the top of it, racing ahead, reaching. I don't know how long I lay there trying to wake myself up completely or to dream about something else but it seemed like days. Finally Slick yawned in the kitchen and I sat up straight.

I hadn't been dreaming. There was a black crest before my eyes where it shouldn't be. I jumped up and grabbed Grandpa's camera from the mantle and took a picture. But as I snapped it the shadow disappeared. I went over and looked at the sill. There was nothing, no reason for a shadow to be there. Especially one so black.

I was suddenly afraid. "Grandpa!" I called, running out the door. "Grandpa!"

We almost collided on the steps. Grandpa was carrying a tray of cleaned fish.

"Grandpa, there's a weird shadow in the window. It comes and goes away and comes back again." I dragged him around the big stone fireplace. The shadow was back, reaching upward with a sinister flickering action. Grandpa just looked at it, his face grave. It faded shortly, as if it had made its point.

"Guy," Grandpa said finally, not looking at me. "It's just a trick of the light. Don't let it bother you none." He put the fish in the refrigerator, walked heavily into the bedroom and lay down on the bed. When I looked in on him later, he was still awake, his eyes staring at the ceiling.

The shadow didn't come back that day and, after a while, I forgot about it. I spent the afternoon swimming and teaching the girls to play army.

That night we had a fish fry in back of the other cabin. Afterward the girls and I sat on the steps eating watermelon and spitting seeds. The trees swirled in the wind and the sky darkened on one side. Uncle Willis played his guitar and the grownups sang folk songs: Peter, Paul, and Mary, Bob Dylan, Joan Baez. Then he played a couple of country tunes I knew Grandpa liked. The women wove flowers for their hair and the men passed around a skin of wine. I felt more calm and happy than I had in a long time, more so when Grandpa finally came over.

"Have some wine, Hanks!" called Uncle Willis. Grandpa laughed and shook his head. He walked over to the truck and got his flask of whiskey out of the glove compartment. The guys cheered.

Grandpa came and joined us kids on the steps. Aunt Irene brought him a plate of food. Little Abby was shy and went to sit on her Daddy's shoulders. She looked back at Grandpa with large, distrustful brown eyes and he winked at her. "I guess no one's interested in what I've got in my pockets," he said, clearing his throat. His straight silver hair gleamed on his forehead above his twinkling eyes. Jill and I jumped at him. Laughing, he gave us each a stick of candy, leaving one for Abby. But Abby wouldn't come.

After he ate, Grandpa leaned back and stretched.

"Daddy, tell us about when you lived in Ellijay. Tell us about how you met Momma," suggested Aunt Remy. The setting sun broke through the clouds for an instant and lit her curls from behind.

"I'll bet you did some courtin' up here, old man," said

Uncle Willis, laughing. Abby slid casually down from his shoulders.

"He did!" Momma said. "And he brought our mother here for their honeymoon. They stayed in the very cabin we're staying in now."

Grandpa smiled, but his eyes were pained. We all thought he was just missing Grandma. The wind picked up suddenly, scattering paper plates and napkins. We began moving at the signal of the storm to get things put up in a hurry. In the confusion Abby crept behind Grandpa and reached a hand toward his pocket. Grandpa got her. Her shrieks and laughter filled the air as the rain finally came down.

The sounds of the storm grew stronger as the night wore on. The wind blew the cabin door open at one point, scaring Slick half to death, and the lightning seemed to dance closer to the cabins each time it struck.

I slept fitfully and woke up early, missing the warmth of Grandpa's body. At first I thought he must have gone to the bathroom and then I started worrying that he'd gone fishing without me. But Slick was still there. He was lying on the rug, his head erect and pointed toward the door. A low growl began in his throat.

I got out of bed and walked slowly into the main room, picking up my bazooka along the way. The hardwood floor felt cold and smooth under my bare feet. When I rounded the fireplace, I stopped short.

Grandpa was standing in front of the window with his back to me. And outside — impossible! — stood a girl, looking at him. She was young, with black hair blowing in the wind. Her eyebrows came down low in the center and her cheekbones were high so that her dark eyes looked narrow and angry, wildly angry. A chill shot through my body and I ducked back into the bedroom before she could turn that gaze on me.

I crept to the window, past the growling dog, and silently unlatched it. I had to see what she was standing on. The ground on that side of the house sloped almost straight down to the lake. Cold, wet air touched my face. I looked out and felt the skin crawl from my scalp straight down to the small of my back. No one was there.

I pulled the window to and backed straight up against the far wall, holding my bazooka in front of me like a charm. Grandpa must have heard me because he came right back into the room.

He was white. He looked at me and I could tell he knew I'd seen it. His eyes searched the room as if he were looking for words. Then his face changed and his right hand came up to grip his left arm in a gesture I'd come to dread. I helped him sit down on the bed and ran for his shaving kit, calling for Momma.

The road was blocked by a 30-foot pine brought down by lightning and the enormous scarlet oak limb it took with it. We didn't even get in the truck. We could see it from the cabin.

Aunt Irene and Momma sat with Grandpa waiting for the nitroglycerine tablet under his tongue to take effect. Aunt Remy gently pried me away from the sight of Grandpa's still, clammy face and took me back to the other cabin where the girls were still asleep. I wanted to be outside with Ross and Uncle Willis, busy with axes and ropes and the truck, trying to clear the road.

"It was the ghost!" I kept telling Aunty Remy. "It was the ghost that scared Grandpa! It was looking in the window!"

Aunt Remy made me take off my wet sneakers and put on a pair of Uncle Willis's socks while she went into the kitchen to make some cocoa. Then, sitting at the table under a bare light bulb with steaming cups in front of us she said, "Now tell me what happened, Guy."

When I looked at my former babysitter in her pink bathrobe and orange hair frizzing around her head I almost felt like a little boy again, telling her about a bad dream. But her face was pale and her hands holding the cup were shaking. As I talked, she seemed to relax as though thinking about the ghost wasn't as scary as thinking about Grandpa's angina. "Are you sure you saw someone?" she asked me only once.

I nodded.

She got up and paced around the kitchen. She began talking in a low voice, as if to herself. "That old apple seller told me that the ghost had never been seen. He said the crying sound began after an Indian girl drowned herself in the lake. That's how they knew who it was. Why would the ghost — if it is one — suddenly make an appearance after all these years?"

"What else could it be?" I asked. "No one could possibly have been standing outside that window. There's nothing to stand on."

"Unless —" Aunt Remy went on as though she hadn't heard me. "Unless the ghost was some connection with Daddy. Eva Fay said the Indian girl killed herself over a man."

Quick, wet footsteps sounded outside and the door opened as we jumped. It was Aunt Irene, muttering to herself as she disappeared into the bedroom:

"O Lord, rebuke me not in thy wrath:
neither chasten me in thy hot displeasure.
For thine arrows stick fast in me,

and thy hand presseth me sore."

She reappeared with a Bible clutched to her breast. "He's all right," she said. "He wants to hear the Psalms. They're so comforting."

I suspected that Grandpa needed a few minutes of peace more than Aunt Irene's choice of psalms and Aunt Remy may have had the same thought because she stopped Aunt Irene at the door and began talking to her in a low voice. Aunt Irene gave me a stern look over Aunt Remy's shoulder and responded in a voice that I knew she intended me to hear.

"It's the excitement," she said. "He probably feels left out with all the attention we're giving Daddy and made up a story. You'd think he was too old for it. I know where he got it too. You're probably too young to remember but when Momma was alive she used to tell us a story about a face in a window. I believe it happened on their honeymoon. They were dancing — of all things without music, just Daddy humming — and Momma thought she saw a girl watching them through the livingroom window. She gasped and made Daddy turn around and look but he didn't see anything. He went outside to look but didn't find anyone, even though Momma thought she heard a cry or something. Guy probably heard the story from Eva Fay. But they both must have some imagination because, as any fool can see, the hill drops away so steeply behind the cabin that there's nothing to stand on!"

She turned and went out the door so fast that Aunt Remy didn't have time to say anything else and we heard her take up the psalm right where she left off. "What did she need the Bible for?" I asked sarcastically. Then I said, "Aunt Remy, Momma never told me that story."

"I suppose she likes the feel of it in her hands," she answered as if she hadn't even heard my last sentence.

Having worried Aunt Remy somehow relieved me of the problem a little and I lay down on the couch, feeling sleepy. Just before I drifted off I said, "That hill wasn't always so steep. Any fool can see it's eroded."

Everyone slept off and on during the day except Ross and Uncle Willis, who worked steadily to clear the road. Jill and I were set to sweeping floors, making beds, loading the truck and taking care of Abby. Against orders I left my camera on the mantel. By the time the afternoon shadows covered the cabins almost everything was packed up except for a pot of stew simmering on the stove. Grandpa had slept straight through.

Uncle Willis appeared in the door, taking off his cap and wiping sweat on his sleeve. "It's clear," he said.

"Daddy's better. He just woke up," Aunt Irene told him. "Guy, fetch Ross and Willis some tea."

Momma was leaning on the counter in the kitchen and sipping from a cup. "Shouldn't we be leaving soon?" I asked her. "It's getting dark."

Her voice was high when she answered and right in front of me she refilled her cup from the wine skin instead of the kettle. "We'll leave right after supper, Guy. It'll be best not to rush your Grandpa now but we'll take him straight to the doctor in Ellijay when he's ready. Don't worry, he'll be fine."

I'd tried to tell Momma about the ghost earlier but she snapped at me. Aunt Remy told me that Momma was just worried about Grandpa and not to mention the ghost to anyone else. Momma didn't look worried.

Aunt Remy was sitting on the floor near the window teaching a clap-hands game to Jill and Abby, her hair like fire in the dusk. "Guy, you come be Abby's partner," she called to me between songs. I came, hoping for a chance to speak to her. I stuck my hands out to let Abby pat them as she would, neither of us knowing how to play.

"Aunt Remy, I need to talk to you," I said quickly when the next song was over.

She got up at once. "Jill, you teach Abby for a few minutes," she said and led me out on the porch.

We looked down at the now-clear road. "We need to get out of here," I said. "Before dark. If —"

Aunt Remy looked at me, her blue eyes sharp in her white face. She's as scared as me, I thought. Our panic seemed like a physical thing, pulsing in waves back and forth from us to the thick woods on three sides of us. Storm clouds closed above the trees. For a minute I imagined they were the shadow of death, coming for Grandpa. I jerked around and looked through the window at the laughing heads of the girls. "Momma won't listen to me," I said, trying to control my voice. "They don't understand the danger."

"I know," she said quietly. "I've tried to talk to them too. They're just so worried about Daddy that those stories about the ghost just don't seem real."

"They don't believe about last night because I'm a kid."

"I believe you. But the best thing we can do is keep the girls busy so your momma and Irene can get your grandpa ready and the men can clean up. Then we'll eat quickly and get on the road. It won't take long." She was talking fast and kneading the porch railing with her hands. I patted her shoulder awkwardly before going inside.

Grandpa was dressed and sitting on the sofa, looking as though he'd spent a quiet day cleaning his guns. He moved his head and I came to sit beside him.

"Have you told anyone?" he asked clearly when the

girls resumed singing.

"Aunt Remy. She's the only one who would listen to me."

He looked over at his youngest daughter then, sitting near the window. It was as though Grandpa were seeing her for the first time.

He finally spoke again. "Your grandma used to look like that. The first time I saw her hair shine in the sun I forgot everything and everyone else. Couple of years went by that way. It can happen."

After a moment he said, "But I never wondered if she was happy."

I shifted cautiously. I'd never heard Grandpa talk that way about a woman before but it seemed to fit in with the rest of the strangeness. "Grandpa, was the Indian girl your girl before Grandma?"

He looked at me in surprise. "Yeah. She was. But how was I supposed to know —"

He stopped and shook his head. A few minutes later he started talking again. "Her name was Winona. They called her Crazy Winona. I guess she was, a little but you couldn't blame her. Her daddy was a white man who brought her here after her momma died — her momma was a Sioux — and tried to raise her as a white girl. But she never fit in. Some people were ugly about her being a half-breed but that wasn't all. She was different." He paused and felt in his shirt for a cigarette. He put it in his mouth but didn't light it.

His speech was slow and awkward. His eyes slid back to me now and then but mostly he looked at his hands. "It's been years since I've thought about it but even then it didn't occur to me what she must have gone through. For her it would have been more than just hurt feelings. She must have thought I was playing a trick, pretending I liked her. I never explained. I never gave her one more thought after I met your Grandma. Like everyone else I thought she killed herself because she was crazy."

I suddenly felt like I'd swallowed an ice cube. "Grandpa, we need to get out of here before she comes back."

He shook his head. "I'm not afraid anymore. I just feel sorry for her. I don't understand exactly — but maybe I could apologize somehow."

"Grandpa, I don't think —"

"Guy!" Momma said. "Come on in here and pour the tea."

I threw Grandpa a desperate look over my shoulder but he wasn't paying attention. He was calmly watching a thin line form at the bottom of the window.

At last Aunt Irene called dinner and everyone filed through the kitchen to fill their plates. "Let's eat outside again," I suggested to Momma as I fumbled a steaming potato around the pot.

She, smiling vacantly, seemed about to agree when Aunt Irene spoke up. "No, Guy, it's getting too cold. The weather seems to be changing again. Listen to the wind."

We ate in the big room. The wind rushed like frightened deer over the mountain and the shadow pulsed slowly upward in the glass.

Ross began to talk about the war with Uncle Willis. Momma stopped eating and looked unhappily out the window. I saw her face take on a puzzled expression and I knew she'd noticed the shadow. But at that moment, Aunt Irene tactfully changed the subject to music and Momma joined the conversation. I sighed in relief.

"Jill, fetch your daddy's guitar," Grandpa said.

"It's packed," said Aunt Irene, surprised. "Daddy, we need to be going now."

"One song for the road."

I looked at Grandpa. We winked gravely and I felt a rush of love for him. I shook my head slightly, pleading. The shadow increased its activity and it was only a matter of time before someone else noticed it. I couldn't eat. Finally, Uncle Willis began tuning his guitar. He sang a few lines of "Roll in My Sweet Baby's Arms." The shadow was flickering rapidly, right behind his head.

I could stand it no longer. I felt I had to distract them, hoping that we'd all leave after the song if no one else saw it. I jumped up, pulling Jill with me and began to dance with her. Uncle Willis picked up the beat. We danced faster as everyone cheered. Jill laughed and held out her hand to Abby, who timidly joined in. We danced faster and faster, my fear giving me energy and the girls picking up on my excitement, when suddenly Momma screamed.

Without turning around I knew why. The walls pulsed with a purplish light. A chill shot through my shoulders and I whirled to face the window. There were more screams and gasps and then an awful silence as those near the window backed away. No one seemed able to move for an eternity.

Then Aunt Irene went slowly down on her knees, tears streaming down her face. "It's a miracle," she whispered. "A sign from God."

"It's haunted! Haunted!" shrieked Momma drunkenly. "Just like the man said."

The line had reached the top of the window, arms branching from it to make a pattern. The outer pieces were purple, with amber, pale green like new grass and blood red in the pieces made by the shadow's curves. It looked like a piece of stained glass in a church. It stayed that way for a while, the room silent. Then it began to move again, shifting colors and patterns like a slowly-moving kaleidoscope. Abby began to cry.

"Momma?" Jill said in a small voice. We looked around but the grownups were like statues. Then we looked at each other and her blue eyes were pleading but I didn't know what to do. Slick growled, his teeth bared. Uncle Willis went to the window and felt the glass with his hand.

Grandpa stood up. "Everyone turn around and walk out of the cabin, now," he said with quiet authority.

There was a pause while we all looked at him. "Don't look at the window," he said. "Just turn around and leave."

I was the first to obey. To my relief, Aunt Remy picked up Abby and followed me. Just as I got to the door Momma cried out again and we all turned back to look. Winona had appeared, and behind her the colors were running together in a nightmarish swirl and pulsing faster and faster. Hatred shot from her eyes.

"Get out!" I shouted, pulling Momma's arm.

Slick fled through the now-open door, smashing through the screen. But Aunt Irene stood where she had turned to look back at the window. I saw Winona beckon to her. She took a step toward the window, then slumped to the floor all at once like a puppet with its strings cut.

Grandpa's lips were moving but no sound was coming out. I thought Aunt Irene had fainted but as we watched in horror, Winona beckoned to Aunt Remy. She dropped where she stood.

"No!" I screamed. My aunts' faces appeared behind Winona's in the window. With sudden horrifying clarity, I imagined the whole window filling up, Momma, us children, then the husbands and at last Grandpa until the window was a giant tapestry of faces as Winona took her revenge. I had to do something. I snatched blindly for my camera and knocked it off the mantel. As I bent to pick it up, I felt Momma going limp beside me. I straightened and snapped the picture.

I had seen a third face behind Winona's through the lens, and the shadow of a small forth. In the moment that the window went blank I threw the camera with all my strength into it and felt it explode.

Grandpa was on the floor but not limp like the others. His body was rigid, his eyes bulged. I ran to him.

"I'm sorry." His voice finally came though Winona was gone. "I'm sorry. Please."

I took the tablets from his shirt pocket, but even as I pushed one under his tongue I feared it was too late. Then I heard a woman's voice behind me. I turned. Uncle Willis and the girls were rubbing Aunt Irene's hands. Her eyes fluttered open. Ross held Momma, who was now crying quietly. Then Aunt Remy sat up and shook her curls.

In relief I spun back to Grandpa. "It was a trick!" I shouted to him. "Nothing but a trick!" Suddenly I put my ear to is chest. His heart still beat faintly but his breathing had stopped. Then Aunt Remy pushed up aside and bent over the old man. I watched her pull up his jaw to breathe air into his mouth.

Momma babbled behind me. "They can't touch us. They're shapes, just shapes. They can't hurt us." They don't have to, I thought feeling tears on my face. We hurt ourselves.

Then a breeze made me look up through the shattered window. The sky above the trees had deepened in twilight, but the storm clouds were gone. ❧

Armada Moon

THOMAS E. FULLER

Beneath your cold, dispassionate Sea,
Exiled here by King's caprice
And Storm's degree,
We sleep, in liquid silence,
We wait, we wait.

Beneath your grey, sunless Sea,
Our high prowed glory lies.
The slowly dissolving canvases
Like midnight raven banners
Salute our lost pride.

Beneath your dark, loveless Sea,
We, the Glory of an Empire,
Masters of Half the World,
Stare with sightless empty eyes
At our own gold embossed bones.

Beneath your Protestant, English Sea,
We move with specter grace.
We feel the movement of keels
Encrusted with decay, pull free
And bubble-rise in vengeance primed.

Above your placid, sundance Sea,
We float, silhouette shimmering
Against the gold Armada Moon.
Ghostly galleons come again
To sunder your sons in dead Philip's name.

Waygift

GERALD W. PAGE

illustration by

DEBBIE HUGHES

It was one among many, a minor worldsong twisted and blended in among the others, an inconsequential song among symphonies and cathedral choruses; yet to hear it was to ignore the others. There was an element to this song, a poignant quality that could not be dismissed by any human who heard it, a note that somehow identified the song of a dying world.

Barbara was a singer, a gatherer and giver of worldsongs to the younger races who cannot as yet walk the Way as Earthmen can. My name is Duncan. There was no purpose in me, not a special one as singing was to Barbara, not then, not then. I heard the songs, of course, and I walked the Way. I was as changed by the Way as any human is, deepened and straightened. I tasted of Unity and became more and more myself.

To me the songs were things used to pick my course from world to world. But to Barbara they were more; it was her Waygift that she heard them as I never could. Later, after her walks, she would take what songs she heard and sing them. The natives of the worlds we visited would gather and listen to her, hypnotized by the beauty and force of her singing. And me, I would listen just as hypnotized as anyone else. I envied her that gift, just as I relished her for herself and her beauty. The songs she sang were not a beauty that just came out of her now and then but part of the beauty that had grown around her. Her eyes, her face, all of her being had been touched with the worldsongs and made better by it. We were, I often thought, a strange pair. But she loved me, I realized, as much as I loved her.

Iselinn — is there a world more beautiful than Iselinn?

It's a pastel world. Soft blue skies. Softer pink sunsets and sunrises. Supple, swaying trees. Grass of a green so soft it's as if you viewed the world through gauze. The air was a mixture of gentle gasses that were light and exhilarating to breathe. There was lots of water, the fresh of it, cool and sweet, the salt of it teeming with life and activity. And since it is a world, Iselinn has storms upon its seas and lands, has deserts and snow fields and its animals prey on one another in nature's way. The people are people, which I sometimes suspect is a most wondrous thing; they're no more cruel to one another than humans used to be, and probably less so. For although they have never walked the Way and been touched by it as humans have, they have heard the worldsongs sung by those like Barbara who have the Waygift. They know — as humans never knew until they found it — that the Way exists. The people of Iselinn are philosophers and already suspect the nature of the Unity. They wait patiently for the day when they will learn to walk the Way. It will come at a long time after humans are gone, I imagine. The Iselinn will have a need by then to hear the worldsongs for themselves.

Barbara and I were living by the sea on Iselinn's largest continent, enjoying mild days and a pleasantly warm sun. Barbara would sing and I would listen, marvelling, or we would swim, or walk the beach to hunt shells. Frequently we were visited by people of Iselinn, eager to hear the worldsongs. Many times there were Earthmen with us, who had stopped for a visit either because we asked them to or because they had heard of Barbara and wanted to hear her songs. The most frequent of our visitors was our friend Roman.

"Duncan," he once told me, "she sings like no one else. Like the Way itself. I think the Way must have touched her more deeply than any of the rest of us have been touched. She's a vessel. The Way has filled her to the brim and as much as she pours out, the Way somehow keeps her filled."

Sitting beside me on the sand, Barbara laughed.

"It's true," Roman insisted. Roman had a tongue that could lure the worldsongs.

Only what he said about Barbara was true and I never heard it said better. Roman wandered, searching and exploring, looking at the worlds and stars of Iselinn's cluster, seeking out one wonder after another and taking them in like wine. Yet he was never far from Iselinn. We saw him frequently.

One morning I woke early and went out onto the beach and found Roman sitting on a driftwood log, drawing pictures in the sand with a stick. It had been weeks since we had last seen him.

But he was a man you knew would burst in on you in the night if he came then, a man who knew he would be welcome and wasn't shy about it. Yet there he sat, drawing pictures in the sand, after weeks of absence, and he'd not even bothered to wake us and let us know he was back.

He looked around and saw me.

I'd never seen his eyes like that, not in all the time I'd known him. I stopped and said, "What's the matter? Can you talk to me about it?"

With the end of the stick, he wiped out the sand drawing. "I can talk about it," he said.

"All right."

He stood up, looked at me. Those eyes of his — "Duncan, have you ever heard a worldsong change?"

"Sure I have."

"No, not that way. Not a song change. Not a change of melody or pitch or anything like that."

"How else can a song change?"

He stooped to pick up a pebble which he threw at the sea. "I don't know. I guess they can't, except like that." After a moment he added, "I'm talking about a song that feels differently from how it used to feel. If you understand that."

"How did it used to feel?"

"I don't know. I mean, I don't know how to say it. It was never much of a song. Just one of the ones you heard. Only, the feeling of it is different now, the mood's gone — changed. It never was a song I'd really paid attention to. You neither, I'll bet. Duncan, I'm embarrassed coming here like this. I feel like a fool."

"You should never feel like that," Barbara said. I hadn't heard her come out of the house. There was a look on her face that was related to what was in Roman's eye.

Barbara didn't have to be in the Way to hear world-songs. Some people — singers for the most part — have that talent. The songs just come to them, not just the song of the world that they're on — even I can hear the song of the world that I'm on — but the songs from other planets, sometimes from other parts of the galaxy; some say even from outside.

"I heard it last night," she said. "It just came drifting, very faintly. It just came and I heard it."

"I never noticed something troubling you," I said apologetically.

"I didn't hear it until we were asleep. It was faint but it woke me. Not the noise of it — I could barely hear that. But it woke me."

"I know what you mean," Roman said.

"I listened to it in the Way for a while, then came back," she said. "It's such a small song. I can't even guess what the world is like."

"I was there once," Roman said. "A long time ago. It's not much."

"It's dying," Barbara said quietly. "That's what the song is saying now. The world is dying."

Roman nodded his head, admitting what he did not really want to say. After a while he said, "It's a small, almost airless rock. It's the only planet orbiting its star. The others all broke up, all became asteroids. I don't even know why this one didn't."

"It won't last much longer," Barbara said. She turned and started back toward the house. Halfway there she turned and looked at Roman and me. "I want to go there," she said.

"Why?" I asked.

"Maybe the people need help there."

"It's a lifeless world," Roman said.

"Then because it's dying," Barbara said.

"But we can't help a planet," I told her.

"Please."

Oh, I didn't want to go there. But she was letting me decide the issue, and I didn't want to disappoint her or add to her sorrow in any way. And in a way, maybe I'd have been disappointed, too. I nodded.

In the Way I could hear the song. I had heard it a thousand times before and never paid it any heed. It was one among many, but now it had the difference that coming from a dying world would give it. We started toward it, treading across the Way, among the organ songs of gas giants, the whisperings of moons, the windchimes of voices or gongs of the solid planets, the shrillness of the stars. At last we reached a planet where we heard the glass bell

songs of thousands, perhaps more than thousands of asteroids. Still, the poignant, nondescript song of the dying
world persisted and we approached it. And came to it
finally.

We stood on the rocky surface of a small and moonless
world, circling a minor star. The only planet of a star where
stellar abortion after stellar abortion had scattered fields of
asteroids where there might have been whole planets.
There was air, though it was very thin, and the only life we
could see was a sparsely growing orange lichen that covered a rock here, a rock there. The horizon was close and
there were jagged mountains. There were craters as well.
Barbara was standing at my side and though I did not
glance at her, I knew she was shaking with the things she
felt. So was I. I reached for her hand and she moved closer
to my side.

"You see a lot of asteroids in star clusters like this,"
Roman said, though not as if he believed the explanation
mattered. "Sometimes the stars are so close that the stresses are too great to permit planets. The cooling gasses break
up rather than form full-sized planets. You get asteroids."

"This planet formed."

"I know. It's a freak, that's all. For some reason it
resisted or avoided the stresses that destroyed the other
forming worlds."

"But why is this world dying?" I asked.

"Maybe the sun's about to go nova," Roman said.

"No. It's the world, not the star. The starsong's normal."

"Roman was right, I think," Barbara said. "The world is
dying because of all the stresses in this part of space. The
star's too close, the asteroids and meteors are constantly bom-
barding it. It's not a strong world." Her voice trembled. I
tightened my hold on her hand. "Listen to it's song. Its all

there."

As though her words were a signal, the ground trembled. It shook for almost thirty seconds, then the shaking died down. The world was quiet again, except for the distant agony of the worldsong.

I turned to Barbara. "Well?" I asked.

"I've never heard a song like that before," she said. "I've never heard a song that expressed such loneliness before."

"A world can't think," I said. "It has no feelings."

"I know that."

She pulled her hand free of mine and started off. She stopped and turned to look at me. I saw what was in her face, sure enough, but there was nothing then and there I could do about it. Later perhaps, but not then.

I sat on a rock and waited.

The song was burning into my memory as no other song ever had. Roman stood close by, staring at the ground, waiting to leave but unwilling to do so while we stayed. Barbara looked around, not wildly, not hysterically, but unable to find a purpose to her looking just the same.

And all the time I was thinking, here we are: humans, the race that walks the Way. The beings highest on the evolutionary scale of any creatures in this galaxy, the ones who hear the worldsongs, the ones touched and changed by the Way, the ones with the secrets of Unity. Here we are, three of us as close as any three people can be to one another. Only just now the three are as alone — and lonely — as it's possible to be.

After a while I called out Barbara's name. She came over, face sober and strained. "I think it's time to go," I told her.

"Yes," she agreed. "There can't be much more time, can there?"

"It's already beginning," Roman said. He pointed. There was a fissure spreading across the surface of the planet, slowly, ever so slowly, with the dignity of coming death.

We were never in danger, of course. All we had to do was reach out and open the fabric between space and the Way, step onto the concourse and let the opening close behind us. We were humans and humans had walked the Way and been changed by it. Humans could breathe almost any sort of air, stand almost any gravity, almost any atmospheric pressure. Though there would have been a risk, I suppose, our chances were good we could have stayed there through the planet's break-up and then, floating in space among the world's floating debris, still have time to reach the Way before being harmed. And if we were harmed, short of being dead, the Way would heal us.

But we didn't wish to stay. I reached out and touched my fingers to the fabric of space and made the opening. There was a rush of sound, the glassy-bell-music of the asteroids and the more distant songs of the stars and planets. I held the opening for Barbara and Roman, then followed after them. I found Barbara standing on the concourse of the Way and sensed something of what she felt. I took her in my arms and held her. I think she must have been crying. After a time we started back.

We heard the end of the nameless planet's worldsong. There was no rise in the sound of it, no sudden burst of protest or agony.

It was that the song did not really end —

It changed. The pallid worldsong, with its undertone of anguish, ceased to be. But it smoothly changed to something else. The world broke apart and as it did so, the worldsong fragmented also. Song became songs. The new songs were small and bell-like, graceful. There was a dignity to them. The planet and its songs were gone, but the death had been a birth of asteroids and a song for each of them.

I saw Barbara crying this time. But the tears were not the same. We returned to Iselinn.

And that comes to the end of it, I suppose. Except that after a time Barbara came to sing a worldsong of that nameless planet. She was careful who she sang it for, of course. Most would be troubled by that song, though humans aren't — not once they hear its ending, the way the anguished song becomes another sort of music. Humans sometimes come from as far away as Aelaerto or even Blessed just to hear that song. And sometimes Barbara will sing it to the people of Iselinn — to a certain select few of them, at least. They can understand it also. I do not think they can be too far from learning to walk the Way. ❧

La Belle Dame

JACK MASSA
illustration by
HARRY O. MORRIS

"Have you ever found yourself someplace and not known how you got there? I mean, or even remembered who you are and how you came to be there?"

I looked up from my newspaper, startled to find the girl sitting on the same bench as me. I hadn't noticed her sitting down, and the park was nearly empty. Besides, she was the kind of girl who normally would have caught my eye right away.

"I'm asking because it's just happened to me. Just now, I found myself walking along the path here. This is Boston, isn't it?"

She had that frail, helpless look I always find disarmingly attractive. Her face was thin and fair, almost glossy. She had long, fine, dark hair, and big eyes that stared at me with a strange, feverish look.

A drug-user? No doubt. Maybe a hooker with a novel approach to landing customers?

"Yes. This is Boston." I turned deliberately back to the sports page, retreating into the hard, secure defenses of the seasoned city-dweller.

Towers of concrete and blue glass jutted up around us. We sat at the north end of the Common on a Tuesday afternoon. A chill, intermittent drizzle had kept the usual lunchtime crowds away. It was early October, and the leaves had already begun to fall.

I kept staring at my paper, trying to concentrate on the

print. I expected the girl to get up and leave, to find someone else to hit up for change or solicit or whatever it was.
But she just sat there, staring at the ground with a miser-
able expression.

I studied her from the corner of my eye. She wore a
bulky sweater, blue jeans, tennis shoes. Hardly the work
clothes of a hooker, even of the younger, poorer sort.

She caught my looking at her. She seemed ready to
cry.

On reflex I glanced down again, but it was too late. I
looked up immediately, feeling awkward for having been
caught. "You really are distressed," I said.

"Yes." Her voice was angry and frustrated. Like it
should have been obvious to me. Which, I guess, was true.

"You don't remember who you are or how you got
here?" I said.

She shook her head, gazing at the asphalt.

I noticed she didn't have a purse. "Have you got a
wallet? Anything with identification?"

Apparently this hadn't occurred to her. She checked
through her pockets, but found nothing.

"Can you remember anything before you got to the
park?"

She looked at me, her eyes confused, intense. "I think
it was raining. Someone was calling me . . . needing me."

"What name did they use?"

"I don't remember. It was more like I felt them calling.
Oh, God. I must be crazy."

She started to cry. I put down the paper and moved
toward her, feeling self-conscious, as I always do around
women I'm attracted to — even though she wasn't looking
at me.

I sat close, but I didn't touch her. "Don't worry," I said.
"This kind of amnesia is really pretty common. And it's

almost always temporary."

"I'm sorry." She wiped her eyes. "I'm sure you've got problems of your own."

"Everybody's got problems."

I looked at my watch. I was due back at the office in ten minutes, but I could always stretch out the lunch hour. Keeping the same dull job for six years did have a few advantages.

"Listen, my name is Gary," I said. "Gary Curran. There's a Muffin House down the street. I'll buy you a cup of coffee."

"No. I better not."

"It'll warm you up, give you a chance to relax and remember. Don't worry, I'm not trying to hit on you. Just a cup of coffee." I stood up, but suppressed the impulse to offer her my hand. "I mean, chivalry is not dead, entirely."

For the first time, she smiled.

The lunch-hour business at the restaurant was trailing off, so we got a table right away. At first, she just asked for hot tea. But I convinced her to try something to eat, so she added vegetable soup to the order. I ordered coffee.

She asked what I did for a living. I figured talking about me would keep her mind off her dilemma, and I imagined that her memory was more likely to come back by itself if she didn't try to force it.

"I'm a copy editor for Billings-Schumann. In the text-book division."

"You edit books? That must be really interesting."

"Naw. Mostly I sit in a cubbyhole all day and look for mistakes in manuscripts. Misspellings, punctuation errors. Sometimes I'm lucky and find a logical inconsistency between paragraphs."

She didn't see the humor. "You don't like it," she said.

What was to like? Monotony, low pay, zero prestige. And after six years in the same job it was obvious I wasn't going to rise any higher in the company. I had had ambitions to become an acquisitions editor once. Then again, I'd had ambitions to become a novelist too.

But I wasn't going to lay all that on her.

"It's okay. I get to read a lot. Last month I did a psychology text. That's how I found out what I told you about amnesia being so common."

Actually, I made that part up, but it sounded good, and I thought it would make her feel better to think I knew what I was talking about.

Instead, I could see by her look that it just reminded her of her problem. Typically, I had said exactly the wrong thing.

I tried to cover. "Right now, I'm working on a poetry anthology for the college market. British and American Romantics."

"Do you like it?"

"Some of them are okay."

She smiled faintly. "Are you a romantic?"

I must have blushed, because her smile widened.

Our order came. We talked some more about poetry. She didn't seem to know much; mostly she asked questions and let me do the talking. She was easy to open up to. I told her about my education, my attempts to be a writer, the freelance editing I sometimes do. I mentioned that one of the publishers I freelance for does occult books, and that sparked her interest.

"Are you into the occult?" she asked.

"Not really. I just work for them once in a while. Moon Spirit Press, they operate out of a bookstore over on Newberry Street."

"But you're not a believer?"

"No. Well, I keep an open mind."

"Meaning?"

I shrugged, a little embarrassed. "I guess I believe there are forces that science doesn't understand yet. Maybe some occult practices can put people in touch with those forces. Who knows?"

I couldn't tell whether or not she thought me silly. She turned her attention back to the soup.

By the time she had finished and laid down her spoon she looked better, less fragile and pale.

"I've decided what to do," she said. "I'll go back to the park and walk around, see if I can find anything to jar my memory. Does that sound like a good plan?"

I hated thinking of her wandering the city alone, with no money and no place to go. Besides, I was really enjoying her company. What did I have to lose but a boring afternoon at work?

"Listen," I said. "I'm going to call in sick to work and go with you."

"Oh, I couldn't ask you to do that."

"I want to."

"But I feel like I'm disrupting your life."

"Don't worry. My life needs some disrupting."

I used the pay phone at the back of the restaurant to call the office. I told them I had a touch of flu and was going home to bed.

As I hung up, an idea occurred to me. I looked through the phone book under Boston City Government and found the number of the Police Department Missing Persons Bureau. I called them up and told them I had seen this girl walking in the park and looking disoriented, and I gave them her description. They checked, but they had no report on anyone like her. When I went back to the table and told her this, she seemed almost relieved instead of disappointed.

The sky had lightened some and the drizzle changed to mist. We spent the afternoon tracing the footpaths in the Common and wandering around downtown. We walked as far north as the Court House, then back down Tremont Street and through the Public Gardens. A few times she stopped, staring around as if something had struck her as familiar.

But each time she shook her head after a moment and looked at me as if to apologize. I was just glad she no longer seemed so upset.

By late afternoon we were on Commonwealth Avenue, a couple of blocks from the Pru Center with its sharp-edged blue skyscraper. That stretch of Commonwealth has a mall, a wide strip of green set in the middle of the lanes of traffic. We sat down to rest on a bench. It must have been about four, because traffic was getting thick, the smell of exhaust heavy in the wet air.

The girl stared at the ground and shook her head. "It'll be dark soon. I guess there's nothing left but to turn myself in to the police. I guess they'll put me up in some kind of shelter, at least for the night."

Her voice was toneless, resigned. But I sensed desperation at the edges.

I didn't know if she'd accept, but at least I could offer. "Look, my apartment's only about a mile from here. It's not much, but I'd be happy to put you up for a while."

"That's really nice of you. But I've taken too much advantage of you already."

"It's no big deal. I just don't see any reason for a girl like you to have to sleep in some shelter with all the human debris. It'll just be till you figure out who you are. I really wouldn't mind."

I heard a strange note, like pleading, in my voice and wondered where it was coming from. She just smiled and shook her head, like she was overwhelmed by my kindness.

"Just for a day or two," she said. "If I haven't remembered by then, I'm going to have to leave anyway."

"That's fine." I stood up and she did too.

"You really are a good guy," she said. "You were right about chivalry not being dead."

We started walking again, through the noise of the traffic and the fading light of the afternoon. My heart started racing with an adrenaline rush. Here I was with a young girl of the frail, disarmingly attractive sort, taking her home for the night. I tried to remind myself that an evening of romance was probably the last thing on her mind.

It didn't help when, crossing the street, she took hold of my arm.

We got to my building just after dark and rode the elevator up to the sixth floor. I had a sack of groceries in my arms. We had stopped at a market and bought the makings for spaghetti. I decided to cook in, a demonstration that things were normal, that she wasn't disrupting my life too much. Of course, if not for her, I wouldn't have bothered with the Italian bread or the Chianti.

While I cooked, she sat at the kitchen table and watched me with a deep, vacant stare. I got the feeling she was really hungry, but when the food was ready she hardly touched it. I ate a lot, mostly out of nervousness. We hardly talked at all.

Afterward, she insisted on doing the dishes, so I took my wineglass into the living room. I turned on the stereo and stood for a long time trying to decide what record to play. Finally, I switched on the radio and tuned to the classical music station. I sat down on the couch, wondering what was going to happen. I heard her finishing up in the kitchen and my heart started pounding again.

She came in and sat next to me, her leg pressed against mine. Smiling, she took the glass from my hand, swallowed down what was left in it, then leaned over and kissed me on the mouth. Her lips opened and I could taste the wine on her tongue.

It had been a long time since I kissed a woman. But as much as I wanted her, I didn't want to feel I was taking advantage.

She pulled back and searched my eyes. "Have I embarrassed you?"

"No. But are you sure you want to do this?"

She sat up straight, avoiding my eyes. "I hope you don't think I did that just to thank you or something. I hope you think better of me than that. I may be confused, but I'm not that confused."

"I didn't mean to offend you. It's just hard for me to believe a girl like you could be interested in me."

A tender look softened her features. Her hand caressed my cheek. "You're wrong."

This time I kissed her without hesitation. I put my hand on her breast and she moaned and covered it with her hand.

I led her to my bedroom. She opened the shades to let the lights from Kenmore Square shine in, then turned off the overhead light. Smiling at me, she started to unbutton her blouse.

Feeling awkward, I turned my back while I undressed. When I turned to face her again, she was standing naked beside the bed. In the pale light her body looked even whiter than her face. Her breasts were small and round, her waist and hips very narrow. I saw almost no hair between her legs.

I walked toward her, self-conscious about my movements, my body. But her eyes were fixed on my eyes with such intensity that I soon forgot all about myself.

She fell asleep, cuddled in my arms. I lay on my back, staring at the gleam of light on the windows. My euphoria slowly drifted away, leaving me wondering why she had jumped into bed so willingly.

I've never had great success with women, a fact I've analyzed endlessly and fruitlessly. The few women I had any relationship with to speak of all seemed to please me less and less as time went on. One of them told me that I couldn't accept a woman as a human being, that I insisted on holding her up against some ideal in my mind. Maybe she was right. Anyway, as I got into my thirties I sought women out less and less. I was tired of the disappointment. As with writing novels, it was easier not to try.

Now this mystery girl had walked into my life, literally out of nowhere. It seemed too good to be true, much too good.

As I lay in the darkness, paranoia took over. I developed the fantasy that it was all some elaborate setup, that she was going to wait until I was asleep, then rob my apartment. For a long time I stared at the ceiling, determined to stay wake and catch her if she made such a move. But eventually I fell asleep.

In the morning I found her beside me, and I could hardly believe it. I stared at her for a long time, oblivious to the fact that I had to go to work. When I finally moved to get out of bed, she woke up.

"Where are you going?" she asked.

"To work. I've got to go to work."

"Stay with me." She grabbed my wrist and pulled me down on top of her. She kissed me hungrily and I hardened right away.

"Call in sick," she whispered.

"I can't do that every day."

"Just today."

I didn't need much convincing. We spent the morning in bed. Her appetite amazed me, and so did my body's capability to respond.

But by noon I felt drained and exhausted. I was afraid she'd want to make love again and I wouldn't be able, so I decided to go on to work.

I arrived at the office around one. On the way to my desk, I passed my boss, Miriam, in the hall.

Miriam is the motherly type, white-haired, soft-spoken. Her gray eyes examined my face behind her glasses. "I wasn't expecting to see you in today, Gary. Are you feeling better?"

"Yes. Thank you."

"You look very pale. Are you sure you should be here?"

I smiled. It was all I could do to keep it from breaking into a wicked grin. "I'm fine, Miriam. Really."

I walked to my cubicle, sat down and stared at the open manuscript on my desk. It was the poetry anthology; I was about a third of the way through. I picked up my pencil and stared at the page: the even stanzas of Wordsworth's verse, the cramped prose of the anthologist's footnotes.

I couldn't get my mind on the work. The characters on the page leaned into one another and blurred. My thoughts kept flying back to the girl in my apartment, the feel of her skin, her scent on my fingers. My memories of her seemed more real than the Formica desk top, the carpet under my feet.

Paging through the manuscript, I stumbled on a poem that seemed to describe her. It was one of Wordsworth's later poems, called "She was a Phantom of Delight." If you looked it up, you'd probably decide it's terribly sentimental, and really, only the first part expressed what I felt about the girl. But I was like a fourteen-year-old in love that day. I mulled it over a while, then called her on the phone and read her the first stanza.

"Come home soon," she said.

I don't remember much of what happened the next couple of weeks. In the daytime I sat in my office, thinking about her, scarcely able to think of anything else. At night we made love in the dim, frosty light from the windows, and I reveled in her warmth and smoothness, the taste of her breath. Afterward, I would hold her in my arms and talk to her, babbling on for hours, pouring out my heart while she cuddled against me and murmured in reply.

We didn't try anymore to find out who she was or where she came from. She didn't seem concerned or worried enough to bring it up. As for me, I only dreaded the moment when her old life would reappear and she would leave.

I realized that my infatuation with her had deepened into an obsession. But I was happier in that obsession than ever before in my life. I even started writing again, short poems about her, and about the emptiness I had felt before finding her. The poems were nothing great, nothing I would show to anyone. But the simple fact that she inspired me to write again seemed like a miracle.

In the midst of all this happiness, I felt more and more tired. At first I attributed the fatigue to overexcitement and lack of sleep. But even when I slept ten or twelve hours a night, the weariness grew worse.

One Monday morning I could barely drag myself out of bed. I would have thought it a bad case of the flu, except there were no other symptoms but this unbearable exhaustion. I couldn't concentrate on my work at all. I finally gave up and went home.

When I got to my apartment, she was there, wearing my robe. She put me to bed right away. I fell asleep with my head pillowed on her breast.

I went to the doctor the next day. He examined me and ran some tests, but he didn't seem to know what was wrong. He prescribed vitamins, scheduled more tests, told me to rest.

After the appointment I felt a little better, so I went in to work. I could tell by the expressions on people's faces that I must have looked like hell. I went into the bathroom and the face I saw in the mirror scared me.

I looked fifty instead of thirty-five. My skin was pasty, forehead wrinkled, eyes dull. My cheeks had gone loose and hollow, as if the flesh were being eaten away from inside.

Weird suspicions rose in my mind, curled like smoke and coalesced. I remembered a book I had edited once, about Chinese magic and folklore. The book recounted several stories of fox spirits who took the form of beautiful maidens. Under mysterious circumstances the spirits appeared to young men and seduced them, gradually draining them of their life force, until they died.

With a cold lump at the pit of my stomach, I walked back to my desk and searched through the anthology manuscript. There was a poem I wanted to find, one I barely remembered though I had read it only a few days before. After some searching I found it, one by Keats called

"La Belle Dame Sans Merci." I scanned the lines, my lips moving as I whispered the words.

A pale and haggard knight, found wandering beside a lake, tells how he met a faery woman who seduced him and lulled him to sleep. In his sleep, he dreams of an army of other knights.

> I saw pale Kings and Princes too,
> Pale warriors, death-pale were they all;
> They cried, "La belle dame sans merci
> Thee hath in thrall!"

This is getting out of hand, I thought. This is paranoia taken to the extreme. Nonetheless, I made a photocopy of the poem and put it in my shirt pocket, like a talisman.

Over the dinner table that night, I stared at her face, comparing it to the face I remembered from the first time I saw her. She no longer looked so white and thin. Her cheeks were rounder, less gaunt. Even her shoulders seemed wider, her breasts more full. Only her eyes were the same, still with that lost, feverish look.

When I finished eating, I asked her if she had had any memories come up from her past. She seemed disturbed by the question and shook her head.

"Maybe we should try the missing persons bureau again," I suggested. "It's been two weeks. They might have gotten a report on you."

"I guess we could try."

"You don't seem very enthusiastic about the idea."

She searched my face for a moment, then gave what seemed like a forced smile. She came over, stood behind my chair, wrapped her arms around my chest.

"I guess I'm afraid of finding out about my past. I'm afraid it might change what we have now, with each other."

She kissed me on the neck. I shoved the chair away from the table and stood up.

"What's the matter?" she said.

"Nothing. Nothing." I took the folded paper out of my shirt pocket. "I came across another poem today that kind of reminded me of you. I thought you might like to hear it."

"Okay."

Leaning against the table, I read her the poem. My voice cracked in a couple of places. I kept glancing up to check her reaction. Her lips stayed pressed together, as if to contain her feelings. But in her eyes I saw recognition, and a shadow of something else. Was it guilt, or pity?

"What do you think?" I said. "Scary, isn't it?"

She blinked, then raised her eyes to confront me. "I feel sorry for them, and for her."

"What do you mean?"

"For the knights, because they lost their lives, and for the lady, because she has to steal her life from those she loves."

My mouth had gone dry. "What makes you think she loves them?"

She shrugged. "I don't know. Just my opinion."

She glanced down then, and started to clear the table.

I walked out of the kitchen, still holding the poem in my hand, feeling numb inside. I stopped in the middle of the living room and wondered what to do. I wanted to run, to leave the apartment and never come back. At the same time, I wanted to go and take her in my arms, to apologize for my suspicions, to tell her that nothing mattered to me except what I felt for her.

Somehow, I ended up at the living room window, staring out into the darkness. For a long time I watched the lights of the traffic flowing up and down Kenmore Square.

Next day I sat at my desk, reading and rereading the Keats poem, trying to convince myself that it couldn't be true, that it was all just paranoid delusion.

The doctor's tests will uncover what's wrong, I told myself. Something reassuringly simple, like cancer. But I couldn't believe any organic disease would have come on so quickly. And it wasn't just the fatigue, it was the lapses of mind, the inability to concentrate on anything but her.

Enchantment, I thought. La belle dame thee hath in thrall.

I left work in the early afternoon, took the subway to Copley Square and walked down Newberry Street. Most of the brownstone buildings there have storefronts on two levels, up a flight of steps to the first story, down a flight to the basement. In a basement near the corner of Exeter Street is the occult bookstore which is also the headquarters of Moon Spirit Books.

The man at the cash register was not one who worked in the publishing end of the business, and he didn't know me, which was fine. The first thing I did was hunt up the book on Chinese magic I had edited. I read over all the stories about the fox spirits. The descriptions of their victims made my belly squirm.

For a long time I stared at the bookshelves without seeing them, my thoughts racing round and round. If my suspicions were right, if she was some inhuman thing sapping away my life, then I needed to act, and soon. If not, if it was all just paranoid fantasy, then my mind had swerved pretty close to the edge. In that case, what harm in swerving a little closer?

I went to the section on witchcraft and practical magic and read through all the books on the shelves till I found a spell that sounded right. It was in a trade paperback published by some little press in Indiana. The title was

Practical Esoterica for the Modern Witch.

I brought the book up to the cash register, picked out a white candle from a bin on the counter, and a brass candlestick to hold it. Since I don't smoke and never use candles, I had to stop at a drugstore down the street to pick up one of those throwaway lighters. Then I went out to the mall on Commonwealth Avenue, found a bench and read over the spell about eight times, till I knew all the steps almost by heart.

When I got back to my apartment, she was in the kitchen. She had just started fixing dinner.

"You're home early," she said.

I avoided looking at her eyes. "I'm going into the bedroom for a while. To be alone, all right?"

"Are you ill?"

"No. I'll see you later."

Without waiting for her answer, I went to the bedroom, shut the door and locked it. I spread the book out on the rug, but since it was a paperback, it wouldn't stay open. I tried creasing the spine, but that didn't work. I looked around for something heavy to weigh down the pages, but couldn't find anything that would do. By now I had started sweating, worried that she might knock on the door and try to come in before I was ready. Finally I just tore the few pages I needed out of the book and spread them on the floor.

The spell was titled "Exorcism for Troublesome or Tormented Spirits." It was written in verse, filled with a lot of Germanic and Latin-sounding names. I read it through in a low voice, bowing my head where the book indicated. At the proper point, I blessed and lit the candle. Several more verses brought me to the place where you call up the spirit to be exorcised.

I went to the door, unlocked it and pulled it open a

crack. I called her and asked her to come into the bedroom, then hurried back to my place behind the candle.

I heard her footsteps draw near. She pushed open the door, and I saw that she was naked. Stepping into the room, she glanced at the candle and the torn pages, then gazed at me with a look that showed no surprise, only sadness.

"You didn't have to resort to this," she said. "All you have to do is tell me to go, and I will."

I felt ridiculous. "I know this looks crazy," I said. "But I have to be sure. If I blow out the candle and you're still here, I'll know everything is all right."

"If you blow out the candle, I won't still be here."

My whole body coiled like it wanted to run. "Then it's true?"

Her eyes shone in the candlelight. "The poem you read is about one like me."

It seemed all the more incredible to hear her confirm it. "And from the moment I saw you, you were leading me along, planning to . . . use me. "

"No. I didn't know myself at first. We come to this world not knowing what we are. It helps us bond to the one who calls us."

She took a step forward. "Stay away," I warned her, and poised myself over the candle.

"I said, you don't have to do that. If you tell me to go, I will go. I'm not evil. I exist only for you."

"What do you mean?"

"The poem doesn't tell the whole story. The yearning in your soul brought me into being. Haven't I made you happy?"

"Yes. But you're killing me."

"If you keep me," she said slowly, "you will die sooner than you might otherwise. Because you will share what life you have with me. If you send me away, I will die now. I will cease to exist in this form, and you can never bring me back. Never." Her hands, at her sides, turned palms toward me, a gesture of pleading. "That is your choice: a longer life alone, or a briefer one full of love."

She moved toward me, the candlelight rippling over her skin. In panic, I drew in my breath to blow out the candle.

Then I thought of my life before, the loneliness and failed ambition, the creeping self-hate. What would I be giving up? Years of becoming more desiccated and brittle, of slowly dying inside.

She stood over me, gazing into my eyes. "I'm only here because you wanted me."

Her graceful arms reached down for me. Dreamlike, without feeling the effort of arms and legs, I rose to her embrace.

We stood holding one another, I don't know how long. Then, her eyes bright with love and tenderness, she led me to my bed.

A long time later, the candle burned itself out. ❧

Precursor

DONALD M. HASSLER

> . . . changed their lives in some
> profound way that no one else
> had ever done.
> > W.J. Bate, SAMUEL JOHNSON

My father truly changed my life, gave hope,
And made the world a better place to live.
For instance, on his desk he left a note
The night he died so fine that I would give
Ten quatrains for. Biscuit, our puppy, dead
Had led my dad to sentiment. "Keep chasing
Squirrels. No one can hurt you now," he said.
And much more critics find embarrassing.

So my poems ought not to wax so blatant
On the nature of this man but rather turn
Upon themselves to forge lines independent
Of this note or that act. But if I learn
Such artifice detached from filial strife,
He dies again for art who died for life.

❧

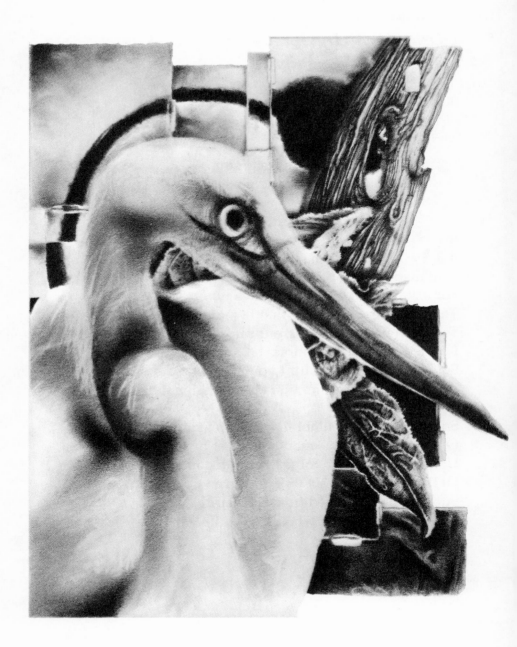

The Egret

MICHAEL BISHOP
illustration by
RODGER GERBERDING

As usual, the telephone rang at dinnertime. McGruder cringed, and from their places around the table Polly and the kids gave him pleading looks that meant, Please don't answer it — for once just let the damned thing ring.

As usual, McGruder ignored their silent pleas, rose heavily from his meal, and spoke a grudging hello into the mouthpiece of the instrument of torture on the kitchen wall.

"Did I call you at dinner?" Harry Profitt's reedy voice wanted to know. "Too bad. But at least you got somebody to make it for you, don't you, Stork? Me, I eat out of tin cans or fry up cheap fixings for myself. A one-eyed fella, a guy more than half blind, never had a leper's chance to find him a helpmeet to do that kind of sweet domestic stuff. And you know whose lousy goddamn fault that is, don't you? Don't you, Stork-O?"

"You're never going to let me forget, Harry."

"Damned straight I'm not. Why should I? You ruined my life, you bastard. You've got a wife and kids. You're a big-shot ranger out at the state preserve. You wear a uniform and swagger around. Me, I got nobody. I got no position. The birds I like to watch fly over — sometimes I can't half tell them from tatters of smoke or cloud. And it all goes back to you, doesn't it, Mason? Forgive me — Stork the Dork."

McGruder took it. He took it every time that One-

Eyed Harry Profitt called. Still guilt-ridden after thirty years, he could find no easy way to lay the specter of his culpability.

As a tall, skinny thirteen-year-old, Mason "Stork" McGruder had shot the fateful BB. It had been a bitter-cold December day, and the boys had all worn thermal parkas or heavy coats. The idea had been to score war-game points by making their BBs go *kerthunk!* in the folds of their enemies' winter clothes. That evening, hearing this news, McGruder's father had taken off his belt and repeatedly walloped his son before everyone in Harry's family. But Harry had lost his eye anyway, and an infection had settled in the other one, heaping even more guilt on the young McGruder.

So thirty years later he answered the phone every time it rang and resignedly took Harry's abuse. Tonight, after enduring a good five minutes of it, he said, "I'm really sorry about what happened, Harry, but it's time you shut up about all that and did something with the days you've got left."

"Like what?" Harry replied. "A job? I can't see worth a mole's butt. And I get dizzy spells. They grab me when I'm not expecting them. If it wasn't for my social security, I couldn't keep body and soul together." McGruder knew that this was true. Harry spent some of his money on bird seed — watching birds was just about his only healthy recreation — but a helluva lot more of it on cheap bitter beer in long-necked amber bottles.

But at last Harry was tiring. "Damn you to very Hell, Stork!" he concluded, as he usually did, and slammed his handset down with such force that the tiny bones in McGruder's inner ear began to vibrate. Polly, meanwhile, looked across the dinner table at him with reproach in her eyes.

One morning, slurping a mug of lukewarm instant coffee on the top step of his tumbledown back stairs, Harry Profitt thought he saw something moving in the weeds at the far edge of his yard. He had to squint, one-eyed, to bring this living object into focus, but the focus he got made it hard to see much but a cushion-sized white torso floating above two spidery gray legs. A serpentine neck, also white, coiled up from the torso, and atop the neck was a narrow head with a feathery crest pointing one way and a daggerlike beak the other.

"A snowy egret," Harry muttered. "What's it doing in my back yard?"

Usually, like herons and ibises, the egrets just flew over — long-legged tatters of soiled silk on the china-blue sky, winging inland to their rookeries. Never, in Harry's experience, did any of these birds drop down to scout the weedy terrain of his two-bit barony. Now, though, the realization that one of the graceful egrets had *landed* on it truly fretted him. About fifty yards away, after all, lived a pair of tigerish yellow toms who, when it came to birding, took no prisoners. They were too thin and impatient to toy with their victims. Already this summer, Profitt had seen them butcher a mockingbird, three brown thrashers, four robins, a gray catbird, and a couple of bluejays. Pecan trees full of squawking relatives couldn't keep those toms at bay, and Profitt himself was too achey and slow to scare the blood-thirsty critters off.

"Egret, they'll catch you," he said, squinting at the small, long-legged bird stepping daintily through the woods. "If you're hurt, you're damned well doomed."

He set down his mug and went to see what he could do.

Shuffling to keep from pitching headlong into the ratty bushes marking his yard's far boundary, Profitt stalked the egret. (It was definitely an egret.) The bird, prissily high-stepping, eluded him, but without panicking or trying to fly. It *couldn't* fly, the man decided; something had happened to one of its wings. So their pointless do-si-do continued, the long-legged bird moving to escape Profitt as the half-blind man reached out lurchingly to hug nothing but egretless air.

"To hell with this!" Profitt shouted. He straightened, turned his back on the bird, and limped back to the house. Once inside, he thought, only a real sonuvabitch would leave an egret out there to fend for itself with those damn toms around.

Finally, it came to him to telephone Stork McGruder and ask him how best to handle a downed bird of this sort. Even if it meant calling the joker for some other reason than to remind him of how McGruder'd ruined his life, he'd do it to save the egret.

Profitt dialed the number of the ranger station at the preserve and asked for McGruder. A woman on the other end told him that the ranger hadn't reported today, that he'd come down with a virus and was at home. Great. Profitt could inconvenience buddy-boy Stork and do something for the downed egret all at the same time.

Profitt dialed again. Mrs. McGruder answered. She recognized the voice of their tormentor and told him angrily that Mason could not come listen to his abuse.

"I'm so sorry to hear that," Profitt said. "But this is urgent enough to get poor Mason up. Tell him who's calling."

"Good day!" Mrs. McGruder said, and Profitt knew that she was getting ready to hang up with one of his own receiver slams — when McGruder himself intervened to take the phone from her.

"What is it this morning?" the ranger asked, and he

did sound weak.

Profitt, pretty clearly to the ranger's surprise, told Stork about the snowy egret in his yard. He asked McGruder's advice. He wondered if maybe someone couldn't come out to his house and get the poor bird before those damned marauding cats did.

"*You've* got to do it," McGruder said, warming to a problem that for once had nothing to do with a thirty-year grudge. "Listen, Harry, *you've* got to go out there and fetch in that egret."

"Damn it, I've tried. I'm better than half-blind, as you damn well know, and that sucker, hurt like he is, dances away from me every time I try to grab him."

"You got any meat in the house?"

"No filet mignon, Stork. No tidbits of tenderized beef."

"Some hamburger? A can of sardines, maybe?"

"Well, I've got some raw bacon that's just abut gone bad on me. That the sort of thing you're looking for?"

"It'll do Harry, it'll do. Take a strip of it and sort of duck-walk out there holding it in your fingertips. Your egret's probably hungry. Somebody's shot it or something, and it's been tiptoeing around your back yard looking for vittles. If you go out there and feed it, you'll be able to grab it while it's lifting up its head to swallow your little peace offering."

"What do I do once the bird's in hand?"

"Carry it inside, Harry. You've got to get it out of the yard. Snowy egrets're valuable birds, and they're legally protected, but those cats over your way don't know that and probably wouldn't care even it they did. I'll call the preserve and tell 'em to send somebody over to take custody of the egret."

Profitt cradled the handset with mocking gentleness,

found a strip of nearly rancid bacon in his refrigerator, and went down the back steps, squinting out into his lot for some sign of the egret. Ah, there it was. With the greasy bacon extended as bait, Profitt hunkered and began duck-walking awkwardly toward the bird. The hungry egret scented the bacon and began stepping gingerly toward the strange one-eyed man approaching it. . . .

McGruder, exhausted, slumped to the couch beside the telephone stand. He was grimacing, but in his grimace, his wife thought, was something disturbingly akin to a smile.

"What is it?" she asked him. "You feeling sick again?"

"Much better, Polly. Much better. I might as well be hung for a hit man as a horse thief, hadn't I?"

"I don't understand."

"He'll never stop calling."

"He would if you wouldn't listen to him, Mason."

"I *have* to listen to him. I put out the crackpot's eye. I *deserve* to hear what he tells me. Some of it, anyway."

"That's foolishness, Mason."

"Well, from now on, it'll be easier to take — a whole helluva lot easier to take."

"What are you talking about?"

"It's instinct, Polly. It's biologically dictated egret behavior from years and years back."

"Do you still have a fever? You're not making sense."

"They go for the eyes, that's all I'm saying. They take their daggerlike beaks and go straight for the glistening eye."

It took about an hour for the phone to begin ringing again, but when it did, McGruder insisted on answering it himself. ❧

Grey Men

JOSEPH PAYNE BRENNAN

Grey men are groping in my garden tonight,
faces amorphous, hands like sopping leaves.
They shake their heads and hide among the stalks.

When the moon climbs, they crawl along the shrubbery,
nodding to one another. They meet and whisper.
I waited too long — they are crawling up the walks.

❧

Gothic

JAME A. RILEY
photo by
ELIZABETH A. SAUNDERS

Balconies, balustrades, and the long,
Hard faces of gargoyles; horns and teeth.
Eyes bulging from the basaltic stone.

Ivy climbs the blood-brown brickwork
Inch by tangled upward inch.
Reaching toward dark, turreted towers.

Mullioned glass refracts lightning flashed
Splendor about the interior of this
Mammoth dwelling from centuries past.

The past hanging in its tapestries;
In its cracked oils, gilt-framed.
Individuals flash-frozen on canvas.

Stairways haunted by shadows —
Candle flame slithering from step to step
Caressing each spindle with fingers of light.

Lightning captured in crystal chandeliers
Shatters upon the marble floors
Like momentary sparks of fragmented glass.

Books, thick as dust, infest the walls
Holding snatches of thought trapped in
Cracked leather covers; gold lettered spines.

Their messages and dreams seeping
Out like whispers into darkness, only to be
Trampled by the echoes of thunder.

In the vast rooms and corridors,
The dead continue to act out their
Partially forgotten lives, for all of time.

さ

Not by Blood Alone

MILLEA KENIN

"Anna, I am at your window,
yes I, your lover; let me in!
I faint for want of your dear blood —
Anna!"
           "— No longer. It's a sin"

Claws scrabble, and the casement rattles.
She shakes her head; her lips are stern.
Weakly the bat's wings flap and flutter;
with a faint despairing cry, he turns,
flies slowly into the reddish darkness
where the steel mills pollute the night.
Anna stands stiff before the window,
staring until he's lost to sight.

Smiling, she sits before her mirror,
loosening and brushing her long black hair.
Slowly her pale reflection dwindles,
the cold smile last — then nothing's there.

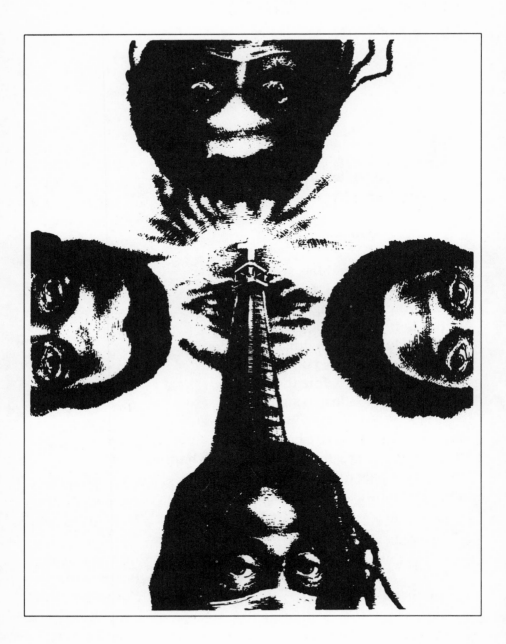

Moving

JAMES ROBERT SMITH
illustration by
RODGER GERBERDING

Gordon Hughes wasn't an evil man. Not really. But he was a very rich man, and influential, and he did not like to be stymied. In fact, he never had been stopped in any endeavor since he'd lost a fist fight as a boy. No. It is doubtful that Gordon Hughes ever went about his business with the idea that harming another or causing them pain was the main thrust of his activities. He was, though, a covetous man.

As stated, Hughes was very influential, probably the most powerful person in all of Woodvine, Georgia. When Senator Talmadge himself had come stumping through the county, the Hughes home was the one place he stopped to make his pitch. It was a hell of a sight, red galluses everywhere. Almost everyone thanked God that Gordon Hughes was a citizen of Woodvine, and all walked about with their chests puffed out for weeks afterward. Neither was Gordon Hughes a hated man.

But greed was part and parcel of what Mr. Hughes was. If he saw what he wanted, he bought it, as cheaply as he could. If he could not buy it, then he took it, by hook or by crook. Nobody stood in his path for long.

Across the way from Gordon Hughes' fine house was Mount Zion Church. The grounds of that church were a pretty thing. The oaks there were greater than any others in the town, and all festooned with spanish moss that hung to the earth in heavy tendrils. All about the place, and among the cemetery with its headstones, the wild azalea grew fat and full, their blossoms ripening huge, pink and white, in the spring air. Easily, it was the prettiest spot in the whole county.

After Senator Talmadge's visit, Mr. Hughes complained to Lydia, his wife, that it was a damned shame that they didn't have a better home to have showcased for Georgia's most powerful man. Yes, Mrs. Hughes had replied, that was just too bad. But, she had added, their home *was* the finest in town.

And all the while she talked, Gordon Hughes stood at his big picture window and gazed across at the church and the property about it. He could see a new structure standing over there in place of the old, graying church. A new house. His house.

That church across the road was a Baptist church. (Was there any other kind in the county?) Its members were old folk who attended services every Sunday and every Wednesday and whenever else the minister said "Be here!". They were good, industrious folk. And they were black.

Again, Mr. Hughes was not truly an evil man. He did not hate the people whose church stood across the road from his fine home. Their minister, Reverend Coggin, was many times a guest in the Hughes house; although he entered and exited through the kitchen door, as was deemed proper in those days. And Gordon Hughes enjoyed those times when he sat by an opened window, listening to the music passing from that church to his ears. Still, the idea that he wanted the property upon which the church stood grew in his mind. He would have it.

So, he sent word to Reverend Coggin that he wanted o speak with him. Shirley Bassey, who cooked for Mr. and Mrs. Hughes, took the letter to her minister when Sunday

came. He accepted the invitation, of course, and made the
journey to see the county's most important citizen on a
bright winter's morning when the air was but cool and the
sun sparkled. He went into the Hughes home.

Gordon Hughes invited Reverend Coggin into his
parlor, and there they sat to pass the time for a bit, while
the wealthy man built up to the subject at his heart. For his
part, Reverend Coggin waited, listened, made his small
talk, and wondered what was about. He was calm, but he
was more than a little anxious, for he could think of no reason why he should be so summoned. The Klan was quiet
(and to his credit, Mr. Hughes had done much to shut
those boys up), and it was not yet time for church homecoming when white folk came to visit. But he waited
patiently. He was an old man, and experienced in dealing
with Gordon Hughes, had known his father well.

Round and about went the conversation until, finally,
Hughes made his pitch. The Reverend listened, did not
become upset.

"Besides the money I will pay for the land, I will also
pay, in full, the cost of moving the church. I own a large
plot at the intersection of Lee and Bull. I give it to the congregation title-free. It's but a mile down the way." His eyes
sparkled in the sunlight that gleamed through curtains and
lace.

"We're an old church," Reverend Coggin said after
waiting in thoughtful silence for a moment. "We have a lot
of history attached to that place. We, as a church, have put
down roots there. Our families are buried there." He said
nothing more, having completed his oblique refusal.

"I understand," Hughes told him. "I do. That is why
I'm more than happy to give the church more land than
they would be giving up. That is why I will be happy to
pay for everything to relocate your church." He smiled.

"You *will* put it to the congregation?"

"Of course, Mr. Hughes." A shake of hands, a slap on the back, and Reverend Coggin was gone from the house of Gordon Hughes, a good deal sadder and a little more afraid than he had been before he'd gone in. He knew what the congregation would say. He knew what they would say to Mr. Gordon Hughes, owner of almost everything in the county. The answer would be *no* and Mr. Hughes would become angry. Coggin hunched his old shoulders as a shiver snaked its way up his spine.

The congregation heard what the reverend had to say. They sat in the pews on a mild winter's evening, their black faces turned up to see their preacher, to hear what he was telling them. They fell uncharacteristically silent for such a Sunday meeting, the realization sinking in. It would be futile to refuse the white man what he wanted. It would do no good to say no to his request. But they said it anyway, and the reverend felt both proud and sad at the same time.

The wealthy man was not pleased that Coggin's flock did not see things his way. He could not understand how they could so easily turn down his most generous offer. But he did not worry overlong about the situation, for Woodvine, Georgia was his town. The people who had said no to him worked in his saw mills, his warehouses, his stores. Everyone answered to him. Everyone. He owned Woodvine. Even its spirit. It was the easiest thing in the world for him to have the church building condemned, the land it had stood upon for so long forcibly sold. He did it and he bought it all.

Although it hurt then, the people of the church bowed before the law that was wielded against them. No one did anything foolish. No one tried to stand up to the city father any more than they already had. None of them did anything, and no white folk stepped forward to take their part.

Once more, Gordon Hughes had what he wanted. He was generous in his victory, and still adhered to what he had originally offered to the good people of Mount Zion Church. A mile down Bull, where it crossed Lee, Hughes signed over a parcel of land to the soon-to-be-moved church. He hired a builder from Waycross who came up, put the old building on blocks and wagons, and had it moved carefully down to the new site. He paid for it all, and improvements. To salve his conscience.

Too, as he had promised, and as Reverend Coggin had feared, the cemetery was moved, remains and all. The church was completely uprooted. Erection of the new Hughes home began at once.

For his part, Reverend Coggin made the most of the situation. He kept quiet, even among his family, of the dealings with Mr. Hughes. He even invited the generous Gordon Hughes to the dedication of the new church, which the latter attended with smiles and good humor.

Soon after, before the completion of Gordon Hughes' fine, new home, the old minister passed away, and was the first new tenant in the new cemetery. The house went up.

Almost a year after construction began, Mr. and Mrs. Hughes were able to move into their big house. It was much finer than their old one; they now had a ballroom (the only one within four counties!) and more space than they knew what to do with. They held a massive celebration to honor the completion of the great house. The mayors from half a dozen towns were there, and two congressmen attended. The place was full of light, and life, and cheer. Hughes was pleased.

Winter had come 'round again, merely chilly, as it does in the southern part of Georgia. Gordon Hughes awoke one fine, sun-filled morning, stepped out upon the wide porch that girdled his house. He strode out, onto the heart-of-pine planking, smelling the good air, watching the fog slowly lift as the sun burned it off. He looked down the way, where Bull Street veered to the east, and decided that it was a good day for a stroll. In fact, he could walk down to where he had a stand of slash pines, to check the harvest. A brisk walk. It would be good.

He started off, his hard soles clacking upon the paving stones bought and sold to the town by one of his companies. The road, all dark and sandy, was empty of traffic, and the dew clung to it, holding down the dust that would later rise beneath passing wheels. Moving quickly, Gordon Hughes made good time, coming to the place where Bull Street bent like a crimped pipe. There were not many houses this far out, and the paving stones faded to rough grasses that bled into the stands of pines that stood on every side. He went further toward Lee.

And, looking that way, he stopped short.

He could have *sworn*. He could have bet his life that the Mount Zion Church had been moved to the *southwest* corner of Lee and Bull. But it wasn't there. It stood, amidst the pines and the mist, on the *northwest* corner of the intersection. Gordon Hughes blinked. He stared. He took a deep breath, turned about to make certain he had not somehow got headed the wrong way, and looked again. Northwest it was. In some confusion, he moved toward the church, slowly, then quickly.

One big front door, a year-old coat of white paint just beginning to fade, opened wide as he neared it. Gasping, he half expected to see the old figure of Reverend Coggin coming down the steps. But it was only Parley East, the new minister; he spotted Hughes, greeted him.

"Hello, Mr. Hughes! What brings you here at such an early hour?" He moved down a step.

Still puzzled, the white man took a moment to reply. "A walk. I was just out for a walk, Reverend."

"Well! A good day to you, then." The black man went toward the cemetery, taking long steps to match his long legs.

"Reverend?"

The other turned back. "Yes?"

"Have we . . . *moved* your church lately?" He gazed across at the opposite corner where twenty-year-old pines lifted up their green, green branches. He could smell sap draining into pans.

"*Moved*, sir?" He tried not to seem disrespectful to Woodvine's first citizen, especially considering how good the man had been to the church.

"Yes." Hughes was perplexed, gawking. "Moved."

"Not in a year, sir. Not since before I came here." He smiled, not knowing exactly why. "Anything else I can do?"

"A year ago. Of course." He faced back toward Woodvine. "Nothing else, Reverend. Nothing else." With an absent wave, he headed back. He had to go to his office uptown, and look at the records there. The deed, the deed.

Sawyer Long knew just where to look to find every deed of any piece of property his employer had ever owned. He had worked for the Hughes family for almost fifty years, and his memory served him well. "Yes sir, Mr. Hughes! I can look that up for you in an instant." He went to a long row of filing cabinets, all brown and woody there in the musty room. True to his promise, he plucked it free of the drawer in which it had rested for over a year. With a flourish of dust, he handed it over.

Gordon Hughes pulled the document out of its envelope and eyed it. Carefully. Yes. Yes. He had been mistaken. The lot he had given over to Mount Zion was precisely where the church now stood.

"Anything wrong?" Gray eyebrows perked below a balding pate.

"No. Nothing wrong, really. I just seem to be losing my memory a little younger than Father did," he admitted.

With shaking hand, he gave the deed copy back to the employee. Later, out on the street with the sun shining brightly, the avenue full of traffic, he felt better. He went home, and did not think about Mount Zion Church, or tried not to. Although he stayed away from that part of Bull Street, his dreams were sometimes filled with images of the plain, frame building. Reverend Coggin would come out, smile and nod at him.

Weeks passed; no one noticed how Gordon Hughes went out of his way to make wide detours around the spot where Lee crossed Bull. One day, though, he had no choice but to drive his new auto down South Street one block from where Zion Church stood. Nervously, as he approached Bull heading down South, he craned his neck to see past the houses that lay between the intersection and the church. Almost, he did not notice the church at his right, on the northwest corner of South and Bull.

The rich man's heart thudded; he felt it pounding away at his ribs, trying to get out. He gripped the steering wheel in clenched fists. His face went white. He stared, eyes bulging. It couldn't be. No!

"A quarter of a mile," he breathed. The church had moved a quarter of a mile from where it *had* been. Hughes sighed, forgot about his errand, and sped away from the church, toward town, toward his office and deeds and faithful Sawyer Long.

Gordon Hughes blustered into the filing cabinet-lined office where the smell of paper dominated. His color had returned and his face was flushed a ruddy hue.

"Mr. Hughes!" Sawyer Long, looking every day of his sixty-eight years, could see how upset his employer was. He stood to meet him.

"Sawyer!" He grasped the old man's hands, causing him to drop the pen he was holding.

"Yessir! What's wrong?" His own heart fluttered.

"You remember the parcel that I gave to Reverend Coggin's congregation. Mount Zion. You remember, don't you?"

"Yessir. I remember." He considered. "Is it on fire? Is it burning?" Long took a step toward the door, ready to sound the alarm.

"No! No! Nothing like that."

The old man regained his composure, looked at Gordon Hughes. "What, then?"

"Do you recall weeks ago when I came in here to have a look at a copy of the deed?"

"Yes. I remember."

"Where was it located? The parcel, I mean."

Sawyer Long was confused. "I don't understand, sir."

"Where was it? Where was Mount Zion Church!"

"I . . . I reckon it was right where it is now." He paused, trying to understand. "On the northwest corner of South and Bull."

Hughes stiffened at the words. In a moment, with Long standing by, waiting for the other to say something, Gordon Hughes stepped slowly out of the room, down the stairs, to the street. He went home. He stayed there for days; his wife thought that he was not feeling well, and he did not tell her what was disturbing him.

On a misty morning a week after last seeing the church, Gordon Hughes saw it again. He went out upon the wide front porch to gaze up the street and down, to assure himself that Woodvine was yet normal, and all his.

First, he looked northward, to calm himself. Then he glanced to the south, to the bend in Bull Street.

And there, unmistakably, was Mount Zion Church. It stood there in the crook of the road, where old Widow Hilliard's huge yard had been. There were less than a dozen houses standing between it and Mr. Hughes. For a long, long time he stared at it. He stared while the sun rose up over the pines, melting the clammy fog that hugged the ground. The mists were soon gone. The church was not. Gordon Hughes retreated into his fine, big home.

"Lydia! Lydia!" He shrieked his wife's name until she came hurrying into the wide, polished foyer. In spite of what they knew they should do, Shirley, their cook, and Rae, their maid, came hurrying in also. The three women stopped there, staring at Mr. Hughes, waiting for him to speak. His lips, paled to white on a whiter face, finally parted.

"What? What is it, Gordon?" Lydia moved toward him, so that she could hear his whispered words. She went close.

"The church," he rasped. "It's moving."

And then he fainted.

Mrs. Hughes sent for a doctor, and Doctor Warner came as quickly as he was called. With help, Mr. Hughes had been taken to his bed, there to await his physician. Warner bent over him, poking, prodding, asking questions. He made his diagnosis.

"He needs rest, Lydia. I think that's all that's really wrong with him." He whispered to her, out of earshot of Gordon and the help.

"Tired. That's all?"

"Well, maybe a bit of guilt."

"Guilt? What do you mean?" Her hands fluttered to her throat.

"Something about Mount Zion Church. Having it condemned so that he could buy up this property for the new house. You know," he said.

"I see."

"Well. You make sure that he gets plenty of rest and that he doesn't overtax himself. Okay?"

"Yes. Yes, Doctor Warner. I'll see to it." For the remainder of the day, she watched over her husband, making certain that he had taken the medication the doctor had left. Mr. Hughes slept.

Something woke him up. His eyes snapped wide, and he was instantly alert, completely rested. It was night, dark but for the moon, and the house was quiet. In his bed, appropriately huge and soft, his wife slept soundly, her even breathing drifting through the room. Outside, he could hear strange noises; noises that made him afraid to go to the window to look out and see just what was causing them. He waited, gathering his courage. The noises came and went with the wind: footsteps in the sandy soil (many of them), wood grating against wood; toil in the cool, moonlit night.

Courage gathered, the master raised himself from his downy spot; his base feet found his slippers at his bedside. Quickly, before his nerve could fade, he shuffled to the window and flung the sash wide.

He saw them. They came up out of the earth and out of the churchyard. From *his* yard, they sprang up from the grass, from between the rows and rows of wild azalea. These were the ones the workers had missed. The ones with no gravestones. The ones who had been buried too deep. They joined their kin who had been, and still were, coming up from the displaced cemetery of Mount Zion Church. There was work to be done.

Annie West, dead these twenty years, tottered out of

the good, black loam, and made her way from house to house. She had been nursemaid and midwife; her touch and her voice had been soothing things to salve pain and banish worry. From one ear to another, she went through the town, whispering. "Sleep," she crooned. "Sleep. And remember that the Church of Mount Zion is where it has always been."

Gordon Hughes heard her as she slithered up the stairs to his room. Tearing his eyes from the sight of the hundreds-strong army in the streets, he watched as the shade floated to his wife's ear. He listened as Annie whispered her sweet words. Lydia Hughes smiled. Gordon moaned in fear. With a contemptuous glance for Mr. Hughes, Annie was gone, a vanished shadow. There were more ears to be whispered into.

From his post, Hughes could see the army as they toiled. There were a hundred dead faces he recognized. There were more that he did not. They went wherever they were needed.

A handful of black men who had worked in the offices of some Hughes enterprise or another went into rooms, into cabinets and drawers, and they fixed paper to read as it now must. With pens and with ink, they stroked and dabbed until everything was right. Then they went back to the street, back to the church, where the real work was going on.

A hundred backs braced. Two hundred legs strained. Arms uncounted pushed and pulled, directing the mass that was Mount Zion Church, the shell of wood that held the souls, the spirit and souls, of a proud, old community. They moved it. Again. While Woodvine slept. But for Gordon Hughes.

And when the church was half a block closer to its roots, the hundreds went and they dug and lifted and heaved till the cemetery was that much closer. Still, they were not done. They returned to the abandoned site, filling in, tamping down, replanting wherever a thing had been disturbed. Then they were done. Then they returned to their beds, for now.

In the morning, Mrs. Hughes awoke to a husband struck dumb. He answered no question. There were no replies for any request directed at him. He rose, ate the breakfast that was placed before him at the table, and he brooded. He retired to his library and he thought, long and hard. After a while, he came out. "We're moving," he told his wife.

"What?" She gave him a look that displayed her genuine confusion.

"We are moving," he said. "Get William Bass and tell him that we'll need as many strong arms as he can muster. We are moving our household." He paused. "Oh. And you and Shirley need to pack your porcelain away. We wouldn't want you to break any of it."

"Moving? Where?"

In reply, Gordon Hughes pointed through the window before which they were standing. "The old place," he said. "It's still vacant. It was good enough then; it's good enough now."

Lydia pleaded with him. She begged. She tried to talk some sense into him. He would not listen. Soon, William Bass and his men were trundling the heavy pieces across the dusty road to the old house. He would not stop. She called Dr. Warner.

"Gordon," Dr. Warner greeted him where he stood on the porch of his quickly emptying home. "Just what are you doing?"

"I think that's pretty obvious." Nothing more. Strong men wrestled with a heavy couch. Even in the cool air, there was the smell of sweat, of hard work.

"Well, then, *why* are you doing this?"

"The church." He gestured toward it. "There's no more empty lots between it any my house. I reckon they'll put it *right here* the next time they take a mind to move it."

"*Who* will move it, Gordon?"

"The niggers, Dr. Warner. All those dead niggers." With that, he strode from the porch, ready to order the placement of each piece of furniture being brought to the old place. For now, he was willing to retreat. At least he would deprive them of physically moving him out. He did not relish the thought of dead hands grasping at him, shoving him, lifting him up while his wife and everyone else slept through it all. No. At least he would deprive them of that.

The doctor went to Mrs. Hughes. "I'm sorry, Lydia. But I think that we'll just have to humor him for now. Just sit tight. Things will be all right." She sighed with no choice but to believe him.

Gordon Hughes and his wife went back to their old house. They went back, and Gordon waited for what he knew must come. It did not happen for a week. But it did.

When it was over, Mount Zion Church was precisely back to where it had always been: across the road from the home of Gordon and Lydia Hughes. Its grounds were gorgeous; a prettier sight could not be had in the whole of the county. Tall oaks spread their gnarly limbs high and low. Thick moss hung from every limb, and flowers bloomed there in spring on healthy bushes. In the heat of the day there was plenty of shade, and the sun dappled the ground wherever it could.

Of Gordon Hughes' fine, new home, there was no trace. No one could remember it. No one could recall it. Save for Gordon, himself.

He did not like retreating. He did not like it. Oh, he had saved himself one small indignity, but it smacked too much of losing. Eventually, he knew, he would come up with something that would even things out; he would gather a bit of revenge for himself. For he still ruled Woodvine. That had not changed. For the time, he was content to wait, and plan.

Almost a month passed before he woke one morning to discover that he had to look one block north to see Mount Zion Church. His house had been moved in the night, and, little by little, the Hughes homeplace edged slowly out of town. 🙶

Some Info on Lotus Contributors

ELIZABETH A. SAUNDERS makes her editorial debut with a remarkable collection. Although she was reluctant to take on this task, books were too much a part of her life and it was inevitable that she would end up creating them. She has worked at a variety of professions in the past, including advertising, doing separations for textile printing, bartender (where she also performed magic and ate fire), cruiseship magician, eating fire with a limbo act in the Virgin Islands, and designing and writing property management and mortgage banking computer systems. She now works as a project leader and tech writer for a consulting firm. She has a small home in a large library.

JAME A. RILEY is a graduate of Kent State University, where he received his BFA in Graphic Design, and, along with Scott H. Urban, founded Unnameable Press. He does all the design for the Press including book design, newsletters, and advertising, and does the same things for other people to make his living. Jame has exhibited his work in several gallery shows and numerous conventions, and is a member of the Dreamsmiths Artist Guild. His work has appeared in *Critical Mass, Scavenger's Newsletter, Blazing Armadillo Stories*, and *Centauri Express Audio Magazine*. He is Art Director for *Centauri Express* and has done all of their package and advertising design.

ROBERT R. McCAMMON One of the hottest American horror writers at the moment, Robert McCammon has written a dozen books, including the novels, *Bethany's Sin, They Thirst, Mystery Walk, Usher's Passing, Wolf's Hour* and the award winning, *Swan Song*. His short stories have been adapted for television's *Darkroom* and *Twilight Zone* series. He has appeared in numerous anthologies and magazines, and many of his stories are collected in the single author anthology, *Blue World*. He makes his home in Birmingham, Alabama.

BOB GIADROSICH Since 1987, Bob has been a regular contributor to TSR's *Dragon Magazine* and *Dungeon Adventures*. Other work includes, *L. Ron Hubbard Presents Writers of the Future, Vol. 5*; I.C.E.'s gaming module, "Pirates", and Flying Buffalo's, "Cityscape: Book 4." Bob has also appeared in *Critical Mass, Pulsar!*, and *Easyriders*. He publishes his own work through Sharayah Press in Atlanta, GA.

JOHN GREY An Australian-born poet, playwrite, and short story writer, John performs his original music in various Providence clubs with his band, House to Let. His latest chapbook is "Devil in the River" from Nocturnal Publications.

SUSAN MacTABERT has had fiction and poetry appear in *Amazing Tales, Literary Magazine of Fantasy and Terror, Dark Horizons, Weirdbook, Moonbroth,* and *Dark Words/Gentle Sounds.* She has also had artwork published in various small magazines. She has two stories placed with Yarnia Press and is currently at work on a novel. Susan lives in Mission Viejo, CA where she currently works for Orange County as Children's Librarian Assistant at the Mission Viejo Library.

RODGER GERBERDING With two illustrations in our previous anthology, *All the Devils Are Here,* this is Rodger's second appearance in work by Unnameable Press. Rodger has appeared in numerous magazines, including, *The Horrorshow, New Blood, Horrorstruck, Weird Tales, Fantasy Tales, The Mage,* and many others. New and forthcoming books illustrated by him include: *Obsession,* ed. by Gary Raisor, from Dark Harvest; *The Spider,* by H.H. Ewers, *Infinity's Child,* by Chas de Vet, and *Colossus and Others* by Donald Wandrei, all from Jwindz. He has also written critical articles on Howard Wandrei and Frank Utpatel.

TODD RILEY This is Todd's fifth appearance in Unnameable Press publications. He did the illustrations for the very limited poetry folios, "In the Mist of Visions" and "Homecoming." He was in both of our previous anthologies, *All the Devils Are Here* and *Minor Apocalypses and Other Small Horrors.* Todd is a graduate of Ohio State University, and lives with his wife Terry in Columbus, Ohio, where he makes his living in the computer industry.

THOMAS E. FULLER This man is amazing. It is a shame that, like so many of us, he has had to spend far too much time in positions where he is underpaid and unappreciated. In spite of this, he has had about 24 hours of material broadcast on radio, 18 different plays produced in 22 different places, written three novels, a handful of short stories and vast quantities of intelligent, thought provoking, and readable poetry. Thomas has created and edited 6 issues of an audio magazine called *Centauri Express* which is a delight to listen to, has written a screen play for a western being filmed in Georgia, instructional videos, technical manuals, outdoor dramas, TV scripts, and other assorted stuff. Someone give this man some money before he quits doing it.

P.J. MEACHAM This is Jack's second appearance in an Unnameable Press collection. He did two illustrations for *All the Devils*. Jack grew up in Oklahoma and California, has a BA in sculpture from the California College of Arts and Crafts, and additional schooling in illustration and design from the Portfolio Center in Atlanta. He has exhibited his SF and Fantasy work at the Austin NASFC, Atlanta Worldcon, and numerous conventions throughout the Southeast. Jack is also a founding member of the Dreamsmiths Artist Guild, was their first president, and has participated in the Dreamsmiths gallery exhibits.

RON LINDAHN & VAL LAKEY LINDAHN are a husband and wife team who have done many great covers for *Isaac Asimov's SF Magazine* and *Analog* plus numerous black-and-white interiors for these and other publications. They have done book covers and interiors for Dark Harvest, Bluejay, and Scream Press. In addition to the illustration work, Ron does equally great design and printed work. Ron and Val live and work in the mountains in Rabun Gap, Georgia.

CHARLES L. GRANT has won multiple World Fantasy Awards as well as a couple of Nebulas and several other awards. He is the author of dozens of novels, both under his own name and several pseudonyms. Charlie is also the highly acclaimed editor of the *Shadows* collections and many other horror anthologies. His recent novels include *The Pet* and *In a Dark Dream*.

JOSEPH PAYNE BRENNAN One of the last great writers discovered by the original *Weird Tales*, Joe received the Grand Master Award for fantasy, and was one of the foremost dark fantasy poets of this century. The author of more than 500 short stories, 15 books, and several thousand poems, his story and poetry collections include *Nine Horrors and a Dream*, *Nightmare Need*, and *Stories of Darkness and Dread* from Arkham House and *The Borders Just Beyond*, *Creep to Death*, *The Adventures of Lucius Leffing* and *An Act of Providence* from Donald Grant. We were pleased to present several of his poems in *All the Devils Are Here*. Joe spent much of his life working for Yale University Library. Unfortunately, he passed away in late January of this year. He will be missed.

MICHAEL BISHOP is easily one of the best American writers currently being published. Michael has won the Nebula award for both best novel and short story, and has been nominated for both the Hugo and Nebula a number of times. He is a recipient of the Rhysling Award for SF poetry. His novels include *Transfigurations, No Enemy But Time, Ancient of Days, The Secret Ascension, Unicorn Mountain* and others. His short story collections include, *Blooded on Arachne, One Winter in Eden,* and *Close Encounters With the Deity.* His short fiction has been widely anthologized and has appeared in numerous Best of the Year collections. Michael, who lives with his wife and two children in Pine Mountain, GA, has been published in all the top markets for SF including *Omni* and *Playboy.*

MICHAEL N. LANGFORD has appeared in the anthology *Afterlives, All The Devils Are Here,* and *Critical Mass* magazine. A member of the Science Fiction Writers of Cobb County (as are several others included in this list), he lives in Athens, GA, which isn't that close to Cobb County.

JACK MASSA Jack's first novel *Moon Crow* came out in 1979. Subsequently, several of Jack's short stories have been published in *Critical Mass, Full Spectrum, The Best of Omni,* and the British Best of the Year, *Orbit SF Yearbook.* Jack is a freelance documentation specialist in Tucker, GA, and he is looking forward to the publication of a couple of novels.

BRAD LINAWEAVER Author of the Prometheus Award-winning novel, *Moon of Ice,* Brad has a regular book review column in the *Atlanta Journal and Constitution.* Brad has been a Nebula finalist for short story and has had appearances in a number of anthologies; among them, *Friends of the Horseclans, Magic in Ithkar II,* and *Tales of the Witch World 2.* He has had work in various magazines including *Amazing, Fantastic, Reason, New Libertarian* and *National Review,* and has also been involved with *Centauri Express* and *Horror House.* Brad lives in Atlanta.

GREGORY NICOLL Another Atlanta writer, Greg has had several stories published in collections such as *Cold Shocks,* ed. by Tim Sullivan, *Ripper!, There Will Be War, Vol. VI, The Year's Best Horror Stories, Series XVII,* and has collaborated on the Lucasfilm computer game, *Forge.* Greg was a contributor to *The Penguin Encyclopedia of Horror and the Supernatural* and *All the Devils Are Here.* He is currently polishing his novel, *Gorehound.*

CLAY CROKER A full time and freelance Atlanta animator, Clay has the largest collection of cartoons we've ever seen. He has done some illustration, comic, and model work, and has built himself a full-body Godzilla costume that looks as good as any that ever shambled through a Japanese sound stage. Clay has recently been working on new intros for *Tom and Jerry* cartoons.

GERALD W. PAGE Jerry has been widely published in many magazines and anthologies including *Weirdbook, Analog, Fantasy and Science Fiction, Whispers,* and *Light Years and Dark.* He was the editor of several volumes of *The Year's Best Horror* and also edited the collection *Nameless Places* for Arkham House. He has produced a number of issues of a fanzine titled, *Spicy Armadillo Stories . . .* formerly *Blazing Armadillo Stories.* Jerry is a resident of Atlanta.

HARRY O. MORRIS One of the foremost innovators of a new type of Horror and Dark Fantasy illustration, Harry has been featured in almost every horror magazine in the last few years as well as several books from Scream Press. He appeared in Clive Barker's *Books of Blood* with J.K. Potter. The publisher of Silver Scarab Books, Harry also illustrated many of them. His work was featured in the final issue of the magazine *Night Cry* and on the dust jacket for the Arkham House collection *Polyphemus,* by Michael Shea. Harry lives in Albuquerque, New Mexico.

KAY MARIE PORTERFIELD A Denver writer, Kay is the author of five non-fiction books, the most recent of which is *Violent Voices,* a guide to healing from emotional abuse, published by Health Communications, Inc. Her articles have appeared in many publications including *Cosmopolitan* and *New Age Journal,* her fiction has appeared in *Redbook,* and her poetry has been published in a number of literary magazines. Currently she's at work on a book about cults and religious addiction. When Kay's not writing, she's teaching English and Journalism at Metropolitan State College and raising her teenage son, Dylan.

JAMES ROBERT SMITH A resident of Charlotte, NC, James has been published in several small press magazines, and is also involved in the creation and marketing of several comic books. He has a couple of North Carolina comic shops and sends out a Dark Fantasy book catalog.

BOBBY G. WARNER His fiction has appeared in numerous small press publications, including *Fantasy and Terror* and *Fantasy Macabre*. Always honored to share the contents page with one of his favorite writers, Janet Fox, Bobby makes his home in Wedgefield, SC.

GLEN R. EGBERT is a district psychologist in Lancaster, CA. He has had fiction published in several small magazines and anthologies. His story, "Niche" was the lead story in *All The Devils Are Here*.

JANET FOX Her short fiction and poetry has been widely published in the small press, and she has made appearances in *The Year's Best Horror*, *Twilight Zone*, and *Sword and Sorceress*. She is the editor/publisher of a writer's market report, *Scavenger's Newsletter*. Janet lives in Kansas.

ERIC TURNMIRE has been working much of his life to break into the SF/Fantasy field in some fashion. Finally, with his photography, he may have found the way. A life-long friend of the art director for Unnameable, we are sure that this appearance is only the first of many. Eric makes his home in Urbana, Ohio . . . and, as several contributors to this collection can assure you, it's one of the dullest places in the midwest.

SCOTT H. URBAN One of the original founders of Unnameable Press, Scott has been featured in many of our publications. Since leaving his post as first editor, Scott has placed his short stories and poems in many other publications, including *Fantasy and Terror*, *Noctulpa*, *The New Kent Quarterly*, *Atlantis*, *Scream Factory*, *Nightmare Express*, and others. He has several chapbooks forthcoming, including *The Chute* from George Hatch. Scott is a founding member of the October Society and a graduate of Kent State University with a degree in telecommunications. After several years in radio, he went back to school, got his teaching certificate and is now teaching American Lit in North Carolina where he lives with his wife and two daughters.

G. WARLOCK VANCE One of the original founders of the October Society, Warlock was a vital catalyst in the creation of Unnameable Press. This is the fourth of our publications in which he has appeared. Warlock has applied a degree in Art from Kent State University to several jobs in the Cleveland, Ohio area. No, his name isn't really Warlock, that's why the G. appears at the front. However, those of us who knew him in college will always know him as Warlock.

DARRYL ELLIOTT A member of the Dreamsmiths Artist Guild, Darryl has exhibited his illustration work throughout the Southeast and at many regional SF cons. This is the first genre publication of Darryl's work, which amazed the art director to no end. In the day-to-day world, Darryl is a renegade freelance advertising art director.

CHARLES SCOGINS Leaving his home in San Francisco, Charles moved to Atlanta in the hopes of expanding his advertising illustration career. He seems to be doing well, but can't wait to move back to California. Charles has exhibited his work with the Society of Illustrators, both in Atlanta and San Francisco, and with the Dreamsmiths Artist Guild. He is also busy being a father on a horse farm in Stone Mountain, GA.

ELIZABETH CONKLIN A resident of Lawrenceville, GA, Elizabeth has been published previously in *Ellery Queen's Mystery Magazine* and *Critical Mass Magazine*.

DONALD M. HASSLER Currently the editor of the SF research journal, *Extrapolations*, Mack (as he is known to anyone who doesn't have him as a professor at Kent State University) is a past president of the Science Fiction Research Association. He is a professor of English Literature at KSU, a former Dean of the Honors College there, and has had poetry and criticism published in many literary reviews and journals.

JANE YOLEN One of the most respected names in both adult and juvenile fantasy fiction, Jane has had over one hundred books published and has won the World Fantasy Award. Her fantasy works include *Sister Light, Sister Dark, The Booke of Merlin, Cards of Grief*, and the Pit Dragon Trilogy. Her children's books include, *Neptune Rising, The Girl Who Cried Flowers, The Girl Who Loved the Wind, Dream Weaver*, and more. These have been illustrated by such critically acclaimed artists as David Wiesner, David Palladini, Barry Moser, and Michael Hague. Jane was recently a president of the Science Fiction Writers of America, and lives with her husband in Hatfield, Massachusetts.

MARY ELIZABETH COUNSELMAN One of the most popular woman writers in the original *Weird Tales*, Mary's short stories have been widely anthologized in the past fifty years. Her story, "The Three Marked Pennies" is one of the most reprinted Dark Fantasy stories written this century. Mary's poetry has appeared in *The Saturday*

Evening Post, Collier's, and the most recent issue of the new *Weird Tales.* She lives in Alabama.

MICHAEL D. PARKS Part time illustrator, part-time sculptor and model-maker, part-time book dealer, and part-time musician, Mike is also a full time father and husband. Mike had an illustration in *All the Devils Are Here* and will continue to contribute to Unnameable projects . . . as long as there is time. He is currently playing in a band and creating original "Mad Lab Models." He lives in Columbus, OH with his wife and daughter.

WENDY WEBB comes from a family of writers. The daughter of Sharon Webb, who appeared in our last book, Wendy has been published in *Shadows 10, Women of Darkness, Final Shadows,* and *Sea Harp Hotel* (in which her father also has a story). She was the female lead in the S.P. Somtow film, *The Laughing Dead.* Wendy writes full time in Stone Mountain, GA and has recently finished her second book.

DEBBIE HUGHES recently had two paintings exhibited in the show, "Into the Future" at the Park Avenue Atrium in New York, and has several scheduled to appear in another show there in the Spring of '91. She has three covers coming out on Baen Books. Debbie also had a cover on the Apr. '89 issue of *SF Chronicle.* Her home and studio are in Knoxville, TN.

MARK MAXWELL Another Knoxville artist, Mark has had work traveling in an International Space Art Exhibit which spent some time in several Canadian and Russian cities, including Moscow and Kiev. The exhibit will go to the Smithsonian Air & Space Museum next. Mark has new astronomical work appearing in *Visions of Space* by David Hardy from Paper Tiger and in *The Stream of Stars* from Workman Publishing. Mark is currently at work on a brochure for a new NASA project.

MILLEA KENIN has had both her poetry and fiction widely published in the small press. She has appeared in the anthologies *The Writing on the Wall* and *Mothers and Other Lovers,* and her short story "Scarlet Eyes" appeared in *Sword and Sorceress III.* Ms. Kenin lives in Okland, CA.

CARLTON GRINDLE After several years writing non-fiction, Carlton once again ventures into the fantasy field. He has previously appeared in *Anubis, Spaceway, Witchcraft and Sorcery* and *Perry Rhodan.*

BRAD STRICKLAND A resident of Oakwood, Ga, Brad has had five novels published, including *Moon Dreams, Nul's Quest, Shadowshow*, and, most recently, *Children of the Knife*. Brad's short story "Through the Door to Might-Have-Been" was presented in *All The Devils Are Here*. In his day-to-day existence, Brad is an assistant professor at Gainesville College. He lives with his wife, Barbara, and his children, Amy and Johnathan.

MARVIN KAYE A well respected and award-winning author, Mr. Kaye is also the editor of several collections of fantasy including *Masterpieces of Terror and the Supernatural* and co-wrote several novels with Parke Godwin. He is an assistant professor of writing at New York University.

WHEN THE BLACK LOTUS BLOOMS has been released in three simultaneous editions: Two-thousand, two-hundred softcover; four-hundred signed, limited edition hardcovers — three-hundred-fifty of which are for sale, the remaining fifty are contributor and presentation copies; and fifty-two de-luxe, signed, lettered, boxed copies. The type is Palatino, both roman and italic. The titles and initial caps are set in Arnold Böcklin. The type was set by American Composition & Graphics in Atlanta, GA. The paper in all editions is 60# Booktext Natural which meets archival standards. The binding cloth is black Roxcite C cover. The printing and binding was done by BookCrafters, Inc. in Fredricksberg, VA.